I0611574

Also by Ray Hobbs and Published by Wingspan Press

An Act of Kindness	2014
Following On	2016
A Year From Now	2017
A Rural Diversion	2019
A Chance Sighting	2020
Roses and Red Herrings	2020
Happy Even After	2020
The Right Direction	2020
An Ideal World	2020
Mischief and Masquerade	2021
Big Ideas	2021
First Appearances	2021
New Directions	2021
A Deserving Case	2021
Unknown Warrior	2021
Daffs in December	2022
A Worthy Scoundrel	2022

Published Elsewhere

Second Wind (Spiderwize)	2011
Lovingly Restored (New Generation P ublishing)	2018

Fatal Shock

Ray Hobbs

Wingspan Press

This book is a work of fiction. Names, characters, settings and incidents are either the product of the author's imagination or used fictitiously. Any resemblance to actual events, settings or persons, living or dead, is entirely coincidental.

Published in the United States and the United Kingdom
by WingSpan Press, Livermore, CA

The WingSpan name, logo and colophon are the trademarks
of WingSpan Publishing.

ISBN 978-1-63683-033-9 (pbk.)
ISBN 978-1-63683-973-8 (ebook)

First edition 2022

Printed in the United States of America

www.wingspanpress.com

This book is dedicated to the memory of my late uncle, Squadron Leader Wilson H 'Bombs' Charlton, GC, RAF, sometime Commanding Officer 5131 Bomb Disposal Squadron and therefore Officer in Charge of RAF Bomb Disposal in Great Britain, France and the British sector of Germany.

RH

Sources and Acknowledgements

Turner, J. F., *Service Most Silent* (London, Harrap, 1955. Reprinted Barnsley, Pen & Sword Books Ltd, 2008).

Cashford, N., *All Mine!* (Sheffield, ALD Design & Print, 2002).

Lincoln, A., *Secret Naval Investigator* (London, Kimber, 1961. Reprinted Barnsley, Frontline Books, 2017).

When duty calls to risks unknown,
When help must come from Thee alone,
Protect her from the hidden rock,
From war's dread engine's fatal shock,
O hear from Heaven our sailors' cry,
And in their peril, be Thou nigh.

A hymn for the commissioning of a warship.
Words by L. M. S. Pasley (dates unknown).

As ever, I wish to acknowledge the invaluable assistance of my brother Chris in the preparation of the manuscript of this book.

RH

Author's Note

During the Second World War, the warning sign *Danger UXB* was an all-too common feature. 'UXB' stood for 'Unexploded Bomb', although the same sign was used to warn the public of unexploded mines. It must have seemed unnecessary to create a separate symbol for the parachute mine as, if the worst came about, the result would be exactly the same.

By its very nature, the parachute mine was inaccurate. Even a moderate wind was capable of blowing it off-course, so that, instead of finding its way into a river or an estuary, it was often found on dry land, and sometimes in a location that was barely accessible.

Not all mines were designed to sink ships. Some, like many of the bombs that fell but failed to explode immediately, were intended to create a nuisance, to make normal, day-to-day, city life impossible until they could be made safe. Others were intended simply to kill anyone who tried to uncover their secrets. The magnetic mine was Hitler's first secret weapon and a foretaste of the malevolent ingenuity that the war was to foster.

RH

1

An Unlikely Candidate

Portsmouth, March 1940

Commander Todd's unusually large hands seemed to dwarf the foolscap service document they held. By contrast, those of Lieutenant-Commander Ghyll were slender, the hands of a man accustomed to dismantling the delicate but lethal contrivances of a spiteful enemy. Both he and Todd had read the document, and were about to interview the officer whose record it represented.

'Your date of birth was the twelfth of July, eighteen ninety-nine. That makes you forty years old. You're a bit old for a lieutenant, aren't you, Reid?' Todd glanced unnecessarily at his fellow senior officer, as if seeking agreement.

'I suppose I am, sir.' Vincent was a man of medium build, with naturally crinkled, light-brown hair and eyebrows that rose very slightly towards the centre, giving the appearance of an air of concern. 'You're not the first to have commented on that, but if our paths had crossed ten months ago, you'd have considered me rather old for a sub-lieutenant, because that's what I was.'

'Really? I see you were a leading seaman before you were commissioned. What's your explanation for this belated ascent of the commissioned ladder?'

A pair of angry seagulls outside the office window distracted Vincent for the moment, but he'd been asked the question so many times that he could answer confidently and without sounding defensive. 'My wife died in childbirth six years ago, sir, and I felt after a while that I needed the distraction of male company.'

'Didn't you work with other men?'

'Yes, I did, sir, but they were academics and intellectuals. It's hard to explain to anyone who's not had the same experience, but I needed company of a worldlier kind.'

'I'm heartily sorry to hear of your bereavement, Reid.'

'Thank you, sir.'

Ghyll nodded his head in joint sympathy.

'All the same,' said Todd, 'that doesn't really answer my question.'

'I'm coming to that, sir. You see, having served in the RNVR during the last conflict, I decided to re-enlist, mainly for the comradeship. I had no immediate thoughts of promotion. It was only later that, because of my experience in minesweeping, my commanding officer persuaded me to apply for a commission. It was granted in nineteen thirty-six, when I was thirty-seven years old. Does that answer your question, sir?'

'Yes, Reid, it does. Todd looked further into the document. 'I see you served from nineteen-sixteen until a year after the war, and that shortly before your discharge you were awarded the DSM for defusing a mine that had become parted from its mooring and drifted inshore. You were a leading seaman at the time. How on earth did you come to be entrusted with that?'

Vincent was unable to hide a modest smile. 'There was no officer available, sir, and the lives of people too infirm to be moved were in immediate jeopardy, so I borrowed some tools from the local blacksmith, a most obliging chap who didn't mind turning out in the middle of the night once the situation had been explained to him. Having done that, I carried out the task I'd observed on so many occasions when assisting an officer. The process was really quite straightforward.'

'I can assure you, Reid,' said Ghyll, 'that it's not always so straightforward.' He smiled at the commander, as if sharing a secret joke.

It was Ghyll's turn to scrutinise the service document. He was younger than Todd, with dark hair and an immaculately-trimmed set of whiskers that gave him a disconcertingly severe appearance. He said, 'You're some kind of professor, I believe, Reid.'

'In peacetime, I teach history of music at the London Institute of Music and Theatre,' Vincent confirmed.

Todd sighed heavily. 'I'm very impressed by that, Reid, as I'm sure Lieutenant-Commander Ghyll is, but I don't see how, even with your experience of minesweeping and your remarkable intervention in the case of the drifting mine, you're likely to be of any use to us in solving our immediate problem.'

Vincent had anticipated scepticism. The world of the music scholar must have seemed entirely foreign to that of a naval officer trained in underwater warfare, but it was up to him to put forward his argument as convincingly as he could. 'Your notice calls for officers with certain transferable skills, sir,' he pointed out. 'In particular, you mention the need for an analytical mind, and I believe you're welcoming applications from members of the legal profession.'

'Yes.' Todd nodded impatiently. 'You're not a barrister, though, are you? The reason I want to hear from such men is that they have the kind of mentality that enables them to sift through evidence until they arrive at the truth. They are able to determine which facts are germane to the case, and which are immaterial or, even worse, red herrings. That is the only way we're ever going to understand the designs and overcome the inevitable anti-handling devices currently being devised by the enemy.'

'I can do that, sir,' Vincent told him confidently.

'I'd like to know how.'

'When I analyse a piece of music,' Vincent explained, 'I have to decide on what features I'm looking for. I ask myself, am I searching for a new theme or a new key, or perhaps both? Am I looking for maybe more than one theme? Am I so convinced that I'm looking at a certain established structure that I fail to recognise a new one, or simply a new development on an existing one? Those are just a few of the analytical questions I have to ask, and I can see no difference between them and the search for evidence that you describe.' Pointing to his service document, he went on. 'As you can see, I was working with mines as early as nineteen-seventeen, I've continued to keep abreast of the developments to which the RNVR has been made privy, and you will also see from my service document that in June of last year I completed the diving course at *HMS Excellent*.' He added, as an important afterthought, 'Being a widower, of course, I have no marital ties. That, I recall, is also one of your prerequisites.'

Commander Todd had been following Vincent's argument, sometimes with apparent difficulty, although he looked up sharply at the mention of diving. He placed the service document flat on his desk and said, 'I have to ask you to leave us for a little while, Reid, and allow us to give full consideration to what you've told us. You'll find a seat in the passageway. If not, speak to the Wren on the desk and she'll make sure you're given one.'

'Aye, aye, sir.' Vincent took his leave of the two senior officers and found a wooden chair in the passage. He sat back to examine his surroundings. He was aware that the Torpedo School, as it was known during the previous war, had been moved ashore in the early twenties, and that the name *HMS Vernon* had moved with it. The assembly of hulks that Vincent had known was sadly no more, but they had always given an impression of impermanence, and he had to admit that the new premises on the Gunwharf site were probably more practical.

He cast his eye over the portraits of *Vernon*'s past commanding officers and wondered a little about the Navy's preoccupation with its history. Pride and tradition had been integral features of the service for a long time, and now, he'd arrived at *Vernon* with a proposition that called for fresh thinking, one that must have sounded, at the very least, implausible. Putting himself in Todd's position, and Ghyll's, if it came to that, he could even sympathise with their train of thought.

On the other hand, he reflected, Todd had taken the unprecedented step of considering transferable, rather than service-based, skills, an initiative that was a clear indication of a mind open to new possibilities. He pondered that for a while, until Lieutenant-Commander Ghyll came out of the office to speak to him. Vincent rose to his feet and came to attention.

'Will you join us again, Reid?'

'Aye, aye, sir.' Vincent followed him into the office.

'Take a seat, Reid.' Commander Todd looked up at the clock and said, 'I should be able to smell coffee, but my nostrils have not so much as twitched this morning.'

'I'll chase it up, sir.' Lieutenant-Commander Ghyll got up and left the office.

'Is coffee acceptable, Reid?'

'Most acceptable, thank you, sir.' It was an encouraging sign. At least, they weren't going to dismiss him out of hand. They might even have it in mind to give him a second hearing.

The door opened again and Ghyll entered, followed by a Wren with a tray of coffee things. 'I caught her in the corridor,' he said.

The girl placed the tray on Commander Todd's desk and asked, 'Would you like me to pour it, sir?'

'No, thank you, my dear. I can do that. Carry on.'

'Aye, aye, sir.' She made her exit.

'How do you take your coffee, Reid?'

'White, please, but without sugar, sir.'

Todd poured the coffee before ending the suspense. 'Neither of us understood a word of your musical gobbledegook, Reid,' he said, 'but I'm going to give you the opportunity to prove your worth. We're not going to rush into things by recruiting you immediately into Mine Investigation, but we do need divers with mining experience, as well as extra manpower with the mines that have drifted inland, of which there are many. We're going to put you to work on some of those horrors.' He extended his hand and said, 'Welcome to RMS, Reid.'

'RMS, sir?'

' "Rendering Mines Safe". That's our function, and now that you've talked your way into it, it's going to be yours as well.'

After coffee, Lieutenant-Commander Ghyll took Vincent into the laboratory building to show him a magnetic mine.

'It presented us with a barrage of unexplained calamities,' he said. 'That was until we learned that is was magnetic. Until then, it could have been activated by pressure, sound, or even black magic, for all we knew, and we were losing ships at an alarming rate.'

'So it's magnetic, but how does that work, sir?'

'The idea is that the mine picks up a ship's magnetic field and explodes directly beneath it without the need for contact of any description. These,' he said, indicating a collection of parts, 'are from the first Type "A" to be defused, and we owe that and much more to Lieutenant-Commander Ouvry, whom you will possibly meet in your travels.'

'What's the magnetic tolerance of such a mine, sir?'

'Think of it as completely *in*tolerant, Reid. When we approach one of these things, we remove every vestige of ferrous metal from our persons, and we use only the approved non-magnetic tools.' As if the question had only just occurred to him, he asked, 'Do you wear spectacles at all?'

'Only for close work, sir.'

'Better get them checked. If the hinges are steel, they'll need to be replaced with brass, gunmetal or stainless ones.' With a playful smile, he added, 'As you can imagine, the need for non-magnetic tools rules out borrowing spanners, hammers and pincers from the local smithy.'

The joke was harmless enough. Vincent returned Ghyll's smile and examined the mine's casing. He found four access ports, two on each side.

'Yes,' said Ghyll, 'it's vitally important to deal with the anti-handling device, the booby-trap, if you prefer it, first.' He lifted the device from the bench to show Vincent.

'Whatever it's called,' said Vincent, 'I shall be inclined to handle it carefully. How is it made safe?'

'Ouvry reached inside and found these two electrical wires,' he said pointing to them. 'He twisted them, and they parted – it's usually a good idea to break an electrical circuit – and then he insulated the broken ends with tape to keep them from getting up to mischief.'

Ghyll went on to describe the other triggers contained within the mine. 'If the mine hits dry land, the timer triggers it to explode after twenty-five seconds. This one was washed ashore, and it should have exploded in shallow water, but it somehow failed to do that, which is why we were able to work on it.'

'What if it falls into water, sir?' It seemed the most appropriate place to lay a mine, and Vincent's curiosity was aroused by Ghyll's reference to shallow water.

'If it falls into a depth of more than about eight feet, the magnetic trigger will be automatically armed. If it's lifted into shallower water, it's likely to blow up immediately, and that's why we occasionally need a diver, whose job it will be to defuse and disarm the wretched thing under water. I'm sure you'll see now why your diving qualification captured Commander Todd's attention.' He smiled again. 'For all we know, your musical analytical skills may yet come to the fore, but neither the Commander nor I knows a symphony from a swansong, so we decided to give you the benefit of any remaining doubt.'

'I'll try not to disappoint you, sir, if only for the sake of my own survival.'

'Quite.' Ghyll looked thoughtful for a moment, and then asked, 'Do you possess a motorcar, by any chance?'

It seemed an odd question. 'Yes, sir. I have a Riley Monaco.'

Ghyll raised his eyebrows appreciatively. 'Very nice indeed.'

'It's at my London home, laid up for the duration of hostilities, sir. Why do you ask?' Fuel rationing was particularly stringent, and it left nothing for private use.

'We can get you an official allowance for petrol. The Luftwaffe are dropping parachute mines all over London and the home counties, so you'll need it. Otherwise, until we get our own transport, we have to rely on the civil service pool, an arrangement that is far from satisfactory.'

'I can have my car back on the road very quickly, sir.'

'I'm glad to hear it.' He looked at his watch and said, 'I make it close to lunchtime. You'll take lunch with us in the wardroom, I trust, Reid?'

'Thank you, sir, I'd like that very much.'

'Good, because this is now your base.'

2

The Sword of Damocles

The parachute mine menace was so pressing that training was necessarily brief and hurried, and it wasn't long before Vincent was sent to London, where most of the mines were falling. He arrived at the address he'd been given in Wapping to find his assistant, an able seaman, waiting for him.

The rating saluted and said, 'Excuse me, sir. Are you Lieutenant Reid?'

'Yes.'

'I'm here to assist you, sir. Able Seaman Riddle.'

'I'm glad to meet you, Riddle.' Vincent shook his hand.

A warden approached and asked, 'Have you come to deal with the landmine, sir?'

'We both have, warden. Where is it?'

'It's hanging by its parachute from one of the loading hoists over the wharf, sir.'

'Its parachute got caught on it, sir,' explained Riddle. 'The release mechanism must have failed. The actual mine is only about two feet above the wharf.' He pointed, and Vincent was able to see the mine, suspended as it was above the narrow pathway that ran beside and above the wharf.

'Like the sword of Damocles,' remarked Vincent, 'but fortunately suspended by something more substantial than a human hair.'

'That's what I thought, sir,' said Riddle.

A policeman joined them to say, 'The warehouse is empty and the area is cordoned off, sir.'

'Well done. Come with me, Riddle.' When they were alone, he said, 'I imagine everyone calls you "Jimmy"?'

'Yes, sir.'

It was inevitable. 'Do you mind that?'

'No, sir. It's followed me around since schooldays, and there are worse things they could call me.'

The warden shouted, 'Have you got everything you need, sir?'

'Yes,' Vincent told him, 'Now, be a good chap and leave us to concentrate.'

The two men descended the stone steps to the dock and approached the mine. Vincent put his glasses on. They were for close work, and it seemed to him that work couldn't get much closer.

'At least, this way, I have access to everything,' said Vincent, examining the four base plates and realising that the mine was a Type 'A'. 'Just leave the tools, Jimmy, and go back to the safety point.'

'Aye, aye, sir.' He looked as if he knew the drill.

'Okay, with any luck, I'll see you in a short while.'

'Good luck, sir.'

'Thank you.' Vincent opened the bag of tools, which resembled a plumber's bass, and took out a stethoscope. With shaking hands, he placed the stethoscope against the casing and listened. There was no sound from within. 'Good,' he said to himself, 'it's still asleep.' His mouth was dry, and his tongue felt like carpet felt. He replaced the stethoscope and took the four-pronged spanner made specially for RMS. Using both hands to hold the tool steady, he pushed the prongs carefully into the corresponding holes in the locking plate and applied anti-clockwise pressure. It wouldn't budge, so he leant his weight against it and pushed as hard as he could, fearfully conscious that he was standing next to seven hundred kilogrammes of high explosive. Eventually, the cap began to turn. Encouraged, he continued to apply the wrench, pausing briefly to wipe the perspiration from his forehead. Finally, he took the cap from its socket and placed it in the tool bag. As he did so, he noticed that the tool had left indentations in his hands. He wasn't surprised.

Next, he lifted the aluminium arrangement slowly and carefully out of its housing, using a brass rod as a lever. It was one of those occasions when a longer reach would have made the job much easier, but he held the anti-handling device in his right hand, conscious as ever of the trials of being left-handed, while he fumbled in the bag for a knife. Sweat was pouring into his eyes again, and he transferred the knife to his pocket while he removed his recently-modified glasses, realising he would be able to see better without them. Taking the knife from his pocket, he began cutting through the wire. Being bronze, the knife wasn't particularly sharp, and it took some effort before he was able to part the wire.

Once more, he had to reach into the bag for insulating tape, and with some difficulty, he managed to cut two small pieces. He blinked as perspiration ran from his brow and into his eyes. Even in the fiercely cold, March wind, he was perspiring freely. Blinking again, he covered the ends of the wires. Relieved so far, he unscrewed the gaine, which he understood to be a kind of detonator, from the device and placed both items in the bag. 'One down, three to go,' he told himself, 'but that was the really nasty one.' For some reason, he found it helped to talk to himself.

With the anti-handling device now disarmed, he could approach the remaining three devices more confidently, but with no less respect.

The neighbouring plate appeared to conceal a hydrostatic valve, which he removed without difficulty. Having done that, he made his way to the other side of the mine.

He took a quarter-inch screwdriver and began removing the next plate. It was held by only four screws, and he removed it to find a threaded plug with an arrangement of two crossed bars, which he was unable to move by hand. The only way to loosen it was with a brass rod and a four-ounce hammer. He hadn't anticipated the need to use a hammer. The thought of it caused his pulse to quicken and perspiration to bead all over his body. His shirt was already soaked.

He placed the rod firmly against one of the bars. It was now or never, and he tapped the end of the rod with the hammer. There was no movement, so he tapped harder. The plug began to turn. Quickly, he put the tools down and picked up the stethoscope. He had to be sure. He held the stethoscope against the mine and was relieved beyond words that the only sound he could hear was that of his blood pounding in his ears. He put down the stethoscope and picked up the rod and hammer again. One gentle tap and it moved easily, so he loosened it by hand and removed it. As far as he could make out, the villain that lay exposed was the main detonator, and its removal called for the biggest screwdriver in his toolkit.

Carefully, he used it to lever the detonator out. It was attached to five wires. Sweat was rolling off his forehead, and he steadied the detonator with one hand while he drew an already sodden sleeve across his brow.

Laboriously, he severed the wires, finally placing the detonator in the bag.

The final task was to remove the priming charge, which still presented a challenge. Once more, it called for the four-pin spanner, which he applied to the locking ring. It turned more easily than its predecessor, and he was able to remove it without difficulty.

He drew out the primer, which came attached to a long coil spring. The final part of the job was done, and Vincent was alarmed to find that his hands were now shaking uncontrollably. He also felt decidedly queasy.

'Jimmy!' He beckoned his assistant, who hurried to his side.

'Well done, sir.'

'Thank you, Jimmy. We'd better report to the warden, and then I think we should find a cup of tea. Just take the tools and everything back to my car, will you?'

'Aye, aye, sir.'

Jimmy disappeared up the steps hardly a second too soon, as a wave of nausea overpowered Vincent, and he vomited over the side of the wharf. According to Lieutenant-Commander Ghyll, it was a normal occurrence, especially after a defusing debut, but he hoped nevertheless that no one had seen him.

When he was satisfied that he'd left the entire contents of his stomach in the dock, he climbed the steps and spoke to the warden and the policeman. 'It's safe,' he told them. 'A party will be along shortly to remove it.' He added, perhaps unnecessarily, 'It's not going to hurt anyone now.'

'Thank you, sir' said the warden. 'On behalf of everybody who lives in this neighbourhood, thank you, sir.'

'I'll second that,' said the policeman.

'I expect you and the sailor would like a cuppa, sir,' said the warden.

'That would be very nice, thank you. Mine's with milk, but no sugar. You'll have to ask Jimmy what his preference is.'

Several minutes later, Vincent and Jimmy sat on a low wall, drinking tea from enamel mugs.

'Where do you live, Jimmy?'

'Bloomsbury, sir.'

'That's handy.' It would be, too. RMS officers and ratings were paid a generous ration allowance for living out, and he would be able to call on his family as well. 'I'll give you a lift home if you like. That way, I'll know where to come when I need you.'

'Thank you, sir. That's very kind of you.'

'What did you do before the war?'

'I was at school, sir.'

'I'm sorry. That was a silly question. I should really have asked you what you would have been doing had the war not created a diversion.'

Jimmy gave him a wistful look. 'I wanted to study clarinet at one of the music colleges, sir, but Hitler put a stop to that.'

'Yes, he's a Wagnerite, they tell me, and he has an unreasoning dislike of Jewish composers. At the mention of Mendelssohn, he tears his hair out and chews the carpet.' He shook his head disapprovingly. 'In my book, there's no room in music for politics or hatred of any kind.'

'Are you keen on music, sir?'

'Yes, I am. Believe it or not, the Kaiser played the same trick on me.'

'Really, sir?'

'Yes, I was going to study piano, but the war came along, and it's not easy to put the practice in when you're serving in a minesweeper.'

Jimmy eyed him sadly, but said nothing.

'After the war, I joined the academics. I went to university and took my degree. I taught analysis and history of music at the London Institute before the war. They let me teach some piano as well, and I even managed a few recitals.' He smiled encouragingly. 'So, you see, things didn't turn out too badly, and the same may well apply to you after this war.'

'Thanks for telling me that, sir. I feel better for it.'

'That's the spirit, Jimmy.'

Jimmy finished his tea and emptied the leaves on to the ground. 'If you don't mind my asking, sir, have you been doing this for long?'

'That was my first since nineteen-nineteen,' confided Vincent.

'I'm glad you didn't tell me that earlier, sir.'

'It would have been unkind,' he agreed. 'How long have you been doing this work, Jimmy?'

'Since October last year, sir. Mr Penny and I got into it right from the beginning.'

'What happened to, er, Mr Penny?' As the question left his lips, he knew he shouldn't have asked it.

'He got blown up, sir.'

'I'm glad you didn't tell me that earlier, Jimmy.'

After dropping his assistant in Bloomsbury, Vincent drove back to his house in Holborn, where he made a phone call to Commander Todd, reporting that the menace had been made safe.

'You've done well,' said Todd, 'How do you find the rating we sent you?'

'He's excellent, sir.'

'I wondered, because he was present at one shortly before Christmas that went wrong, and he had to do the seventeen-second sprint.'

'So I gather, sir, but it doesn't seem to have unnerved him unduly.'

'Good. Well, stay where you are, and we'll know where to find you. I've no doubt your services will be required again shortly.'

'Aye, aye, sir.'

When the commander had rung off, Vincent went to the kitchen and found a quarter-pound of tea. It was treasure trove and sorely needed, and he put the kettle on, hoping he would stay awake long enough to enjoy the tea. A night of little sleep and the reaction after the morning's tension had left him drooping.

He actually enjoyed two cups of tea before heading wearily to the bathroom.

His father, who had previously owned the house, had been a man of ideas and fancies, and one of his more welcome initiatives had been to have a 'gentleman's shower', as the manufacturers called it, installed in the spacious bathroom. It was a matter of self-indulgence for Vincent to undress and shower before giving in to sleep.

3

The Woman From the Ministry

Vincent and Jimmy were called to several mines in the days that followed. There was certainly no shortage of them, and to attend to two, and sometimes three, in a day was quite normal. Most of them were as routine as unexploded mines could be, but Vincent was called to one in Leamouth that called for all his training and presence of mind.

'It's believed to be a Type 'A', and it's submerged in four fathoms of Thames water,' he was told. 'A mobile diving unit is on its way from Chatham. Hopefully, you'll have everything you need.' It seemed to Vincent to be a particularly silly thing to say. His informant also said something else, that Vincent didn't catch, about a ministry of some kind, but he was more concerned with the mine itself.

'I don't know that there'll be much for you to do,' he told Jimmy when he picked him up, 'but my orders are to bring you.'

'I've attended a diver before, sir.'

'Have you?' He was tempted to enquire further, but good sense prevailed. Jimmy's past experience was not a matter to be probed too deeply.

When they arrived at the scene, they found that the lorry from Chatham had already arrived. Its driver had reversed it as close to the wharf as it could go and still provide room for access to its interior. A petty officer appeared to be in charge.

'The warden says the mine's stuck in the mud and leanin' against one of the pillars, sir, although his eyesight must be better than mine, because I 'aven't seen it yet.'

'Is there a way down, PO?'

'Yes, sir, there's the iron ladder, here, at the end of the wharf.' He pointed unnecessarily to the place where the timbers of the wharf terminated, giving way to a stone pillar. 'I reckon the mine's just about as close to the ladder as it can get without being triggered.'

It was obviously the case, but Vincent refrained from pointing that out. 'Right,' he said, 'I'll go in and change. Able Seaman Riddle will assist me. You can supervise the air pump and lines.'

He and Jimmy entered the lorry, where a diving suit and its accessories were laid out neatly beside a wooden crate thoughtfully provided as a seat for the diver.

Vincent stripped down to his underwear, donned the diving suit and put his feet into the weighted boots, tying the heavy laces with quick-release knots in case he had to make a rapid ascent. Having done that, he sat on the crate while Jimmy tucked in the neck ring to protect Vincent's shoulders where the brass corselet and lead weights hung. They weighed fourteen pounds each and were suspended fore and aft from the corselet. His weighted belt also carried his tools.

Next, he made his way laboriously to the iron ladder. His leaden boots made his movements clumsy and deliberate, but he descended partway, clinging to the top rung while Jimmy placed the brass helmet complete with lines and air pipes over his head and locked it on to the corselet. The air pump started up, pumping air into the helmet, and Jimmy completed the ensemble by screwing the faceplate into place. Vincent was now enclosed in a watertight suit, and he resumed his journey down the ladder. After a dozen-or-so rungs, he ran out of ladder, so he seized the shot rope, the stout, anchored rope that would be his guide to the surface, should he find himself unable to locate the ladder again.

He came to rest on the bottom and adjusted his air intake, so that the balance of air in the suit against the lead weights enabled him to move with relative ease.

Switching on the torch situated on his helmet, he located the mine, which was propped on its nose, just as the warden had described, almost vertically against the stone pillar. He made his way towards it, negotiating the detritus of the years, but had to wait for the water to clear, as each footstep raised a cloud of mud and silt that left it opaque.

After a while, he was able to examine the mine and discover where the plates were situated. Two were clearly on view, and that was a blow, as it meant that the others would be inaccessible. He felt around the back of the casing, and his suspicion was confirmed. Access to them was impossible.

As he removed his hand, he thought he felt the mine move slightly. His heart pounded as he considered the implications. One sharp movement could trigger the mechanism, and he would have no means of escape. For a moment, he wondered if he might have imagined the shift; it was easy to imagine anything in those murky conditions. Even so, he resolved to return to the surface and warn everyone to evacuate the area. Clearly, the mine was incapable of being rendered safe.

As he turned to reach for the shot rope, he saw the mine move again, and it was clear that imagination had nothing to do with it. He reached again, and was conscious of movement in the water, like a current, except that currents did not exist in docks. It was cloudy, and he couldn't see a thing. He'd lost the shot rope, and the ladder was a long way above his head. In any case, if the mine was going to explode, it would do it before he could reach the surface. He could only wait and pray fervently.

Eventually, the sediment settled, and he saw both the shot rope and the ladder. More dramatically still, he could see the mine, not as it had been, propped against the pillar, but now on its side. Best of all, more than seventeen seconds had elapsed since the disturbance, evidence enough that his guardian angel hadn't deserted him.

Gingerly, he crept over to the horizontal mine and waited again for the water to clear, not that murky water was the only impediment, as the faceplate had misted up, no doubt as a result of his accelerated breathing. He touched the small water inlet valve to fill his mouth with water, which he squirted on to the glass window, clearing the mist. That done, he considered the polluted state of the water in the dock and spat again.

When the muddied water had settled, he felt carefully over the surface of the casing and, for the first time since he'd left the ladder, he felt that things were happening in his favour. The mine had fallen, leaving its plates exposed on both sides.

With increasingly cold hands, he set about removing the anti-handling device, the detonator, the primer, and lastly, because he now knew it for what it was, the hydrostatic valve. There was nothing new, which was just as well, because he'd had enough shocks for the time being.

Having located the shot rope, he groped around his helmet with a frozen hand until he found the air valve. Relieved again, he opened it to increase the air intake, and therefore the buoyancy in his suit. Within seconds, he felt himself being borne slowly upwards until he reached the ladder and was able to manage his own ascent.

Jimmy was waiting on the wharf to remove the helmet and help him into the lorry. Vincent stopped beside the ratings on the air pump and lines to say, 'Thank you, everyone. It's good to see you again. PO, you'll be relieved to know that I didn't pee in the suit. Being well brought up, I did it before I left my house.'

'Thank you for telling me that, sir.' The petty officer blinked with embarrassment.

Vincent left them looking puzzled and joined Jimmy in the lorry.

'Divers are required to wash and dry their suits personally for just that reason, Jimmy,' he explained. 'I can't imagine what he'd have done if I had been caught short. I suppose they'd have got some unsuspecting Wren or a defaulter to do the honours.'

As Jimmy helped him off with the weights, the corselet and the lead-weighted boots, he asked, 'How was it, sir?'

'Cold, but fairly straightforward.' He didn't see why anyone else should be alarmed.

Presently, he emerged from the lorry, dressed warmly in his uniform and a seaman's jersey, and still grateful to be alive.

'I'll see if I can find a wet, sir,' said Jimmy. 'Someone must be grateful enough to put the kettle on for us.'

'That's a good idea.' Vincent was content simply to lean against the wall and recover, if not from a thousand natural shocks, at least from a few of an unnatural kind.

He stood there for a while, just letting the world slip out of focus and breathing welcome fresh air after his ordeal, until he heard voices at the entrance to the wharf. Jimmy had arrived with a tray bearing several mugs of tea. Also, a woman was speaking to the policeman on duty and showing him, presumably, her identity card and other credentials. He had no idea why she should be doing that, nor did he care, because more important to him by far was the fact that Jimmy was handing him a mug of tea, which, at that moment, he expected to taste like champagne.

'Thank you, Jimmy,' he said with a great deal of feeling.

Suddenly, he was aware of another person, the woman who had used her identification to enter the restricted area.

'Lieutenant Reid? I'm Hazel Wythenshawe from the Ministry of Information. As you know, I've come to —'

'Madam,' he said, 'it's not my custom to be rude, especially to a lady, but I really don't care if you're from Buckingham Palace, Westminster Abbey or Lewisham Mechanics' Institute. Please leave me in peace.' It was a shame, because she was very attractive, with lustrous brown hair and, initially at least, an engaging smile, but he needed solitude more than anything else.

The smile was now gone. 'There seems to have been a misunderstanding,' she said. 'I was told you were expecting me.'

'You were wrongly informed, madam. In less dramatic circumstances, I might easily have welcomed your company, but not this morning, I'm afraid.' He turned to the petty officer, who had now recovered from his earlier embarrassment, and said, 'PO, kindly escort this lady to the gate.'

'Aye, aye, sir. Please come this way, madam.'

'Oh, very well. There's obviously been a mistake. Good day, Lieutenant.'

'Good day, madam.' Vincent returned his attention to his tea, which tasted rather better than champagne now that he could enjoy it in peace.

He tried telephoning Commander Todd, who was elsewhere, so he spoke to Lieutenant-Commander Ghyll.

'I have to report that the menace at Leamouth is now safe, sir.'

They were on an insecure telephone line, so it was necessary to speak in cryptic terms.

'I'm delighted to hear it, Reid, but I've had the Ministry of Information breathing fire and brimstone because you sent one of their people away with a flea in her ear. What were you thinking of?'

So that was the reason the woman had been able to enter the restricted area. Vincent took a long breath and said, 'I'd just spent the best part of an hour in cold, muddy water in the company of a particularly unpleasant character that marked my arrival by toppling from its original position and hitting the riverbed with disconcerting force, sir. When the waters cleared and I realised I had neither grown wings nor acquired a harp, I resumed and completed my task. Not surprisingly, I reached the surface feeling somewhat drained. I changed into my uniform again, and I'd just accepted a mug of tea from my assistant, when I was accosted, quite without warning, by a young female. You ask me what I was thinking of, sir. I was incapable of coherent thought, but that didn't prevent me from being bloody angry.'

'I'm sorry, Reid. I didn't know about the thing shifting. That must have given you a bloody awful shock.'

'It was one of those moments that will accompany me to the grave, sir.'

'No wonder you were displeased. That's how Miss Wythenshawe described you. She said you were civil but displeased.' Ghyll sounded as if he were reading the indictment.

'I ask you, sir, what should I have done?'

'Ideally, you should have received a message informing you that an employee of the Ministry would contact you. That you didn't is not your fault in the slightest. It's just bloody unfortunate.'

Vincent thought about the telephone call he'd received that morning. 'Actually, sir,' he said, 'the officer who alerted me to the Leamouth mine did, I believe, make a vague and passing reference to a ministry, but I was more concerned at the time with preventing part of the East End from being restructured.'

'Quite. Just to fill in the details, the Ministry of Information are making a documentary film about our current task and our response to our visitors. I've no doubt it will amount to little more than propaganda designed to boost public morale, but I'm told it has the Prime Minister's blessing, and who are we to argue with Mr Chamberlain? At all events, the Ministry simply wanted you to give an interview to go with the film they'd made—'

'Film, sir?' The whole business was descending into a farce.

'Yes, they filmed your descent and your return, all from a safe distance, of course.'

'The buggers! I'd no idea they were doing that.'

'It might not have helped your state of mind had you been aware of it, Reid. Look, I'll explain the circumstances to the Ministry. Leave it an hour, and then call them yourself and speak to this woman. Arrange to meet her and, without breaching the Official Secrets Act, tell her… something. You can describe life on the riverbed if you wish, but do try to get them off our backs.'

'Do you mean you have a war to wage as well, sir?'

'There's no need for sarcasm, Reid, but I'll allow you some slack in the circumstances.'

'What's this woman's name, sir, and which department enjoys the dubious benefit of her services?'

'She's Miss Hazel Wythenshawe, and I'm sure the switchboard operator will be able to locate her. I'll give you the Ministry's number. It's Bloomsbury two seven six one-to-four.'

'Thank you, sir.'

'And, Reid?'

'Yes, sir?'

'Well done this morning. It can't have been easy, or pleasant, for that matter.'

'It's in the past now, sir.'

'So it is. Goodbye, Reid.'

'Goodbye, sir.'

Vincent replaced the receiver and sat down. The more he thought about it the more farcical it sounded. He and many others were trying their hardest to save the country from obliteration by parachute mines, and a bunch of civil servants wanted to make a hooray film about it. On a whim, he set about thinking of a suitable collective noun for that type of civil servant. The first to occur to him was An Unreality of Civil Servants, and then A Remoteness of Civil Servants. It was a game his father used to play. One of his favourites was A Delay of Solicitors, and another that Vincent recalled was An Obfuscation of Defence Counsel. Being a judge, he was naturally kinder to those of his own calling. Vincent looked up at his photograph and wondered what he would have made of a film about parachute mines, that showed a diver entering the water and then, much later, emerging without appearing to have done anything in between. He mused about that and about other things until it was approximately time to speak to the unspeakable. He dialled the Bloomsbury number and waited. Eventually, he was rewarded.

'Ministry of Information. Which department do you require?'

'Whichever department it is that employs Miss Hazel Wythenshawe, please.'

'And who shall I say is calling?'

'Lieutenant Vincent Reid, RNVR.'

'Is this a private call?'

She sounded very disapproving, and Vincent was tempted to tease her, but he resisted the urge. 'It most certainly is not.'

'Very well. Hold the line, please, whilst I try to connect you.'

He waited, and eventually, a friendlier and younger voice said, 'Lieutenant Reid, this is Hazel Wythenshawe.'

'Miss Wythenshawe, I realise now that I owe you an apology.'

'No, no, I should apologise to you. In the circumstances, my intrusion this morning was insensitive and unforgiveable.'

Caught on the back foot, Vincent could only say, 'But no more so than my rudeness.'

She gave a rather nervous laugh. 'Now that we've both apologised, or at least tried to,' she said, 'can we agree that we're both reprobates and move on?'

'I should hesitate to call a lady a reprobate, Miss Wythenshawe.'

'As long as you don't call me "madam" again, I really don't mind.'

This was not the conversation he'd envisaged. He'd picked up the telephone with the intention of being distantly polite, if only for the benefit of his superiors, and now he was warming to the woman. He heard himself ask, 'Are you smiling, Miss Wythenshawe?'

'At this very moment? Oddly enough, yes. Are you?'

'It's a rare occurrence, but yes. As we're clearly of one mind, shall we move on?'

'Oh yes, please. Have your people explained what this is about?'

'In essence, yes. I'm told you want to make a propaganda film about our work.'

'Not "propaganda", Lieutenant. "Public information" is the official label, and yes, I'm rather keen to interview you. That is, if you're completely in agreement.'

'I must confess, I'm flattered. I never imagined I was so interesting. When shall we meet, Miss Wythenshawe?'

'Whenever is convenient for you.'

'My evenings are usually free. I find it safer to do all my work in daylight. Are you free… tomorrow evening?' Something from his dim past reminded him that a lady usually preferred some notice.

'I can be.'

'Where do you live, Miss Wythenshawe?'

'Where do I…? In Bloomsbury, near the Ministry. Why do you ask?'

'That's a coincidence. I was in Bloomsbury twice today.'

'Were you/'

'My assistant lives there. I had to pick him up and drop him off. If you'd care to give me your address, I'll pick you up, too, and take you to a highly respectable restaurant where we can talk freely, largely because, whilst I may be able to provide you with some useful material for your film, I shall avoid divulging any classified information. Is seven o' clock all right?' He thought he was coping tolerably well, for a man who'd isolated himself from female company for several years.

'You're very kind, Lieutenant.' She sounded hesitant.

'Nonsense. Call it my olive branch.'

'In that case, how can I reciprocate?'

'By accepting my invitation.'

'Very well, Lieutenant. Seven o' clock tomorrow evening, then.'

4

A Happy Return

The lift stopped at the third floor, where an arrow sign told Vincent that the flat he wanted was to the left. In fact, it was only a matter of yards along the passageway. On reaching it, he rang the doorbell and waited.

The door opened, and Miss Wythenshawe appeared in a buttoned-front russet dress with a narrow white collar. The short, puffed sleeves were also trimmed in white.

'Good evening, Lieutenant.'

Vincent removed his cap. 'Good evening, Miss Wythenshawe. If you don't mind my saying so, you look absolutely charming, and your dress is exquisite.'

'It's very kind of you to say so. Please come in while I get my hat and coat.'

He found that the room was decorated and furnished in the Art Deco style, in contrast with his home, which owed its character to an earlier age and more particularly to his parents' taste.

Miss Wythenshawe returned with her coat over her arm. She wore a fedora hat with the brim turned up at the side and to the front.

'Let me help you with your coat,' he offered.

'Thank you, Lieutenant.' She inserted her arms into the sleeves. As he drew the coat up to her shoulders, she said, 'I'm quite taken aback.'

'By what?'

'By your lovely manners. They're a rarity in my life.'

'I'm sorry to hear that, Miss Wythenshawe.'

She hesitated, and then said, 'As this is an informal occasion, do you think you could relax a little and call me Hazel?'

'I'm sure I could. My name, by the way, is Vincent.'

'That's a suitably upright name,' she said, taking her door key from her purse, 'for a man who is reliable, trustworthy and courteous.'

'If those are your expectations, I'll try not to disappoint you, Hazel.' He stood in the passageway while she locked the door.

They took the lift down to the street, where Vincent offered her his arm. 'It's not far,' he assured her.

'The restaurant?'

'No, my car.'

'Where are we going?'

'Emil's in Covent Garden.' He opened the passenger door and held it for her, waiting for her to gather her skirts, before closing it.

As he settled into the driving seat, she asked, 'You've used the restaurant in the past, presumably?'

'Yes,' he said, starting the engine, 'I go there quite often.'

'You must lead a busy social life.'

'On the contrary, I go there alone. Living a solitary life, I think it would be too easy to fall into slipshod ways. Food is naturally important, and I go to some trouble over it, whether I do the cooking or leave it to a chef,' he said, turning carefully into Southampton Row.

'Have you always lived al…?' She caught herself and said, 'I'm sorry. That's not the kind of question to ask when we've only just met.'

'No, I haven't. I've been a widower for six years.'

'Oh, Vincent, I am sorry.'

'I survived,' he assured her, turning right into Queen Street before negotiating the lesser streets that led to Covent Garden. 'Part of that survival was due, as I said earlier, to maintaining standards and not letting myself adopt careless ways.'

'Even so,' she murmured, clearly at a loss for anything meaningful to say.

'I'll tell you about it, and then you won't think of it as a taboo subject. My wife died in childbirth and the baby was stillborn. It was a wretched time, but I learned, with a lot of help from friends, to cope with it. Let's leave it there and spend the rest of the evening enjoying ourselves.' He pulled up at the side of the road and switched off the engine. 'Emil's awaits,' he announced cheerfully, adding, 'Emil himself is no longer with us, but the name and the quality he brought to the restaurant both live on.'

The elderly head waiter greeted him warmly. 'Good evening, Professor Reid.… I beg your pardon. I should say, *Lieutenant* Reid.'

'Don't rub it in, Jean-Claude. Good evening to you.'

As Hazel removed her gloves, the waiter glanced surreptitiously at her left hand and said, 'Good evening, *mademoiselle*.'

'Good evening.'

'Your usual corner table is at your disposal, monsieur, but first, allow me to relieve you both of your outer garments.'

With that out of the way, he summoned a waiter to show them to their table, which he did, leaving them with the menu and assuring them that everything was available. 'An aperitif, perhaps?'

Hazel shook her head. 'Not for me, thank you,' she said.

'Nor for me,' said Vincent. 'I have to drive through the blackout.'

'Then I shall leave you with the menu.'

When he was gone, Vincent said, 'My father, who was quite eccentric, used to grade French waiters according to how well they spoke English. He could be embarrassing at times.'

'He must have been quite a character.'

'He was an amiable pedant, but not an entirely fair one, as he was usually in an unassailable position, being a judge. He would correct barristers, witnesses and almost anyone whose grammar was less than perfect.'

Hazel smiled at his description. 'I get the impression you were fond of him,' she said.

'Yes, I was fond of both my parents.'

'Have you any brothers or sisters?'

'No, my only brother was killed in the last war.'

'Oh, Vincent.' She closed her eyes in shame. 'Every time I ask you a personal question I open a wound.'

'Not really. It was twenty-four years ago. Let's look at this menu and make a decision.'

In the end, they both chose the fillet steak, if only because, like everything else, it was sure to be in short supply before long.

'There,' he said, 'you managed to do that without feeling guilty.'

'No, I didn't. There are people in this country who won't see steak for a very long time.' Lowering her voice, she said, 'As a matter of fact, there's talk – only talk at this stage, mind you – of restrictions being imposed on restaurant pricing so that people like us won't be at an unfair advantage.' She looked uncertain for a moment and said, 'That was wrong, wasn't it? "People like us"?'

'I can hear my father turning in his grave, but I'm not as fussy as he was, so don't worry. Tell me instead about your family.'

'There's nothing much to tell. I'm an only child, and my parents are retired. They live in Kent.'

The waiter returned to take their order and ask about wine, thereby rendering further information unnecessary. 'Since the war began,' he explained, 'we have had no wine waiter. We perform the task ourselves.'

'And you acquit yourselves remarkably well,' remarked Vincent.

'You're very kind, monsieur.'

'I'll leave it to you, Vincent,' said Hazel.

'In that case, we'd like a bottle of the Chateau Beaune Villages 'thirty-five, please.'

'It will be our pleasure, monsieur.' With a small bow, he left them.

'Vincent?'

'Yes?'

'When we arrived, why did the head waiter address you as "Professor Reid"?'

He made a small gesture of surrender and said, 'My secret is out.'

'What is your secret?'

'When I'm not battling with giant sea creatures on the ocean bed or starring in lurid public information films,' he told her in a confidential tone, 'I'm Professor of History of Music at the London Institute, although it's a grand title for someone who does something that's quite straightforward.'

'It can't be all that straightforward.'

'It is for me, and that's all that matters.'

'I'm still impressed.'

'Don't be. A professor in a school of music is somewhat lowlier than the kind associated with a university.'

It was clear that she was exploring a new concept. 'So you teach history of music,' she said. 'Do you play an instrument as well?'

'Yes, I'm not a complete academic. I teach piano and I give recitals as well. At least, I did.'

'I'm terribly impressed that you can do all those things as well as what you were doing yesterday morning.'

'Jimmy and I attended another two today,' he told her.

Hazel could only look at him in surprise. Eventually, she said, 'You seem to have an unusually egalitarian relationship with your assistant.'

'Perish the thought. If he gets ideas above his station, he'll be flogged, keelhauled and marooned like everyone else.'

'I mean that you address him by his Christian name.'

'I don't think I know his Christian name. "Jimmy" is his nickname. His surname is Riddle, and all Riddles are called "Jimmy" for obvious reasons.'

Realisation came home to her. 'Stupid of me,' she said. 'Anyway, how did you get into your current line of work?' Looking around the restaurant, she said, 'I suppose we need to talk in non-specific terms.'

'We should,' he agreed. 'I first joined the Wavy Navy in nineteen-sixteen, when I was seventeen, having lied about my age. There was a shortage of men in minesweepers, so that's where they put me.'

'So you've been associated with that kind of work for quite a long time.'

'Off and on. After the war, study distracted me for a while. I had to find an alternative route into music.'

'Why?'

Realising that her world and his were very different, and that he'd taken quite a lot for granted, he explained. 'I wanted originally to study piano, but three years without practice, not to mention tuition, put paid to that.'

'That was cruel.'

'Yes, I agreed with Lloyd George about hanging the Kaiser, but they only shipped him off to Holland, so I swallowed my resentment, went to London University and took my degree.'

'What did you do then?'

The waiter arrived at their table with the wine, which Vincent tasted and pronounced excellent.

'I taught in a school for a while, and I took an external higher degree before gaining a job at the Institute.'

She was looking at him so intently that he couldn't help noticing the colour of her eyes.

She asked, 'Is something the matter?'

'Not at all, and please forgive me if I was staring, but I imagined, quite naïvely, that your eyes would be hazel, and they're actually blue. They're no less lovely for that,' he assured her.

'Thank you. You're very kind.'

'Not at all. A sincere compliment requires no effort whatsoever, and it can do a great deal of good.'

'That's a lovely thing to say, Vincent, but please go on with your story.'

She had to wait, because the waiter arrived with their order. Eventually, though, they were alone again.

'People cope with disaster, bereavement and so on, in their individual ways,' he said, motioning to her to help herself to vegetables and potatoes. 'My way was to return to the war – the last war, that is – and the genuine ties and friendships I knew in the Navy. There was a kind of kinship I'd never experienced at school and that I would never find at the Institute. I had to re-enlist in the RNVR to rediscover that. It was an honest, down-to-earth sense of belonging, and it rescued me and bore me to the surface again.' Her soulful expression prompted him to say, 'Please don't be upset. I didn't bring you here to depress you.'

'You haven't depressed me.' She said, 'It never occurred to me that you'd been in the last war as well as this one.'

'Yes, I really am as old as that.' He touched the ribbons of the British Victory and War Medals on his chest to prove it.

'What's the other one?'

'The DSM. I found it in a ha'penny lucky bag.'

'I don't believe you. Anyway, by my reckoning, you're only forty-one.'

'Not until July,' he corrected her.

'That weakens your argument further. I'm thirty-two, which makes you less than nine years older than me, and you wouldn't call me old.'

'Perish the thought,' he agreed, 'but you astonish me.' He stared across the table at her. 'That's not blandishment,' he insisted, 'I really am surprised. I had you down at about twenty-five.'

'You say the kindest things.'

'And in all sincerity.' Remembering the reason for their meeting, he said, 'By the way, shouldn't you be interviewing me?'

'I've been interviewing you, and I've formed quite a clear picture of the man I'm dealing with. I just want to ask you a few questions about what you do.' She held up her hand and said, 'I know you can't tell me anything that's sensitive, but I'd like to know first of all about diving, and what it's really like.'

He considered the question before answering. Eventually, he said, 'Imagine, if you can, a dim and murky world. There's light above, but the riverbed is covered in mud, silt and the refuse of the ages. I wear lead weights in various items of my clothing, including my boots. They are to keep me submerged and on the river bed, and air is pumped into my suit so that I can adjust my buoyancy and breathe as well. I have to move slowly and carefully, because any movement muddies the water and reduces visibility. My job is to make safe the things the Luftwaffe drop on us, and to do that I need to be able to see what I'm doing. It's just like any other job, really, but sometimes I do it under water with frozen fingers and tools that feel even colder. I also have to do it without the aid of my glasses.'

'Why?'

'Because they mist up, and when they're inside a diving helmet, there's nothing I can do about it.'

'Doesn't the window-thing mist up as well?'

'Yes, it does. There's a tiny valve on the helmet that lets in water. I take some into my mouth and squirt it on to the window. It usually works.'

She grimaced, but whether it was at the idea of him doing something as uncouth as spitting, or the thought of him taking polluted river water into his mouth remained a mystery. Instead of pursuing it, she said, 'But sometimes you have to do it on dry land, don't you?'

'Yes, but that's child's play.'

'You're making light of it, although that's important.'

'To make light of it?'

'Yes. You see my job is to present your work in a way calculated to make the public feel confident, as well as making the enemy believe he's somehow failed in his act of terrorism. Basically, the public need to know they're being protected by highly professional, skilful and versatile people who are more than equal to the task. At the same time, the Nazis need to know that their efforts are being set to naught by resources, both technical and human, that are superior to theirs.'

'I'll drink to that,' he said, topping up her wineglass and his. 'I can't vouch for its veracity, but I realise you're doing it with the best of motives.'

'American Senator Hiram Johnson said, "The first casualty, when war comes, is truth", and how right he was. The British Government's line is that the truth has to be rationed and manipulated for the good of the people.'

'I'm glad my father's not here. He'd have argued with you from now until doomsday.'

'He must have been a virtuous man.'

'I suppose he was, but he also enjoyed an argument. I've known him argue against his own convictions just for the sake of a verbal exchange.' He smiled as a memory came to him. 'Let me tell you a story about him and his sense of humour.'

'All right.'

'He'd not long been made a judge when it happened.' He could see he had her full attention, which was good, because an anecdote could go either way. 'An habitually unsuccessful felon was brought before him and found guilty of attempting to hold up a post office with a child's toy, a carved, wooden pistol. An elderly man in the queue for old-age pensions disarmed him, and the other pensioners held him captive until the police arrived. After the long list of previous convictions had been read out, my father asked, "Have you anything to say before I pass sentence on you?" The prisoner said wretchedly, "No one ever takes me seriously." At that point, my father said to him, "In that case, your luck has changed, because I'm taking you seriously." The prisoner asked incredulously, "Are you really, Your Honour?" "Yes," said my father, "I'm sentencing you to five years' penal servitude." '

'I don't suppose the prisoner found it quite so funny,' she said, amused all the same.

'My father always took the line that criminals entered into a contract with the judiciary. By behaving as they did, they presented themselves as fair game.'

'I suppose he was right.'

'He certainly thought so, but then, he was very much an individual. He resisted all attempts to make him a High Court judge, and when pressure was brought to bear on him, he retired from the bench.'

'What was his objection?'

'He said he would not be a party to legalised murder. That was his definition of the death penalty. He was quite religious in a quiet sort of way.'

'You know,' she said, laying her knife and fork on her almost empty plate, 'I'm growing to like him more and more.'

'People did.'

Their conversation took various turnings, until Hazel looked at her watch and said, 'I don't know about you, but I have to be at the office by eight-thirty tomorrow morning.'

'No,' he said, 'I haven't.'

'You haven't what?'

'To be at your office at eight-thirty tomorrow. I'll probably be called to attend to something nasty that fell out of the sky during the night.'

'Be careful.' She touched his sleeve and then withdrew her hand when she realised what she'd done.

'Oh, I am.'

When he'd paid the bill, they walked out to the car.

'You know rather a lot about me,' he said.

'If you remember, that was the object of the exercise.'

'My object was to compensate you for my ill-mannered behaviour.' He opened the passenger door and held it for her.

'There was absolutely no need, but I'm glad you did, because it's been a very enjoyable evening.'

'I'm glad,' he said, starting the engine. 'Whenever I insult a lady, I try to make appropriate amends.'

'And you do it so often, I imagine, that it's no wonder you're so practised in the art.'

'Mm.' He transferred his attention to the darkness that surrounded them. 'I wonder if we'll ever get used to driving in the blackout.'

Peering through the windscreen, she said, 'Perhaps I shouldn't talk to you when you're driving.'

'No, it's better if you do. I find silence unnerving.' After a short time, he said, 'I was about to say earlier that you know quite a lot about me, but all I know about you is that you're an only child, that your parents live in Kent, and that you work at the Ministry of Information.'

'That's true, but do you really want to know about my uneventful life?'

He braked suddenly to avoid hitting a pedestrian, who continued to cross the road seemingly oblivious to his lucky escape. 'Yes, I do, and I don't believe it's all that uneventful. Only two days ago, you met me in the most peculiar circumstances, and just now, you came close to seeing me kill a jay-walking pedestrian.'

'That's true, although I'd gladly forego the latter.'

'I know what you mean. Will you let me call on you again?'

If she hesitated, it was less than noticeable. 'Yes, I will. What shall we do?'

'What would you like to do?'

'Have you seen *Wuthering Heights*?'

'No, I haven't. Does it appeal to you?'

'Only if you're keen to see it as well.'

'I haven't been to a cinema for several years. I believe they have talking pictures now, so yes, I'd like to do that.'

Ignoring his exaggeration, she said, 'They're showing it this week at the Regal in Old Gloucester Street.'

'It's almost as if they knew we were coming.' He drew up outside Hazel's building.

'Please don't bother to get out. I've only to cross the pavement.'

'Nonsense. When I escort a lady, I see my duty through to the end.' He got out and opened her door. 'Besides, we have to agree on a day and a time.'

'Of course. Thursday's usually fairly quiet.'

'Thursday it is, then.'

'I don't know the times.'

'Neither do I. I'll investigate and telephone you at the office tomorrow, if that's all right.'

'Perfect. Vincent, thank you for a lovely evening.'

'Thank you for being a part of it.' He took her gloved hands and, when she inclined her cheek, he leaned forward to administer a chaste, parting kiss. It felt strange after so long a time, but then, the whole evening had been a return to the kind of life he'd forgotten.

5

Variation on a Theme

Vincent was not called to an incident the next morning. Instead, he was summoned by telephone to *HMS Vernon.*

'Where were you last evening, Reid?' Lieutenant Commander Ghyll sounded impatient. 'We tried calling you, but you were clearly elsewhere.'

'I was out with a friend, sir.'

'Oh well, in future, if you're out for the evening, give us a call in case we need to speak to you.'

'Aye, aye, sir.'

'We were trying to tell you that you were required here this morning. You still are, so jump into your car and get here as soon as you can.'

When Vincent arrived, Lieutenant Commander Ghyll was waiting to acquaint a number of RMS officers with what appeared to be a new type of fuse.

'We discovered this little demon when a Heinkel One-Eleven crashed near Clacton with all its mines intact. It was quite a stroke of luck. It's not exactly a new type,' he explained. 'In fact, you've met this one before now, but in an earlier form.' The fuse he held up looked very much like those Vincent had been removing from Type 'A' mines, except for a blue dot between two of the four holes.

'This one relies on blue polarity. Now, I suppose I could stand here for fifteen minutes, explaining the theory of polarity to you, but I sense that such an approach would be counter-productive. I'm sure you'll agree that it's bad enough that the Nazis are trying to blind us with science, without my adding to the confusion.' Vincent could almost hear the inward sighs of relief around him, including his own.

'Instead,' said Ghyll, 'I'm going to show you how to disarm and remove the device. If any of you would then like to know more about the theory behind it, I'll be happy to enlighten you afterwards.'

He demonstrated the process, showing the class how it was essential that the fuse was kept from touching the casing, and keeping up a commentary that Vincent found infinitely more useful than a scientific lecture, of which he was sure he would have understood very little. When he'd finished, Ghyll had each member of the class perform the same operation under his scrutiny, during which they were made to recognise the knife-edge on which they were working. As their instructor pointed out, had they been handling live fuses, they would have been blown sky-high on six separate occasions. 'Surely,' he reasoned, 'once would be enough.' Their dutiful laughter had a hollow sound.

At lunch in the wardroom, Vincent made the acquaintance of the two Australians in the group. One, a man of about thirty, called Jack Andrews, told him how they had come to be in RMS.

'There was a few of us from Sydney,' he said. 'We were keen to lend a hand, weren't we, Stan?' This was to his fellow Australian, a quiet, serious man. 'We thought we'd volunteer our services, but the Royal Australian Navy couldn't get excited about our offer, so we came over here and volunteered. They put us straight into RMS, as far removed from service at sea as it's possible to get. Still, we're making ourselves useful. How did you get into it, Vince?'

'I served in a minesweeper in the last war, so it seemed the natural thing to do. I must say, I'm impressed with your story.'

'Why's that, mate?'

'Travelling across the world to do this. That's dedication.'

'Nah.' Jack looked across at Stan, who seemed equally amused by Vincent's compliment. 'We were bored.'

'Let me get you both a drink.'

'That's civil of you, Vince. Scotch and soda for me, please.'

'I'll have the same, mate, if that's all right,' said Stan.

Their conversation continued, and Vincent was agreeably surprised by the way in which he'd been accepted quite naturally by the two as 'Vince', as if they'd known him for years. It was the easy and genuine kind of company he'd tried, and probably failed, to describe to Commander Todd at his interview.

Knowing that Jack and Stan were both operating in London, he gave them each one of his cards. 'If you're ever stuck for somewhere to stay in London,' he said, 'give me a call. You'll be very welcome.'

Jack examined his thoughtfully and said, 'Thanks, Vince. That's very generous of you.' He continued to be fascinated by the card. 'Are you really a professor, Vince?'

'Don't be impressed,' said Vincent.

'But we are, aren't we, Stan?'

'Yair,' said Stan, also staring at the card.

'And you're just like an ordinary bloke,' observed Jack with an air of surprise.

'I hope so.'

Vincent wasn't called upon immediately to attend a Type 'B', as the new mine was designated. His next event was meeting Hazel, as they had arranged.

'You spoil me, Vincent,' she said, 'picking me up at my door like this.'

'Not in the least.' He got in and started the engine.

'I like the fact that you're so courteous and formal,' she said, adding, 'and when I say "formal", I mean it as a compliment.'

'I hadn't thought of taking it any other way.' He smiled and said, 'I met two Australians in Portsmouth, who were anything but formal, but they were all the better for it. They'd travelled eleven thousand miles to take part in the war, and they're the most genuine characters you could imagine.'

'Thank goodness for people like them.'

'Exactly.' As they approached Old Gloucester Street, he asked, 'Have you read *Wuthering Heights*?'

'Yes, some time ago. Have you?'

'Yes.'

Something in his tone made her ask, 'Didn't you enjoy it?'

'Yes, I did. I think it's a wonderful novel, but they say it's not a good idea to read a book before seeing the film.'

'I know what you mean, but let's reserve judgement until we've seen it.'

'That's a good idea, Hazel.' He wished he hadn't made his observation, now. Hazel was so fair-minded, she made him feel negative, and that wasn't his normal state of mind. He tried to sound more constructive. 'Who's in it? Do you know?'

'I only know about Merle Oberon, Laurence Olivier and Flora Robson.'

'That's a solid front row.'

'Oh, I just remembered....'

'Who?'

'David Niven. You know, *Raffles*.'

Vincent gave up. 'I told you I hadn't been to a cinema for several years.'

'I thought you were joking when you said that.'

'Hardly. You have to remember that I lead a solitary life, and I do feel that entertainments such as films and plays are much better enjoyed in company.' He parked at the side of the road.

'I agree, and that is as far as I, as a single woman am allowed to comment.'

'It must be an exasperating existence,' he said, opening his door to get out.

'It is,' she said when he'd opened her door, 'and it takes a man of your insight to realise that.' She took his arm, and they walked the short distance to the cinema.

He asked, 'Do you favour the dress circle?'

'There's no dress circle,' she told him patiently, 'only a balcony.'

'How prosaic. Let's go up there.'

They climbed the stairs, and an usherette showed them to a double seat, which appeared to be one of only a few remaining options. Clearly, *Wuthering Heights* was a popular attraction.

Hazel whispered, 'This is one of those double seats for courting couples.'

'Is courting an obligation?'

'I don't think so.'

The supporting film, which seemed to have been set in an American wilderness, ended, to be followed by a short film from the Ministry of Information. Hazel buried her face in her hands as the Minister for National Service made his official statement.

Vincent asked, 'You didn't write his script, did you?'

'No,' she whispered, removing her hands from her face, 'No one but a politician could write a script like that. I'm only guilty of setting the whole thing up.'

Partly out of sympathy and in some way to do justice to the courting seat, he took her right hand and held it. 'I came expecting music,' he said.

'Apparently, the organist has heeded the minister's advice and joined the RAF.'

'I suppose it was the next stage after making his entrance on a lift, although, by that token, you'd think the Fleet Air Arm would have been the more appropriate choice.'

'At all events, they haven't yet been able to find a substitute.'

'That's a shame, but I'm glad he's doing his bit for King and country.'

The main picture was about to begin. Vincent gave Hazel's hand a gentle squeeze and was gratified when she made no attempt to withdraw it.

The film began, as it should, on the wild Yorkshire moors. Vincent wondered if the filming had been carried out on the actual moors, because they looked quite authentic; at least, he thought they did. He'd never been there to know for certain, but the effect was certainly convincing.

Flora Robson was immediately engaging, but the magic really began when Olivier made his entrance, and there were two stars in the scene. Vincent suspected that the film would owe little to Emily Brontë, but that was only to be expected. What the clutch of consummate actors would make of it remained to be seen.

The film progressed, and the company was joined by Merle Oberon, who always exerted a charm of her own. He was thinking about that when Hazel removed her hand to adjust the skirt of her coat. Having done that, she smiled and took his hand again.

When the action moved to the Linton household, Hazel whispered, 'David Niven.'

His was a new face as far as Vincent was concerned, but he seemed to compensate for lack of experience with natural charm. He felt that the plot was about to leave the rails at this stage, but he surprised himself by accepting the fact, reminding himself that he was watching an American romantic film about a novel that the director probably didn't understand, anyway. Maybe he was learning tolerance at last.

The final scene owed nothing to Emily Brontë and everything to Hollywood, and Vincent was surprised to hear a sniff from Hazel. Without taking his eyes from the screen, he handed her the handkerchief from his breast pocket. She took it gratefully, and he wondered, not for the first time, why ladies' handkerchiefs were so tiny, when nature had made them the more abundantly tearful sex.

They left the Yorkshire moors with two sets of footprints telling their own story, they stood during the playing of the National Anthem, and finally, made their way outside to the car.

He asked, 'Did you eat earlier?'

'Yes. Did you?'

'Yes, I thought I'd better check.'

'What did you think of the film, Vincent?'

'Let me think,' he said. 'It certainly departed from Emily Brontë's version of events. Having said that, though, as a romantic film, it does seem to work, and I think we were looking at a very different form. I must say I enjoyed it.'

'I agree. You can't compare apples with bananas.'

'Particularly when there are no bananas to be had,' he agreed.

A few streets later, Hazel said, 'I'd invite you in for a drink, but I'm afraid shortages have left the cupboard embarrassingly bare.'

'That can be remedied.'

'At this time of night?'

'Oh, yes.' He parked outside his house. 'I'll be back in a jiffy,' he said.

There was a bottle of Burgundy he'd brought up from the cellar for ready use, and he took that. Locking the front door again, he returned to the car and handed the bottle to Hazel.

'How marvellous,' she said.

'Not really. There's a cellar full of wine that my father put down in the twenties and thirties.' He started the car. 'Naturally, I don't publicise the fact. You're the only person who knows.'

'And I shan't tell a soul.'

'I knew I could count on you, Hazel.' He drove to her flat.

'Where does your assistant live? You said he lived in Bloomsbury.'

'Just around the corner from you. I may very well be calling for him tomorrow.'

They arrived at Hazel's flat and she let them in, waiting until he was in the passageway before she closed the blackout curtain and switched on the light.

He helped her out of her coat and removed his own while she hung up her hat and coat.

'Let me help you with yours,' she said, turning to him.

'You're too late.' He hung up his coat and cap beside her things.

'Spoilsport. Come through to the sitting room. The blackout's in place. I'll get a corkscrew and some glasses.'

He walked into the room he remembered as her sitting room, and switched on the light. It was naturally as he remembered it, furnished in the Art Deco style. Even the photographs were in the ever-popular geometric, silver frames. One, in particular, attracted his notice. It was of a young man and taken in the last ten years, he imagined. Men's styles of clothing changed so infrequently, that it was impossible to pinpoint the period.

'That was Edward, my fiancé,' said Hazel, coming into the room with the opened bottle and two wine glasses.

'I'm sorry. I couldn't help noticing it.'

'That's all right. I wasn't exactly hiding it away.' She poured two glasses of wine and said, 'He was a foreign correspondent. We were engaged until nineteen thirty-five, when he met his end in Abyssinia.'

'I'm so sorry, Hazel. Was he killed in the fighting?'

'Nothing so dramatic. He caught a horrible disease and died before he could be shipped home.'

'I really am terribly sorry. As I said the last time we met, you know an awful lot about me, whereas I know hardly anything about you. I must seem unforgivably self-centred.'

'Take a seat, Vincent.' She waved vaguely in the direction of an armchair. 'You're not at all self-centred,' she said, handing him a glass of wine. 'The reason I know so much about you is that I was interviewing you in the restaurant, and the reason you know so little about me is that I left you no time to ask questions.' She paused to say, 'Incidentally, I hope you're warm enough. This electric fire is barely capable of heating the room.'

'I'm very comfortable, thank you, but to return to your history, I know that you're a journalist. Where did you work before the war?'

'I spent some time on the *Daily Record* and then *The Sentinel*. The Ministry of Information asked me to join them at the start of the war, and I'm still not convinced it was a wise decision on my part to accept their invitation.'

'Why do you say that?' It seemed important that he knew such things, if only because it eased his feeling of selfishness.

'That little conversation we had about the truth, remember? "The first casualty when war comes is truth". The British people can't be told everything. Some things are too awful for them to know, but there are other instances when I feel that we're lying to them for no better reason than that it's become a habit.'

He nodded, finding no cause for disagreement. 'But you're a servant of the politicians, and politics is, as everyone knows, a mendacious business.'

She laughed. 'How sceptical you are.'

'I've lived through a world war and the political posturing and manoeuvring that followed it. Who can blame me for harbouring doubts about our elected leaders?' A thought, prompted by the evening's entertainment, came to him, and he said, 'That's why I believe it's healthy for us to enjoy the kind of self-indulgence we experienced this evening. The screenwriter's version of *Wuthering Heights* is largely dishonest, but harmlessly so. If we must live in a dishonest society, let's enjoy the innocent side of it.'

Hazel took the bottle and topped up their glasses. 'You're remarkably balanced in your attitudes, Vincent,' she remarked.

'That's the analytical side of me taking charge,' he told her. 'Political connivance is one thing, but artistic creativity is harmless. The corridors of power remain an amoral battleground, whereas Goldwyn's version of *Wuthering Heights* is no less worthy than a piece of contemporary art.' By association, his mind returned to the fuse he'd seen at *HMS Vernon*. 'In essence, it amounts to no more than a variation on a theme.'

6

An Alarm and an Excursion

Curiously, the telephone remained silent until a little after nine, when the caller turned out to be Lieutenant Commander Ghyll.

'Good morning, Reid.'

'Good morning, sir.'

'I want you to pack an overnight bag and go to Hornsea.'

'Where's that, sir?'

'It's a town on the Yorkshire coast, where two examples believed to be Type "B" were washed ashore yesterday.' In an even more guarded tone, he went on to say, 'Unfortunately, there's now only one. The officer who was working on the first was killed this morning.'

'Poor devil. Once more unto the beach, eh?'

'What? Oh yes, I'm afraid so, but it's better that you know the risk involved.'

'I think you made that known during your demonstration, sir.'

'It's good that you were paying attention, Reid.'

'The prospect of instant death does rather concentrate the mind, sir.'

'Quite. You should take your assistant with you. What's his name?'

'Able Seaman Riddle, sir.'

'Yes, take him. Seeing his officer blown to fragments has left the rating involved in this morning's unfortunate incident somewhat affected by it.'

Vincent was hardly surprised. He hoped the service would take a sympathetic line. 'Where are we staying, sir?'

'At a guest house called, believe it or not, "Sea View". The local constabulary will direct you. Apparently, the owners of the guest house opened their shutters at our request, so we're rather grateful to them. I imagine they'll have changed the linen by this time.'

'I'm sure they will, sir.' Vincent could only wonder about their state of mind, having been host to a naval officer, now dead and presumably a rating rendered *hors de combat* by shock.

'Unfortunately, we've had to put both you and your rating in the same accommodation. We had no choice in the matter, Hornsea being sparsely populated and with other accommodation closed for the duration.'

'That doesn't constitute a problem, sir. I'd go as far as to say I welcome it. Able Seaman Riddle is an intelligent, educated and cultured young man.'

'Is he, by Jove? Well, don't let me keep you. Good luck.'

'Thank you, sir.'

It was the work of a few minutes for Vincent to pack his valise and put it into his car.

When he reached Jimmy's address, he rang the bell as usual, but the door was opened on this occasion by a woman.

'Mrs Riddle? I'm Lieutenant Reid, Jim… your son's officer. May I see him, please?'

'Of course. Come inside, Lieutenant.' Raising her voice, she called, 'Philip! Lieutenant Reid's here to see you.' She showed Vincent into a small morning room *cum* sitting room, and said, 'I'm afraid I've no coffee, Lieutenant. Would you like a cup of tea?'

'No, thank you, Mrs Riddle. I'm afraid we must be away.' He made a mental note of Jimmy's proper name.

Jimmy arrived in the doorway and came to attention.

'Good morning, Jim… Riddle.'

'Good morning, sir.'

'I'd like you to pack an overnight bag. Accommodation's been arranged, and we're going to Yorkshire.'

'Aye, aye, sir.' He ran upstairs to carry out the order.

'Yorkshire,' said Mrs Riddle. 'That'll make a nice change. Philip's never been there.'

'We do tend to travel, Mrs Riddle.' He only hoped that Jimmy would return in a fit state to report, however guardedly, on his brief visit.

'Philip enjoys his work but he doesn't say much about it.'

'Good.'

'He tells us you're a musician, Lieutenant.'

'When circumstances allow, yes, that's correct. I gather your son was keen on studying music, Mrs Riddle.'

'Yes, it's an awful shame, but there's nothing we can do about it.'

'It's not bound to be the end of his musical career, as I've already told him.'

'Oh, good.'

Vincent wondered how much Jimmy's mother understood about the life of a music student. Certainly, it was no time to enlighten her, and he was spared the need to make further conversation, when Jimmy came downstairs carrying a canvas valise.

'I'm ready, sir.'

'Very good. We'll be back, probably late tomorrow, I imagine, Mrs Riddle.'

He turned discreetly while Jimmy took his leave of his mother.

Finally, she said, 'Off you go, then. Be careful and mind your manners.'

As they took the steps down to the pavement, Jimmy said apologetically, 'My mum does tend to fuss, sir.'

'It's one of a mother's prime attributes, Jimmy. Be thankful that she cares about you.' He opened his car and stowed Jimmy's valise inside.

Lively conversation made the journey to Yorkshire seem shorter than it was. Vincent learned that Jimmy shared his passion for the Classical era, and they chatted easily about the music of Haydn, Cimarosa and Mozart.

'It was the greatest tragedy for music itself that Mozart died at thirty-five, sir.' They had just entered the East Riding of Yorkshire.

'There's no denying it, Jimmy, but it's almost as sad that he was the engineer of his own downfall.'

'What makes you say that, sir?'

'The most likely cause of his death was kidney failure, and that points in his case to drinking copious quantities of red wine on an empty stomach. He spent most of his adult life in poverty because he and Constanza were jointly and equally incapable of managing their finances. When he had money, he was extravagantly openhanded with it, and when he could afford to eat, he preferred to drink instead.'

'Would you say that makes his early death less of a tragedy, sir?'

'No, that's not at all what I'm saying. I'm just appraising you of the facts.' With a quick smile, he said, 'The real tragedy, as far as you and I are concerned, is that we're denied the music he might have written had he lived longer.'

'By comparison, Haydn lived a full life, didn't he, sir? He gave us full value.'

'He certainly did. You know, there are those who make the mistake of comparing Mozart with Haydn, when they were basically chalk and cheese.'

'Were they, sir?'

'Absolutely. Haydn was a symphonist, whereas Mozart was an opera composer.'

They continued to chat until they arrived in Hornsea, where they found the police station quite easily.

'Follow the coast road, sir,' said the desk sergeant, 'and you'll find an officer on duty. We had to post him there to keep sightseers away from the mine.'

'Quite.'

'It was a terrible business, this morning, sir.'

'Yes, but don't go on about it, or you might have another terrible business on your hands.'

'I'm sorry, sir. It was the first excitement we've had around here, and it turned out to be a tragedy.'

'Thank you, Sergeant. We'll be on our way.'

Jimmy asked, 'Are you going to be all right, doing it immediately, sir? I thought you might like a cup of tea first.'

'It's not a bad idea, Jimmy. I just wanted to get away from that Job's comforter of a sergeant. Let's find the mine, and then you can go foraging.'

'Aye, aye, sir.'

They saw the policeman first. He was standing at the side of the road, and a large expanse of beach and what appeared to be sand dunes had been roped off.

'Good afternoon, sir.' The policeman saluted Vincent as he got out of his car.

'Good afternoon, Constable. When's high tide?'

'High tide, sir? Between seven and seven-thirty this evening, sir.'

'Thank you. Have you any idea where we might be able to find a cup of tea?'

'Yes, sir.'

That was promising. 'Will you tell my assistant while I have a look at this mine?'

'By all means, sir.'

Vincent heard the policeman give directions to Jimmy. Then, he heard him say, 'Tell her PC White sent you. She'll look kindlier on you then.' Vincent smiled, pleased to have found a man of initiative. He changed his shoes for seaboots and then crawled between the ropes and made his way across the sand dunes.

When he reached the mine, he found two of the plates exposed. The other two, which included the all-important anti-handling device, were under what must have amounted to six inches of sand. He walked back to the car and found Jimmy with two mugs of tea.

'Thanks, Jimmy, and well done.'

'Thank you, sir.'

'It's a difficult one. The mine is resting almost on the side housing the anti-handling device, so we need to roll it until both pairs of plates are accessible.'

'I see, sir.' Jimmy accepted the news in his usual deadpan way.

'But first, let's enjoy our tea.' A cup of tea afterwards would be even better, but he was reluctant to make plans so far ahead.

When they'd finished their tea, Jimmy took the mugs back to their owner and returned to the car.

'Bring the non-magnetic spade.'

Jimmy had it already in his hands. Vincent took two coils of rope from the car, and they walked to the place where the mine lay in the sand.

'I want you to start digging on that side so that we can roll it.' He indicated the side where the plates were exposed, and Jimmy began digging gently. Vincent took the stethoscope from his bag and proceeded to monitor the state of the mine. 'If I tell you to run, Jimmy,

I know you've done it before, but run like hell for the sand dunes, and then flatten yourself in the bottom of one and pray.'

'Aye, aye, sir,' Jimmy continued to dig.

When the trench was dug, Vincent examined the nose of the mine and then the tail. 'Now, there and there,' he said, 'so that I can get a line round each end.'

Again, Jimmy dug carefully until about two feet of the nose and a foot of the tail lay exposed.

'Well done, Jimmy. Now, go back to the safety point and wait for me.'

'Aye, aye, sir.' Jimmy retired to a safe distance, while Vincent passed a noose round each end of the mine, securing them with slip-knots, before returning to the safety point, carefully paying out the two lengths of rope as he went.

Vincent was pleased to see the policeman waiting with Jimmy. He asked, 'Do you fancy being a part of this escapade, Constable?'

'Why not, sir, if it's in the national interest?'

'Stout fellow. We're perfectly safe back here, so we're going to haul on this rope and roll the mine over so that it comes to rest over the little trench that Jimmy's just dug.'

'Just give the word, sir.'

Vincent gathered and tied the ropes together, creating a bight that three men could grasp. 'After three. One, two, three, pull!' All three of them hauled on the lines, and a final pull rolled the mine into position.

The policeman asked, 'What happens now, sir?'

'We wait seventeen seconds.' He placed his hands over his ears and the others did the same.

Jimmy was counting. '...four, elephant, five, elephant, six, elephant...' He reached seventeen and his face relaxed into a grin of satisfaction.

'You sounded like Hannibal taking roll-call, Jimmy.'

'It's the way I time a film when I'm developing it, sir.'

'Most effective, I'm sure.' Vincent had learned something new about his assistant, but he brushed the thought aside for the moment. 'Stay here, both of you,' he said. He walked back to the mine and was rewarded by the sight of four exposed plates. He listened briefly, using the stethoscope, and started work on the anti-handling device. The plate came away easily enough, and he was able to sever and tape off the wires. It was the next part that was the most critical. He had to remove the device without allowing it to touch the casing of the mine. There was barely a quarter of an inch of clearance on either side, so he had to work slowly and meticulously. He could imagine only too well how the unfortunate officer who'd tackled the first mine must have made the fatal connection. It was all too easy with shaking hands, but he had to forget about his predecessor and concentrate every microscopic step of the way. By the time he'd drawn it, he was soaked in perspiration. Now breathing properly, but with hands still shaking, he laid the device on one side while he attended to the remaining three.

Eventually, he stood upright and gave the thumbs up sign to Jimmy, who joined him to pack everything away.

'Well done, sir.'

'Thank you, Jimmy.'

They walked back up the beach, over the sand dunes and back to the car, where PC White was waiting for them with three mugs of tea.

'You're a good hand, PC White,' said Vincent, taking one. 'Do you think your sergeant will let me make a trunk call from the station?'

'Only if you observe the correct procedure, sir.' The Constable winked as he said it.

'Someone will come and take the mine away,' said Vincent. 'It's perfectly harmless now.'

When they had finished their tea, they made the return journey to the police station, where the same sergeant was on duty.

'All done, Sergeant,' reported Vincent.

'Oh, aye? Champion.'

'Do you think I might make a trunk call? I have to report to my senior officer in Portsmouth.'

'You'll need to enter it in the book and sign it, sir.'

'After a job like the one we've just completed, I'd be happy to write it on the wall of the heads, Sergeant.' He made the necessary entry in the telephone log book and called the exchange.

'Number, please?'

'I'd like Portsmouth two four two one, please.'

'What number are you calling from?'

Vincent gave the number of the police station.

'That's Hornsea Police Station.' It sounded like an accusation.

'I know. Will you put my call through, please?'

'Hold the line, caller.'

Vincent waited until *HMS Vernon* came on the line, and he asked for Lieutenant Commander Ghyll. He was rewarded a couple of minutes later.

'Ghyll.'

'Good afternoon, sir. Reid here. I'd just like to report that the monster is now safe, and ready to be winched and carried away.'

'Well done, Reid. I must say, we were quite alarmed when we heard about this morning's disaster, so it's a great relief.'

'I can't disagree, sir.'

'Let me know when you're back in London.'

'Aye, aye, sir.'

7

May

Motor Horns and Bicycle Pumps

Once again, Lieutenant Commander Ghyll held up a detonator for the class to see. 'When a mine is taken from deep water and brought into the shallows, an imbalance is created between the pressure inside the detonator and the pressure outside it. That is when it tends to explode.' He looked around the class, as he so often did after a dramatic disclosure, and seemed satisfied that his pupils were suitably impressed. 'As I speak, the people in the laboratory are working on a new device that will equalise the pressures safely, and we expect it to become available soon. Until then, we have to improvise.' He picked up something that looked like a rubber ball. 'You probably recognise this,' he said, 'as the bulb of an old-fashioned motor horn. Under water, it can be screwed on to the detonator housing, and water, obviously at its ambient pressure, can be introduced. On dry land, you will need this.' He picked up a bicycle pump and screwed the connector on to the horn. 'By operating the pump carefully, you will create a pressure of ten pounds through a non-return valve, in the same way. Are there any questions so far?'

There were lots of questions, not all of them facetious, and Ghyll spent some time dealing with the more sensible queries.

Eventually, everyone was satisfied, and lunch beckoned. However, before the class could secure, a Wren entered the room with a sheet of paper which she handed to Lieutenant Commander Ghyll, who held up his hand to the class. It seemed that he had more information to impart.

'As you probably know,' he said, 'a leadership crisis occurred in Parliament when the Labour Party refused to join a coalition government led by the Prime Minister.' Presumably, for the benefit of anyone who'd been out of circulation for some time, he added, 'Mr Neville Chamberlain, that is.' Referring to the sheet of paper in his hand, he said, 'I can now tell you that Mr Chamberlain has resigned from his post as Prime Minister, and that His Majesty has asked our First Lord, Mr Winston Churchill, to form a government.'

There was a hearty cheer, and the class broke up for lunch in the wardroom.

Vincent shared the class's approval. Even though he'd entertained doubts about Churchill's performance in other capacities, the first Lord was the only realistic choice for Prime Minister, he felt, as the only other obvious contender, Lord Halifax, seemed completely devoid of fighting spirit.

'It seems to me,' said Hazel that evening, 'that he's the best of a bad lot. I just hope he doesn't make a mess of things, as he did at the Treasury. I was a student at the time and very young, but I remember it vividly.' They had just eaten at Hazel's flat, having combined some of their rations.

'I see him in a more positive light,' said Vincent. 'He's certainly had his less-successful moments, but this job is different. Chamberlain was ineffectual and far too conceited to be able to inspire anyone. On the other hand, Churchill is aggressive – he's never made any secret of his feelings about Hitler – and with his gift for oratory, he may well motivate the nation.' He picked up the bottle of wine and was about to refill her glass, when she said, 'Let me do the dishes first, and then we can settle.'

'Let me help you.'

'It's been a long time since I had such an offer, but there's very little to do.'

'Even so, I'd like to help you.'

'Very well. I'll wash and you can dry.'

He helped her carry the dishes into the tiny kitchen and picked up a tea towel.

‘It still seems odd, a man doing this kind of thing,’ she said.

‘I do it every day at home. I just hope my guests are similarly inclined.’

‘Yes, I remember you had someone staying.’ She began running hot water into the sink.

‘It was an offer I made at a meeting in Portsmouth. There were two Australian officers there, and I offered them a bed for the night, should they ever need one. Now, this chap, Jack Andrews, has taken me at my word, and he’s staying tonight until he can fix himself up with a *pied-à-terre*.’

‘But shouldn’t you be there as host?’

‘No, he’s enjoying one of the delights offered by the Admiralty.’

‘Really?’

‘Yes, a Wren third officer. I imagine three would certainly be a crowd.’

‘Ah.’ Realisation emerged. ‘You’re a generous soul, Vincent.’

‘Live and let live, I say. In any case, his leave expires in two days’ time, and then he’ll have to be on the telephone and available for work.’

Hazel took the dried dishes and cutlery from him and put them away. ‘Let’s go and finish the wine, Vincent.’

‘Lead the way.’

As he took his seat, she picked up the bottle and filled his glass.

‘Thank you.’

‘Your film should be ready for screening soon.’

‘My film? Will I be invited to the premiere?’

‘No.’

He produced a petulant face. ‘What’s the point in becoming a film star if I can’t attend the premiere of my film and wave to the newsreel cameras?’

‘The whole film is going to be less than ten minutes long.’

‘Don’t tell me you’ve cut the sequence between my descent into the dock and my triumphant reappearance, spanner in hand and fish swimming inside my helmet.’

‘Just a minute,’ she said, picking up a shorthand notepad and a pencil, ‘you’ve given me an idea.’ Hiding the pad from him, she busied herself with the pencil, at the same time speaking the words. ‘Fish… swimming inside… diving helmet.’

'I don't believe you.' He got up to look, but she hid her work from him, clearly enjoying his discomfiture. 'Let me see,' he demanded.

'No, it's Ministry property.'

'Ministry fiddlesticks.' He knew she was playing a game, but he wanted to know what she'd written. 'Show me that page.'

'No.' She moved from her chair to evade him and sat on the sofa with the notepad behind her back.

'You can't avoid me so easily,' he told her, sitting beside her and reaching for the pad.

With mock-censure, she asked, 'Vincent Reid, what *are* you doing?'

'I'm acting with the noblest of motives.' His hand closed on the notepad, and he realised that his face was almost in contact with hers. Their foreheads touched briefly.

In a tone tinged with expectation, she said, 'I believe you'd go to any lengths to find out what I've written about you.' She made no attempt to distance herself from him, so he moved closer, tentatively touching her lips with his. A moment later, she joined him readily, as if, at a long-awaited signal, some physical barrier had suddenly been lowered.

After a while, they parted breathlessly. 'At this point,' he said, 'I'm supposed to apologise and say that it hadn't been my intention, but that I was seized by impulse.'

'You really have been a stranger to the cinema these past few years,' she observed. 'No one says that kind of thing nowadays. In any case, I think it had been on the cards for some time.'

'Only a cad would give way to impatience,' he assured her solemnly.

'And that's the last thing anyone could call you.'

They kissed again, less urgently, but with the special kind of pleasure that comes with a new intimacy.

'Do you still want to see my notepad?'

'No, it doesn't seem quite so important now.'

'Oh, go on. Have a look.' She retrieved the pad from its hiding place and showed him a sketch of a man in a diving suit with his helmet half-filled with water and populated by fish.

'A very accurate portrayal,' he told her.

'I shudder when I think of you under water,' she said seriously.

'Please don't. With any luck, this could be a long war, and you could fret your life away.'

His response seemed to have puzzled her. 'Why do you say, "With any luck"?'

'Because if it were to end soon, the likeliest outcome would be a victory for the Nazis. The longer we can stay at the wicket, the better our chances are.'

'Do you really think so?'

'I do. With the fortunate exception of the Navy, our forces have been starved of funding since the last war, whereas the Nazis have been rearming almost since they took control. Things are going badly in Norway, and our only chance is to stonewall the enemy until our government can persuade the Americans to lend a hand.'

'Oh, dear.' Her expression was glum. 'This is what comes of working at the Ministry, where optimism is compulsory whatever the truth happens to be. Blind assurance is a habit.'

'I'm sorry,' he said, taking her hand between his, 'I didn't really come here to depress you.'

She smiled forgivingly. 'Whatever your purpose was, I'm nonetheless glad you came.'

'And with that thought, I must leave you.'

'Do you think your Australian friend might be back already?'

'Not a chance, but I mustn't be far from the telephone. I've already been told I must call *HMS Vernon* if I'm out for the evening.' He softened the news by kissing her again.

He was called the next morning to a parachute mine that had landed beside a warehouse near Shadwell Dock. Its fall had been broken by its parachute, which now lay, torn and partly suspended from the warehouse chimney. One look at the mine told Vincent that all four plates were exposed, but that its detonator was of the new kind. Accordingly, he took the car horn with its valve, and the bicycle pump, from his car.

'See if you can find some water, Jimmy,' he said, but don't bring a metal bucket or any other container beyond the gatepost.'

'Aye, aye, sir.' Jimmy set off in search of a building where he could get some water. Meanwhile, Vincent examined the motor horn device, which consisted of a large rubber bulb and a lever-operated shut-off valve and pressure gauge. He could only hope that the gauge was accurate. A threaded bush had been brazed on to the valve so that the whole contraption could be screwed on to the detonator. There was also a one-way valve of the kind found on a bicycle inner tube, that enabled the pump to be connected.

After only a few minutes, Jimmy returned with a galvanised bucket filled with water, which he placed beside the gatepost in accordance with his orders.

'Well done, Jimmy. Go back to the safety point.' Vincent looked up at the grey sky. 'If it comes on to rain, you can shelter in someone's doorway. I'll shout if I need you.' Because of the mine, the area had been evacuated, and some buildings had been left with their doors open when their occupants hurried to safety.

He fixed the pump to the bulb and carefully built up the pressure to ten pounds before closing the valve. Then, he took it to the bucket of water and held it beneath the surface to check for leaks. There were none, so he returned to the mine. Still, sceptical, he removed the plate and screwed the device carefully on to the detonator. When it was tightly in place, he opened the shut-off valve to allow the pressures to become equalised.

Despite Lieutenant Commander Ghyll's assurances, it was still with enormous relief that he removed the detonator.

The other three seemed easy enough by comparison, but he was no less careful in removing them.

Eventually, he and Jimmy were able to pack away the equipment and leave the site. He stopped to speak to the police inspector in charge of security. 'It's dealt with,' he said. 'Someone will come to take away the mine, but it's harmless now.'

'Thank you, Lieutenant,' said the inspector. 'It's been quite a cliff-hanger.'

'I can't disagree with that,' said Vincent.

The inspector glanced at the bag containing the equipment and said, 'I imagine you have to carry some very sophisticated instruments in your line of work.'

Vincent smiled. 'You'd be surprised.'

He dropped Jimmy at his home and then returned to the house, where he found the morning's post in its secure cage. He flipped through the bundle of bills and war notices until he came to a buff envelope labelled *War Office – Important. Do Not Discard.* Intrigued, he opened the envelope and took out the letter, reading it twice, because he found its content less than agreeable.

8

Rest and Recuperation – and Removal

With the waiter now at another table, Hazel asked, 'What's the buzz?'

They both smiled at the naval slang expression she'd learned from Vincent and now used freely.

'I'm about to be evicted,' he announced.

Disbelief made her frown. 'Surely, the house is your property.'

'It will eventually be returned to me. It what condition… well, that remains to be seen, but it will shortly be home to a department of the War Office. They're giving me three weeks to find alternative accommodation and to remove whatever furniture and effects I need.'

'That's disgraceful, Vincent,' said Hazel, reaching across the table for his hand. 'There must be empty houses in London that they could use instead.'

'It's felt that one occupant in a house that size constitutes wastefulness, even when the house is my own.' With a weary look, he said, 'It's not all bad news. Jimmy and I are being rested. We've been given seventy-two hours rest and recuperation, which is better than trying to make removal arrangements at the same time as rendering mines safe.'

Squeezing his hand in helpless sympathy, she said, 'Any help I can give is yours for the asking. When are you going to see the estate agent?'

'An Army officer is coming in the morning. I'll begin house hunting as soon as I can push him out of the door.'

'I'll come with you, if it'll help.'

He smiled for the first time. 'I may just need an escort to the estate agent's office,' he said. 'I've never had to deal with one in the past.'

'You'll be safe with me looking after you. What else needs to be done? There's the removal, of course.'

'Rather a lot will need to be put into store.'

'The removal firms take care of that.' After brief consideration, she said, 'Let's make a list of things that have to be done, in order of priority. I'll help you to do that and I'll come over.... When are you expecting the Army officer?'

'He's coming at nine o' clock. I asked them to make it earlier, as I had so much to do, but they're difficult people to deal with.'

'Maybe he needs a substantial breakfast before he can face a dispossessed house owner.'

Captain Connelly looked as if he'd enjoyed many a substantial breakfast as well as lunch and dinner; in fact, Vincent's instant dislike of him was fuelled only partly by resentment at the seizure of his family home, but also by the sight of a well-fed man in time of shortages.

'Wipe your boots, Captain,' he told him. 'That's what the doormat's for.' Connelly had already tried to enter without invitation, and that had also annoyed Vincent.

'Downstairs rooms, how many?' Connelly held a clipboard in one hand and a pencil in the other.

'What?'

'Ah asked ye how many downstairs rooms there are.'

'English is my first language, Captain. By that, I do not mean pidgin English. I'm not a coolie or punkah wallah, so kindly refrain from treating me as such.' He made a mental resumé of the ground floor and said, 'Not counting the kitchen and larder, there are four.'

'And they are?'

'Do I have to tell you again, Captain Connelly, to address me in English?'

'Are ye sayin' that 'cause I'm Scots?' It had clearly been a point of contention in the past.

'It's all too obvious that you're Glaswegian, but even that does not excuse your ill-mannered and aggressive attitude, nor your abbreviated

English. I'm referring again to your irritating habit of communicating in snarled phrases. Now, what do you wish to know?'

Impatiently, Connelly told him, 'Ah need to know what the ground floor rooms are.'

'You had only to ask. They are the morning room, which is where we're standing, the sitting room-*cum*-drawing room, the dining room and the study.'

Connelly looked around him and asked, 'Where's the sitting room?'

'Across the passage.'

'Here?' He pointed to the open door.

'Yes.'

Connelly stood in the doorway, tapping the architrave with his swagger stick.

'I'd rather you didn't do that, Captain. I've no doubt the paintwork will be damaged all too soon, but there's no need for you to make a start now.'

Connelly made no response, but walked over to the piano, gave it a cursory inspection and struck several keys, producing a loud discord.

'Mind your fingers.' Vincent lowered the fall, narrowly missing Connelly's podgy fingers.

'Ah imagine ye'll be leaving the joanna behind?' He spoke the words without a hint of irony.

'Do you hold a commission in the Royal Corps of Red-Nosed Comedians, Captain?' Vincent glanced at the officer's shoulder flash. 'No, I see you're a pay clerk, so I'll make allowances for your ignorance and explain that this piano is of the highest quality. It's a Steinway, the very Rolls-Royce of pianos, and I'm hardly going to leave it for a bunch of drunken pongoes so that they can hammer out "Four-and-Twenty Virgins", decorate the lid with the rings from a thousand whisky tumblers and beer glasses, and stub out their cigarettes on the keys.'

Connelly waved his stick around the room and said, 'This is going to be the officers' mess. They'll need some off-duty entertainment.'

'In that case,' said Vincent, 'they'll have to make their own arrangements, because this piano is leaving with me.'

'Ah'll be leavin' a copy of this with ye. It explains that you're obliged to leave behind certain items of furniture.'

'I'll cross that bridge when I come to it, Connelly. In the meantime, a piano is not and never will be an item of furniture.'

'So ye say.' He perused his form again and asked, 'Is there a cellar?'

'Of course there is, and let me tell you before we go down there, that its contents are also leaving with me.'

'Listen,' said Connelly. 'As far as Ah'm aware, you are wearing the insignia of a lieutenant in some branch of the Navy. Ah'm also aware, if you're not, that Ah'm a captain and therefore superior to you, and Ah'll thank ye to remember that an' address me as "sir".'

'Connelly,' said Vincent, whose patience was ebbing rapidly, 'you'd struggle to establish superiority over a bewildered jellyfish, and you should count yourself lucky that I address you as civilly as I do, because you don't deserve it. Now, will you complete your foul inventory and leave, so that I can start looking for somewhere to live?'

'He actually expected me to leave the piano and the contents of the cellar behind for the troops' benefit.'

'No, surely not.' Hazel squeezed his hand in the way that had become familiar.

'Some of those billeting officers live in their own world,' observed the estate agent from the driving seat.

'It's a disgusting world, wherever it is,' said Vincent.

'I think you'll like the house we're going to view, Lieutenant Reid,' said the agent, changing the subject to a brighter one. 'Its owner left London earlier this year and put all his furniture into store, leaving you a blank canvas.' He pulled into Wilton Road outside a row of houses not unlike Vincent's, at least from the outside, although they were somewhat smaller.

They followed the agent into the house and were pleasantly surprised. There were three rooms on the ground floor, all well-kept, and the bedrooms were in similar condition. The bathroom provided the greatest surprise, however, and Vincent voiced his approval when he saw it. The shower was a modest one compared with the fireclay edifice he was leaving behind, but it was a shower nonetheless.

'You'd be surprised how one item in a house sells the whole place to the right buyer or tenant,' said the agent on the way back to his office. 'It might be a fireplace or an orangery or, in your case, a shower.'

'In this case,' said Vincent wryly, 'urgency also had a hand in it.'

He was able to complete the transaction subject to a banker's reference, which he knew would offer no problem, and he and Hazel addressed the matter of removal and storage that afternoon.

'As you're so busy,' said Hazel, 'you could let the removers do the packing and then all you need to do is label each piece of furniture that's going into store and say which rooms the rest of the stuff is destined for.'

'You're indispensable,' he said.

'I wouldn't say that, exactly.'

'I did, just now, so it's official. Will you let me give you dinner tonight?'

She put her head on one side, pretending to consider his invitation. Finally, she said, 'That's a difficult one to refuse, so, yes, I'd like that. Thank you.'

'I know we seem to dine out more often than in, but these are unsettled times.' He kissed her.

'I think,' she said, returning his kiss, 'that, if Charles Dickens were still around, he would have something to say about that.'

'Do you think he would say something like, "These are the best of times; they are the worst of times"?'

'You took the words straight out of his mouth.' She looked thoughtful for a moment and asked, 'Do you mind if I use your phone?'

'I don't think he'd have said that.'

'No, I'm asking if I might use your phone.'

'Of course not. Go ahead.' He went into the sitting room so that she could make her call privately. After a while, it seemed to him that, with the fall over its keys, the piano looked as if it were sulking, so he lifted it and spoke softly. 'I'm sorry I allowed that oaf to touch you this morning,' he said. 'Rest assured, I shan't leave you to the mercy of the licentious soldiery.' In compensation for the morning's trauma, he played the first of Chopin's 24 Preludes. It was short, no more than a page, but it said what he wanted it to say.

'Do you often talk to your piano?' Hazel's voice came from the doorway.

'Only occasionally. Captain Connelly had the impertinence to touch it this morning without asking, so I thought I'd offer a few soothing words.'

'And a beautiful piece of music. What was it?'

'One of Chopin's Preludes.'

'Is that what they are? Just preludes, with nothing after them?'

'Yes.' She was clearly interested, so he explained. 'A new system of tuning was introduced in the eighteenth century. Until then, some keys had sounded awful and were best left alone, but with equal temperament tuning, every key sounded good, so Johann Sebastian Bach celebrated the fact by writing forty-eight preludes and fugues, using every key, both major and minor. Now, Chopin admired Bach very much, and he wanted to write something similar, but the fugue is such a complex form, he knew he couldn't do it justice. In the end, he wrote twenty-four preludes, using his particular talent to great effect.'

'Fascinating. It's good to be able to think of great composers as fallible human beings.'

'They all were and are,' he assured her. 'Even Mozart frequently exhibited human frailty. I suppose Bach stands alone in that respect, although he had about two dozen children, which makes him human, after all.'

At the mention of 'two dozen', she grimaced. 'Just think of his poor wife. I think that makes him *in*human.'

'Two wives,' he corrected her. 'He wore out his first wife and then expected his second, Anna Magdalena, to bear his children as well as learning the clavichord. He wrote her a book of pieces. It's called *Eine Kleine Buchlein für Anna Magdalene Bach.*'

'If I'd been Anna Magdalena,' she said, 'I'd have taken his little book and bashed him over the head with it.'

'I believe you would have.'

'You can depend on it.' Then, in a gentler tone, she asked, 'Are you going to play something else?'

'All right. What do you fancy?'

'Something soothing after all the dramas of the day.'

'I'll play a lullaby, Chopin's *Berceuse*.' Turning back to the piano, he began the gentle but insistent left hand motif that formed the basis for what was, in effect, a seamless set of variations that, for the next five minutes, took the most elaborate forms before eventually subsiding, as a lullaby should, into a soft and soothing cadence.

'That was beautiful,' said Hazel.

'I'm glad you enjoyed it. It's my belief that, if Bach, who was Chopin's idol, could have heard it, he would have been spellbound by the Romantic composer's treatment of the Passacaglia.'

'What's a Passa…?'

'Passacaglia? It's a set of variations over a repeated bass.' He showed her the left hand figure again and a little of the florid right hand.

'I'll take your word for it, Vincent, because I'd defy anyone not to be captivated by it. I'm just a little apprehensive.'

'About what?'

'I'm wondering if I'll get a lecture every time you play a piece of music.'

'I'm sorry. It's my way of sharing the enjoyment.'

'You share plenty just by playing the music.' Then changing the subject, she said, 'The telephone call was to my boss, to find out if I'm wanted in the office tomorrow.'

'Sunday? Why on earth does he want you to work on Sunday?'

'You work on Sundays, Vincent, and if something important is happening, so do I. As it happens, I'm not required tomorrow, but I had to check.'

Her words had set him thinking. 'Is something important happening?'

'Quite possibly. I'll keep you informed just as soon as I'm allowed.'

9

Evacuations on Two Fronts

Vincent learned about the latest development when he arrived at HMS Vernon in response to a telephone call from Lieutenant Commander Ghyll. The room was filled with RMS officers, all waiting to be enlightened.

'Basically,' said Ghyll, 'the Army's been caught with its pants down. The Nazis have swept through France, and now, the British Expeditionary Force is falling back on the Channel port of Dunkirk. Its evacuation has already begun.'

Not surprisingly, there were muted exclamations from the gathering. What amounted to the defeat of the British Army was a huge blow.

'Everything that can be done over there is being done and, as usual, our destroyers are in the thick of it, but the danger doesn't end there. Hitler is only too well aware that those ships have to return to our shores, and he's already taking steps to welcome them back to Britain. The Luftwaffe has been busy at night, laying mines outside the harbours they expect us to use, and this presents us with a huge task. Those harbours must be cleared of mines. The approaches are being swept, but some of those mines have been dropped in places the minesweepers cannot reach.' He looked around at the expectant faces in the room and said, 'You will each be given a location. I have the list here.' He began reading the names of officers present and their destinations. Eventually, he came to Vincent. 'Reid,' he said, 'you're going to HMS Lynx, which is the headquarters of Dover Command. You'll be provided with the necessary equipment. I believe the rating who assists you accompanied you here?'

'Yes, sir. He's waiting for me outside.'

'Good. Report to Lieutenant Commander Melrose at HMS Lynx, and he'll give you details of your workload. Have you any questions?'

'None that you can answer, sir.'

Ghyll smiled briefly. 'I think we can all say that, Reid. Carry on.'

'Aye, aye, sir.'

Eric Tyndall, Hazel's sub-editor and therefore her superior, appeared in the doorway with the kind of gloomy expression that usually attended a paucity of news.

'The evacuation's going very slowly,' he said, 'and, so far, we've lost four destroyers.' He shook his head at the impossibility of his task and said 'It's not the kind of thing the public need to be told.'

'The last thing they need to be told,' agreed Hazel. 'On the other hand, we could simply lie through our teeth, as usual.'

'Now, I've spoken to you about this kind of thing before,' he said, wagging his finger in a way that would not have been out of place in a scene from *Goodbye, Mr Chips*. 'There is no place for levity or flippancy in our line of work.'

'Of course not, Mr Tyndall. I've actually been wondering about the possibility of a piece on how tradespeople are coping with the trials of war.'

Tyndall's expression suddenly lightened. 'You know, Miss Wythenshawe, your idea has real possibilities.'

'Good, because I've arranged a couple of interviews for today.'

'Have you really?'

'Well, Mr Tyndall, time waits for no man… or woman, for that matter.' It was true. She had to be at Vincent's house in half-an-hour to meet Bennington's, the wine merchants, and supervise the removal of the wine from the cellar. Her other appointment was with Steinway and Sons, who were going to remove the grand piano.

Lieutenant Commander Melrose lost no time in finding work for Vincent and Jimmy.

'It's right alongside the end of Admiralty Pier and on the inside. The diving party will tell you exactly where.' He was an unusually tall and slender man, who seemed to bend and sway as he moved around his office. 'As a matter of fact, there's talk of sinking a blockship there to deter visits from U-boats and E-boats.'

'Well, sir,' said Vincent, 'We'd better get along there before there's a premature sinking.'

'Good luck, Reid.'

'Thank you, sir.'

Vincent left the building and re-joined Jimmy in the car. 'We're going to Admiralty Pier,' he told him. The Boche have planted a mine right at the end.'

' "The Boche", sir?'

'Yes, that's what we called them in the last war, and I don't see why we should lavish respect on the new generation.'

' "Boche" is a good name, sir. I'll borrow it, if I may.'

'There's no copyright on insults, Jimmy. You're most welcome.' Vincent stopped at the entrance to Admiralty Pier and showed his identification to the sentries. They waved him through, and he drove on. 'That's the Lord Warden Hotel,' he said, pointing to the building as they drove past. 'Some of the most famous people have stayed there en route for France. There was Charles Dickens, William Makepeace Thackeray.... Oh yes, and Napoleon the Third.'

'Not a cheap place to stay, then.'

'Not in the slightest, Jimmy, and most exclusive.' He drove as far as the mobile diving unit, which was parked some thirty or forty feet from the end of the pier.

The petty officer in charge looked at Vincent's identity card and explained. 'We didn't want to take the lorry too far, sir, in case it triggered the mine.'

'Good thinking, PO, and I need the exercise, anyway.'

'There's a rope ladder as well as the shot rope, sir. You should be all right in your diving boots.'

'You'll soon find out if I'm not, PO.' He climbed into the lorry, where he removed his clothes, and Jimmy dressed him in the diving suit.

Almost dressed, he sat on a wooden crate beside the rope ladder while Jimmy fixed the brass helmet with its pipes and rope.

'Good luck, sir.'

'Thank you, Jimmy. Put the kettle on in about half-an-hour's time.'

'Aye, aye, sir.' Jimmy closed the window and secured it.

Vincent descended the rope ladder carefully as there was barely enough room in each step for his cumbersome boots. As he did so, he was conscious that the diving party would be watching him, wondering if they would see him again. It wasn't morbid fascination; fatalities were so common in RMS that their interest was more likely to be out of genuine concern for his safety.

When he reached the seabed, he looked around and spotted the mine immediately. His footsteps caused flurries of sand to cloud the water, but not for long. The harbour, at least that part of it, was infinitely cleaner than the London docks, although the water felt just as cold, even in late May.

He examined the mine and found that, whilst the plates were exposed on both sides, the axis was at an angle, which meant that it would be harder to gain access to two of them. Difficulty, however, was a blessing compared with impossibility, and he set to work on the curiously named 'bomb fuse', which was one of the more accessible pair. he was freshly aware that he'd only ever used the car horn on dry land. In the event, however, it proved easier, as the bicycle pump wasn't required. He filled the bulb with seawater, screwed it on to the plate and drew the whole assembly out far enough to break the electrical circuit. Happily, the linen insulating tape still retained its adhesive property under water, and he was able to cover the bare wires. The rest of the job was relatively easy, although he was no less careful, familiarity being the progenitor of negligence, and he was able to re-ascend the rope ladder.

As ever, Jimmy was waiting to help him on to dry land, and he quickly removed the brass helmet. 'Welcome back, sir.'

'Thank you, Jimmy.'

'Tea's on its way, sir.'

'That's the best kind of music,' said Vincent, taking a mug of tea from the petty officer.

'Can we notify Lieutenant Commander Melrose that the mine's been rendered safe, sir?'

'You may.' Vincent's mine was only the second to be de-fused under water using the car horn.

Happily, Bennington's and Steinway arrived within five minutes of each other, as arranged, and Hazel was able to oversee the removal of the wine and the piano. Bennington's were kind enough to give her a lift to the new address, and she chatted happily with the crew on the way. She was, after all, supposed to be interviewing tradespeople. When all was delivered, she locked up the house in Wilton Road and returned to the Ministry to resume her duties.

That evening, Vincent and Jimmy were treated to a remarkable sight, as three destroyers, one after the other, entered Dover Harbour, and countless weary soldiers disembarked on to Admiralty Pier.

'Just think, sir,' said Jimmy, 'you made that possible.'

Smiling good-naturedly at his assistant's naivete, Vincent said, 'Many others have been responsible, Jimmy. There are the crews of those destroyers, Flag Officer Dover and his staff, who are organising the whole thing.... In an operation of this size, and I hope fervently that it's going to be a big one, individuals cease to count. Let's just hope they can go on evacuating the BEF at this rate. That way, we'll stand some kind of chance.'

Vincent attended two more mines in Dover that week before being recalled to London, where the Luftwaffe were creating a diversion by bombarding the capital with land mines.

'Just leave everything to me,' Hazel told him. 'I've overseen the removal of your piano and your wine, and now I'll do the same with your furniture. All you need do is label each piece with either "Store" or the room for which it's destined.' They were in Vincent's morning room, enjoying one of the few bottles of wine Hazel had reserved.

'You're wonderful, Hazel. I'm very grateful, but are you sure all this is not creating problems for you at the Ministry?'

She laughed. 'I'm interviewing tradespeople about how the war is affecting them. So far, I've interviewed representatives of Bennington's, Steinway and Lord's Removals. It's great fun.'

'I just don't want you to get into trouble.'

'I'm a big girl,' she told him. 'I can take care of myself.' Suddenly thoughtful, she said, 'I am going to be busy, though.'

'Am I allowed to ask?'

'You've been involved in it, so yes, it's about the Dunkirk evacuation. You know that the government's called on owners of small boats to lend a hand, don't you?'

He nodded, waiting for her to tell him more.

'We have to call their boats "little ships", because, whilst they're tiny, they're doing the work of grown-up ships, and the public have to know that.'

'In all fairness, they're going close inshore, where the danger is, picking up evacuees and taking them out to the destroyers,' he said.

'I'm not denying that they're doing a wonderful job, but the story has to be *all* about them, because it's likely to fire the public's imagination. Heroic boat owners are going to the rescue of our brave lads.' She rolled her eyes upward. 'It's too silly for words, when the Navy, which has organised the whole thing and done the lion's share of the work, no longer exists as far as the Ministry is concerned. It's all about propaganda.'

Vincent took her hand sympathetically. 'I'd offer to play something soothing,' he said, 'but you've sent my piano to its next address, a deed for which I am truly grateful.'

'Kiss me instead, Vincent. That usually does the trick.'

'I'm so grateful, I can hardly refuse.' He kissed her with a great deal of feeling.

'I hope you've got a better reason than that.'

'Of course I have.'

Distracted again by her thoughts, she asked, 'Did you see any of the troops coming ashore when you were in Dover?'

'Yes, we did.'

'How did they appear to you?'

'Exhausted, basically. It wasn't a pleasant sight.'

'The powers that be want us to show them bloodied but unbowed and defiant to the end. Above all, the public have to see them giving the bloody silly thumbs-up sign to the cameras.'

He'd never heard her swear, and now that she had, it lent force to her grievance.

'I suppose, for the sake of public morale, they need to look defiant.'

'It's just so cruel.' Her eyes were suddenly wet. 'They want us to treat exhausted men as puppets.'

'I know.' He gave her the handkerchief from his breast pocket. 'It's sickening, but necessary. We now have a prime minister who can fuel public resolve like no one else, but he has to have something to work on. Not even Churchill could fire up cinemagoers who'd just seen images of defeated and dispirited soldiers looking as if they want to be anywhere but where they've found themselves, and doing anything but serve in the Army.' He could read the resentment in her eyes. 'What I'm saying is, I respect your feelings, and believe me, "respect" is the word, because you care genuinely about those men, but you have to look at the overall picture. The public mustn't lose confidence in the armed forces.'

'And the silly thumbs-up sign?'

'I wish they'd find something better than that.' He smiled.

'What's so funny?'

'It just seems to me it's only like cheering to order.'

'What on earth's that?'

He dew her closer.

'Is it story time?'

'Yes. During the last war, we were inspected by Admiral Tyrwhitt, who commanded the Harwich Force and who was apparently something of a celebrity. The newsreel cameras were there and, as he approached our motley collection of minesweepers, we were lined up beside our moorings and ordered to cheer him. Most of us had never heard of him, and the rest couldn't care less, but we had to give three hearty cheers, lifting our caps and looking as if we thought he was wonderful. It was the same sort of thing. It was meaningless but necessary, if only to maintain morale.'

She kissed him and said, 'You talk a lot of sense, Vincent.'

'Fiddlesticks. You're the sensible one, organising my evacuation as you did.'

'Organising your what?'

'What did I say?'

'Evacuation.'

'It was a slip of the tongue, but I suppose it was an evacuation, really. You saved my piano and a cellarful of wine from being misappropriated by alien forces.'

She laughed. 'I suppose I did, and now you've bolstered my morale. What happens next?'

'We'll just have to wait and see.'

10

Their Finest Hour– And Their Busiest

Where landmines were falling on dry land, Vincent and Jimmy were dealing sometimes with as many as three in a day. When they fell into water, it took longer to render them safe, firstly because it was often necessary to travel further to the scene, and because preparations for diving were necessarily time-consuming. The news that the Navy had returned more than a third of a million men to Britain from Dunkirk had lifted everyone's spirits, but work had to go on, with the Luftwaffe always ready to add to the burden.

Two RMS officers and a rating had already been killed that week, and Vincent was all the more thankful to Hazel for organising the move and ensuring that he was able to concentrate on his work without distraction.

It transpired that her efforts had not been without incident, as she told him when they returned one evening to his new address.

'I had a visit from a most uncouth character, who described himself as Accommodation Officer,' she said. 'Do you want to hear about it, or would you rather I left you to get some much-needed sleep?'

'Don't worry, Hazel. I'll kick you out when my eyes begin to close. Was this man overfed, overbearing and… assuming?'

'You couldn't think of another "over", could you?'

'After the past week, I did well to think of the first two.'

'Of course.' She gave his arm an apologetic squeeze. 'It was the same man, because he wanted to know the identity and whereabouts of your superior officer. He was hell-bent on having you disciplined for your allegedly disrespectful attitude.'

'Allegedly? No, he was right. I treated him with no respect at all, simply because he deserved none. At the same time, I'm sorry he subjected you to that,' he said, refilling her glass.

'It was water off a duck's back, Vincent. I've dealt with his kind many times in the past.'

'I'm glad to hear it. What did you tell him?'

'I told him it was none of his business. He'd already tried the Admiralty, but with the same lack of success.'

'He has too much time on his hands. I'm too busy even to be offended, let alone to do anything about it.'

Hazel lifted his arm to snuggle closer. 'And you're not at all interested in power, which is clearly what drives Captain Connelly.' After a moment's thought, she asked, 'Did you hear Mr Churchill's speech on Tuesday?'

'No, but I heard about it.'

'Our job is propaganda; we're supposed to be the professionals, but he's a master of the craft. I really think he could make a mouse believe it was a lion. Given his chequered past, we can only hope that this turns out to be *his* finest hour.' Turning her head to look directly at him, she asked seriously, 'How likely do you think we are to be invaded?'

He gave the question some consideration and said, 'I think it depends on whose advice Hitler takes. Raeder would advise him against it on the basis that the German navy's losses in the Norway campaign have rendered it incapable of supporting an invasion. On the other hand, Göring must be chafing at the bit.'

'Why do you say that?'

'Because he's a strutting show-off, who's just seen his Luftwaffe triumph, almost unopposed, in every campaign so far.'

'What about the army?'

'That's commanded by Corporal Hitler himself. In my opinion, he's the unknown quantity, mainly because it's usually anyone's guess what a megalomaniac will do next.' He gave her shoulder a squeeze and said, 'The main thing is to hope for the best, that Hitler will see the error of his ways, or that he'll trip over one of his victims and fall into the Rhine. There's always a chance of that.'

'Does blind optimism run in your family?'

'I believe so, but I'm really too tired to remember.'

Hazel lifted her head from his shoulder to say, 'That's my cue to leave you, Vincent, and wish you a deep and dreamless sleep before, once more, you take up the cudgels, or whatever you keep in your toolkit, against those everlasting mines.'

The second mine, the next day, had fallen outside a food warehouse in East India Dock Road and, for once, its plates were easily accessible.

'I think I have everything I need, Jimmy,' said Vincent. 'Go back to the safety point and keep your fingers crossed.'

'Aye, aye, sir, but I'll do more than that.'

He didn't doubt it. Vincent had already learned that, when duty allowed, his assistant was a choir member at St George's in Bloomsbury, and that was welcome news because, without being at all glib, he needed all the help he could muster. If he'd not already been aware of it, the blue dot on the fuse, signalling blue polarity, told him that.

Marshalling his concentration, he carried out the first stage of the process, and was about to lift the fuse from its pocket, when he realised that his hands were shaking uncontrollably. To carry on with the procedure in that state was out of the question. He stood up to walk around, just to settle his nerves, but as he did, he became starkly aware that he needed to visit a lavatory quite urgently. RMS officers joked about it, but their humour was thin. In their calling, bowel hyperactivity was an unwelcome fact of life.

He entered the warehouse by the nearest open door and immediately gave thanks, because the single word 'Men' on the door that faced him could not have been more welcoming.

A few minutes later, he returned to the mine and composed himself before attempting to draw the fuse. After a few deep breaths, he began lifting it towards the aperture, holding it between his thumbs and forefingers whilst steadying his hands against the casing. Little by little, he moved the deadly apparatus towards him and lifted it clear of any surrounding metal. Then, laying it on the ground beside him, he knelt forward, resting his forehead against the casing, and breathed very deeply, more relieved than ever that he was still able to do so.

The rest of the procedure was straightforward, so that his signal to Jimmy to join him seemed ridiculously casual after the earlier tension.

'I wondered what had happened, sir,' said Jimmy. 'I mean, when you got up and walked away.'

'It was just a call of nature, Jimmy.'

'Oh?' It sounded like welcome news. 'Where are the heads, sir?'

Vincent pointed. 'Through that doorway, and the first door on your left is the gents.'

'I see, sir. Request permission—'

'Granted.' He wondered if Jimmy had been suffering in sympathy, but he naturally left the question unasked.

With the end of the next week came the particularly welcome news that Vincent and Jimmy were to be rested. It was only for seventy-two hours, but dog-tired as they were, they viewed those three days as a beleaguered traveller might see an oasis in a desert.

After one deliriously restful night and one day, Vincent felt sufficiently rested that he would once again be fit company for Hazel, so he drove her to Emil's in Covent Garden.

'We each have our problems,' said Hazel when they'd given their order to the waiter, 'and mine seem insignificant beside some.'

'I suppose we can all say that,' said Vincent. 'Have you a specific problem in mind?'

'Mm. Lily, one of the secretaries at the Ministry and a good friend of mine, was widowed fairly recently. Her husband was killed on the beach at Dunkirk.' For no obvious reason, she added, 'He was a regular soldier.'

'Poor devil. So near, and yet so far. Poor widow, too.'

'Yes, she has two children, but she's denied the benefit of their company. They were evacuated to a place near Tewkesbury, and they're not very happy there.' Clearly, Hazel shared their unhappiness.

'I'm not surprised, losing their father like that, and having to cope with their loss without their mother around to give them comfort. How old are they?'

'Nine-and-a-half and eight. They're both boys.' Clearly involved in her colleague's woes, she went on. 'Lily's considered bringing the boys home again.'

'Who can blame her? At the same time, no one has any idea what's going to happen here. All we know is that, whatever Hitler does next, London's not going to be the safest place in the country.'

'I'm sorry, Vincent,' she said, patting his hand. 'After the fortnight you've had, I shouldn't bombard you with other people's troubles.'

'Of course you should. Your friend Lily's trials obviously trouble you, too. You're quite right to tell me about them.' He squeezed her hand. 'In any case, I welcome the distraction.'

'Bless you, Vincent.' She was unable to say more, because the waiter had arrived with the wine.

Vincent tasted the wine and gave it his approval. When the waiter had left them, he asked, 'Do you like musical theatre?'

'Yes, I do.' She looked at him strangely. 'I wouldn't have thought it was your cup of tea, Vincent. Opera, yes, but not what most people understand by musical theatre.'

'It depends on the show, but you must realise that my days as a classical snob came to an end when I re-joined the RNVR. Thereafter, my appreciation of various kinds of entertainment broadened beyond belief. It was all part of that worldly camaraderie I told you about.'

'Of course, but what made you ask me?'

'I wondered if you'd like to see *Present Arms* at the Prince of Wales Theatre. The music's by Noel Gay, so it should be good. The first night got excellent reviews.'

Surprise and delight paraded across her features. Finally, she said, 'Thank you, Vincent. I'd love to. I must say, this is a complete surprise.'

'You see, I'm very grateful to you for taking care of the move. You made it almost painless – the only pain was in having the house taken from me – and you shielded me from distraction when I was at my busiest, so I wanted to do something special for you.'

'And you have.' Her face was still alight. 'When are we going?'

'I have tickets for tomorrow evening.'

'Wonderful!'

'After all that, it had better be good,' he said with a wry smile.

In the event, *Present Arms* proved highly entertaining, and Vincent felt that his idea had been a good one.

11

August

'...What the Right Hand Doeth'

Hitler had evidently discounted the caution of Grand Admiral Raeder, and taken Göring's advice, which was to send over the Luftwaffe in huge numbers with the object of achieving air superiority. His thinking was clearly that, only when that aim had been achieved would an invasion of Britain be the pushover he anticipated. The battle raged overhead, but naval routine continued and, with the air filled with the vapour trails of opposing aircraft, Vincent and Jimmy were called to yet another imperilled London dock.

'The dock's closed to traffic, sir,' the senior warden on the scene told Vincent, who nodded. 'I should hope so,' he said,

'The first we knew about it was when we saw the parachute caught up on the wharf. We thought it might be an enemy flier at first, but they don't use that sort of parachute, do they?' He was a grey-haired man of middle years, who appeared to have the freedom to execute his ARP duties during working hours.

'Now, there you have me at a disadvantage, Warden.' Vincent turned to the solitary policeman guarding the site and said, 'Very soon, there'll be a mobile diving unit here, Constable. It'll need to go almost to the wharf.'

'Leave it with me, sir,' said the policeman, who appeared to be quietly confident, unlike the garrulous air-raid warden.

'Thank you.'

'We had everybody out by eight o' clock,' said the warden with an air of satisfaction. ‘Of course, being a local councillor gives me an extra degree of authority.’

‘What do you mean?’

‘I’m saying we evacuated the area by eight o’ clock.’

‘I see.’

‘It’s the first thing we do. We—’

‘Warden,’ said Vincent, ‘I really don’t need to know how ARP organise an evacuation. The fact that it’s been done is enough for me. Now, I’m going down to the wharf to see if I can locate the mine from above.’ Sensing that the warden was about to follow him, he said, ‘I want you to stay here, because I must concentrate.’ Ignoring the warden’s injured look, he made his way to the wharf, where he crouched on the edge and peered into the dock. At first, he saw nothing; as usual, the water simply looked dirty and polluted. He looked up to the hoist, where the parachute had become caught, and followed the vertical line into the dock. Then he saw the tailfins of a mine. It was resting, nose-down, against the timbers of the wharf on which he stood. He stared a little longer until he was satisfied that the tailfins were all he could make out in the polluted water, and then crept carefully away from the wharf, anxious not to disturb the mine with unnecessary vibration. He’d noted inconsequentially that the mine was far enough away from the iron ladder for safety. Had it not been, he told himself, there was every likelihood that it would have been detonated when it landed.

When he returned to the safety point, the warden was peering down the road.

‘Here it is,’ he said, as if he’d spotted the diving unit when all others had given up on it, ‘the van from Chatham. Now, if we take down the rope here—’

‘Leave it to me,’ the policeman told him, and go and do something useful.’

‘That’s a good idea,’ said Vincent.

Again, the warden looked affronted. ‘Suddenly, it’s turned chilly ’round here,’ he said stiffly before moving off.

‘I’m not surprised he’s feeling the cold,’ said Jimmy, speaking for the first time. ‘He’s only “dress’d in a little brief authority”.’

Vincent responded with a quick smile.

'It takes some of them that way,' said the constable, opening up the cordon to make way for the diving unit. He made contact with the driver and waved him into the entrance to the dock.

The petty officer in charge of the unit jumped out and saluted Vincent. 'Lieutenant Reid. Sir? I'm Petty Officer Philpott. Do you need a rating to attend you?'

'No, thank you, PO. My assistant will do that.' Over the petty officer's shoulder, he could see the warden hurrying towards them.

'Have you got everything you need?' He seemed to be addressing the whole gathering.

'This officer will have,' said the PO, who seemed to have sized him up already, 'when he's left alone to concentrate.'

'I told you to stay out of the way,' the constable told him.

'I was only trying to be helpful, and I've as much right as the police to be at a UXB.'

The PO confronted him with an uncompromising expression and said, 'I'll tell you how you can be useful, Warden. Stay out of sight where you'll be safe and sound. That'll do nicely.'

'Thank you, PO,' said Vincent, trying not to smile. 'I'll get ready. Come on, Jimmy.'

Vincent stripped off in the lorry and, with Jimmy's help, donned the diving suit. Finally, with the helmet fixed to the corselet, he descended the iron ladder into the dock.

While he waited for the water to clear, he adjusted the air in the suit to give himself maximum ease of movement. Then, with visibility partially restored, he followed the wall of the dock, pausing occasionally until the water cleared again. Eventually, he located the mine and was able to examine it. Happily, and for once, all the plates were accessible, so he began work on the bomb fuse, which required the motor horn. The task never became any easier, and he worked with total concentration, finally withdrawing the fuse.

Next, he tackled the detonator, and he was reaching for his knife to part the wires, when he became conscious of movement in the water. There was no reason why anything should be moving in the dock, and he peered through the murk to see if he could identify the cause. He could see very little, but he became conscious, after a few seconds, of the water becoming agitated, and there was only one possible reason for that. A second later, his suspicion was confirmed when he realised that a vessel of some kind was entering the dock.

He cut the wires as quickly as he could and dropped the detonator on to the bed of the dock while he taped off the ends of the wires. Working with the same speed, he opened the third plate and removed the primer. Mercifully, the vessel had stopped at least thirty feet away, as far as he could ascertain, and he was able to relax to some extent while he removed the hydrostatic valve.

His heart was still pounding, however, as he made his way by stages back to the iron ladder. Giving himself extra buoyancy, he climbed the ladder and allowed Jimmy to help him on to the wharf. When his helmet was removed, he looked across to the far dock and was astounded to see a launch of the Thames River Police. 'So that was the culprit,' he said, following Jimmy into the lorry.

'No one had told the River Police about the mine, sir,' said Jimmy. 'They got as far as the dock gate, and they would have come into the dock, but the PO and I shouted to them to keep clear while the policeman held up the "Danger UXB" sign for them to see. Thank goodness they took the hint. I shouldn't be surprised if someone's whatsits find their way on to the chopping block for this.'

'And rightly so, Jimmy.'

'I'll leave you to get dressed, sir. The policeman sent that air-raid warden to find some tea. Let's hope he can do that without making a feature out of it.'

Vincent finished dressing and walked up to the safety point, where a police sergeant was talking to the constable. When he saw Vincent, he saluted and said, 'That could have been nasty, sir.'

'It's safe now, Sergeant.'

'We're very thankful, sir. No one had told us about the mine, and we have to investigate empty docks for contraband and stolen goods.'

'I gather you're with the River Police, Sergeant.'

'Yes, sir.'

'As you said, it could have been nasty. I was removing the bomb fuse when I realised I was no longer alone, and I had to break all records to get the detonator out before you came any closer.'

The warden joined them, bearing several mugs of tea on a tray. The sergeant handed one to Vincent and then took one himself. 'Whose responsibility was it, Warden,' he asked, 'to notify all relevant agencies of a UXB?'

'It's an ARP function, Sergeant. I did notify the police.'

'He told us at the station, Sergeant,' said the constable. 'That's why I'm here. He just didn't bother to tell your outfit.'

For once, the warden was silent.

'Do you realise,' the sergeant asked him, 'how close this naval officer came to being chewed up by our propellors?'

'If we hadn't all been blown sky-high first,' added Vincent. 'A police launch is quite capable of triggering a magnetic mine, which is what that thing is.' He pointed, quite unnecessarily to the dock.

The sergeant was incredulous. 'Would it really do that, sir?'

Vincent nodded. He turned to the now sheepish chief warden to say, 'The next stage is the removal of the mine. It's quite safe now, and a team of men will take it way, hopefully without any intervention from you, Warden.'

'I still think the police station should have notified the River Police,' said the warden, standing his ground.

'It was your responsibility,' the sergeant told him. 'The one job you got right today was fetching the tea.' He drained his mug and placed it on the tray. 'Here, you can take back the empties.'

In a way that had become familiar, Hazel lifted Vincent's arm and moved closer to him, allowing his arm to come to rest on her shoulders.

'Something's troubling you,' he said, 'I can tell.'

'How not like a man. You're very perceptive, Vincent. That's one of the qualities I like best about you.'

'Thank you for that, Hazel, but aren't you going to tell me what's on your mind?'

'All right. Do you remember, when I was supervising the move to this house, I said I was looking into the way tradespeople are carrying on despite the exigencies of war?'

'I thought that was just a cover for being out of the office.'

'To begin with, it was, but then I decided it was worth following up.' She wriggled so that she was able to look him in the eye. 'Believe it or not,' she said in a tone that demanded disapproval, 'someone else has had the same idea.'

'So, what happens now?'

She snorted. 'He has official approval, so I have to think again.'

'I'm sorry to hear that. Wasn't this chap aware that you were already working on the idea?'

'Not for one moment.'

He had to be tactful here. 'I'm surprised there's no system in place,' he said, 'to avoid duplication of that kind.'

'I did make my intentions known to my sub-editor, if that's what you mean.'

'Presumably, that's not enough.'

'Evidently.'

After a while, Vincent said, 'If perceptiveness is one of the qualities you like best about me, there must be at least one more.'

'At least,' she agreed.

'Do tell.'

'Are you fishing for compliments?'

'Of course I am. Why else would I ask?'

'Let me think.' She furrowed her brow with concentration.

'I was hoping it would be on the tip of your tongue. Instead, you seem to be plumbing the depths of your memory.'

'I've just remembered,' she said triumphantly.

'Is it a secret?'

'Not between you and me, but it's very private.'

'I'm intrigued.'

'Good, because I can't decide whether or not to tell you.'

'All right, I shan't ask.' He picked up the bottle of wine and asked, 'Would you like me to top you up?'

'Yes, please. Aren't you going to ask me what it is?'

'No, I'm going to wait for you to decide whether or not you want to tell me.'

'Honestly, Vincent,' she said lifting her head to remonstrate with him, 'you're not at all easy to tantalise.'

'Is that the quality you were going to tell me about?'

'No, it's not.'

'Good, because, as qualities go, it's not a particularly spectacular one.'

'Kiss me, and I'll tell you.'

'You drive a hard bargain.' He lowered his head and kissed her.

'All right,' she said, 'the quality I had in mind is that you don't take liberties.'

'That's torn it.' He made a gesture of disappointment.

'What's wrong with that? It's an admirable quality.'

'Agreed. It's just that I was about to take a shameful liberty, and then you said that and made me feel that I had to be respectable again.'

'Oh.' She patted his hand consolingly. 'Maybe you could save it for later, when you're not feeling quite so honourable.'

'It seems I have no alternative.'

'Speaking of honour….'

'Yes?'

'That was a rotten trick, pinching my idea about tradespeople.'

'It's really offended your sense of fair play, hasn't it? Mind you, I still think there should be a system for registering ideas.'

'There should,' she agreed. 'Unfortunately, one feature of the Ministry is that, all too often, "the left hand knoweth not what the right hand doeth".'

Vincent recalled the morning's drama and said, 'Believe me, the Ministry's not alone in that.' Having established that they shared that impediment, they kissed fondly while he traced the contours of her breast.

She said, 'I do know what your right hand doeth, and I'm sorry to have to stall you, but….' She whispered a suggestion in his ear.

Once again, he had to agree, particularly in the light of his experience that morning, that some things were best done in relative safety.

12

Double Indemnity

Dinner at Emil's had become a habit, as Hazel pointed out a few days later.

'There are worse habits,' said Vincent.

'I agree, but is it morally right when many people are existing on rations because they can't afford to eat in places such as this?'

'My father would have adored you, although, having said that, he'd still have argued with you.' Even so, he thought he should address her misgivings. 'Our not doing this,' he reasoned, 'wouldn't make it any more affordable for people dependent on rations.'

'I realise that. I just feel uneasy about it.'

'That's very commendable,' he said, 'but I suspect it's not the only problem that's troubling you.'

Looking like someone who has been found out, she said, 'You've done it again, Vincent. You have a nose for worry and preoccupation.'

'Don't be rude about my nose.' He covered it with his hand.

'You know what I mean. You're so perceptive.'

'I prefer "analytical", but would you like to make a full confession?'

'Hardly a confession, but I'll tell you about it.'

'That's the next best thing,' he said, topping up her glass.

'It's about Lily, the secretary at work.'

'The mother of two boys in Tewkesbury,' he confirmed. 'Yes, I remember your telling me about her.'

'Well done again, Vincent. Actually, they're no longer in Tewkesbury.'

'No?'

'No, they suddenly arrived home. They were waiting outside the flat when Lily arrived home from work. They'd run away from their evacuation home, or whatever it's called. I think "home" is too cosy a name for it.'

'If they made their way from Tewkesbury to London without adult assistance, they must be very resourceful as well as, presumably, having a good reason.'

'It wasn't the happiest of placements,' she confirmed. 'Do you really want to hear about it?'

'Now you've whetted my appetite.'

'All right.' She leaned forward confidentially and began. 'The younger boy, who's eight, is called Reggie. The ten-year-old's name is Eric. He's actually nine-and-a-half, but who cares? He's a lovely boy, but it's Reggie who's the more enterprising of the two, and he'd been in trouble with his hosts because of an incident on the way home from school, when Eric was attacked by the school bully. He was completely overwhelmed until little Reggie joined in the fray.'

'I like him already.'

'You would. He's a little charmer.'

'Go on.'

'Reggie has one of those metal, cylindrical gasmask cases, and he swung it at the bully, hitting him for six and laying his forehead open, and then he leapt on him, punching him for all he was worth. The bully went home in tears.'

'I do like a happy ending.'

'Oh, that wasn't all.' Hazel fortified herself with wine and continued. 'The bully and his father came to the farmhouse where Eric and Reggie were staying, to complain. When the father saw Eric, he asked, 'Is this the one that did it?' The boy told him it wasn't Eric, but the little one, Reggie, at which the bully's father smacked his son for telling fibs. "How could a little boy like Reggie," he demanded, "inflict such a blow?" The two went on their way, but the boys' hosts demanded to know the truth, and when Reggie owned up to what he'd done, they punished him by locking him in the woodshed and leaving him there all night. "Respectable boys," they told him, "fight with their fists".'

'Poor little scrap.' Vincent topped up Hazel's glass again, eager to hear more.

'In the morning, their host mother, for want of a more appropriate title, sent the boys on an errand to the shops with money and ration coupons, so Reggie, who'd had more than enough of the farm and its owners, steered Eric to the railway station, where he used the money for the shopping to buy two tickets to London, and that was how they came to be at the flat when Lily came home. I should add that Lily has returned the money and the ration coupons to their owner along with a terse explanation for the boys' sudden disappearance.'

'I can tell you confidently that my father would have let Reggie leave the court without a blemish on his character. Good lad, I say.' He chuckled and then asked, 'What happens now?'

'Lily won't send them away again, and I can't blame her.'

'Of course not.'

'Here's the sensitive part.'

'I'm braced and ready.'

'Lily's not been in the best of health. She had a brush with cancer two years ago and underwent an operation. It seemed to do the trick, but her doctors warned her against complacency, and she has to have frequent and regular examinations. Let's say that her future's not entirely certain.'

'Of course. Where do you come into it?'

Hazel closed her eyes for a moment. 'Vincent, you've done it again.'

'It's not difficult. Has she asked you for help of some kind?'

'Yes, she's asked me if I'll be the boys' legal guardian, just in case things do go wrong.'

'Let's hope they don't, but how do you feel about that?'

'I couldn't possibly refuse her. I couldn't let her or the boys down, so I've asked her to set things in motion with her solicitor.'

He reached across the table for her hand and squeezed it. 'Well done, Hazel. I'm proud of you.'

'Be careful, Vincent. I'm not readily tearful, but you might just set me off.'

'I'll try not to. Instead, I'll drive you home. Yours or mine?'

'After that disclosure, I'd really appreciate your company tonight.'

'Then you shall have it.'

'I have some coffee that I brought from *Vernon*. Would you like some?'

'I think I should. It's been quite an evening.'

Vincent went to the kitchen to make coffee, and Hazel appeared in the doorway. She seemed anxious. 'If the worst happened, and I had to honour my obligation to the children,' she asked, 'would it affect you and me?'

'Of course it would. There'd be four of us instead of two.' On brief reflection, he added, 'That's always provided I stay the course.'

'What do you mean?'

'In my line of work, I'm not what you'd call a good insurance risk.'

'Oh, Vincent, I don't even want to think about that.' She put her arms around him and held him tight until the coffee was brewed.

They took it into the sitting room and sat together on the sofa.

'I made a will recently,' he said as he poured the coffee.

'Did you?'

'I thought it was a good idea. I mean, I'm blowed if I'm going to let the Chancellor take everything.' He handed her a cup of coffee. 'I've no surviving family,' he said, 'so I'm leaving my worldly wealth to you.'

'To me?' Clearly, it was the last thing she'd expected.

'You're the person who means most to me, and an incident that took place a few days ago prompted me to make that arrangement. What's left of the house when the Army have finished with it, the Steinway, my investments, my bank balance, the wine in the cellar and my cricket bat and pads will all be yours.'

She was silent for several seconds. Eventually, still in the grip of surprise, she said, 'I'm tremendously grateful. I never expected that, but let me say that I'd much rather have you alive than inherit your property.'

'In that case, I'll be very careful.'

'You'd better be.' A thought occurred to her, and she said, 'You mentioned something that happened recently that prompted you to make a will. What was it?'

'Oh, it was an isolated case of negligence, a once in a lifetime hitch. It was an anxious moment, that's all.' He was aware that she was holding him more tightly than ever. 'A once in a lifetime hitch,' he repeated. 'That's all it was.'

'I hope so.'

'Are you going to let go of me so that I can drink my coffee?'

'I don't want to let go of you, but I will.' She relaxed her hold on him and sat back.

'Actually, I must take some sheets from the airing cupboard to make up the spare bed. You can help me if you like.'

'Do I have to sleep in your spare bed? I told you how much I'd appreciate your company.'

'Are you sure? You've just had quite an emotional time.'

'And what better way is there of following it? It's the next logical step.'

'Is it safe now?'

'I went to the clinic this morning,' she confirmed.

'That can't have been pleasant.'

'It was all right. There was only me and a female doctor.'

'You're at the mercy of a man, now.' He kissed her.

'I know. Isn't it good?' She returned his kiss.

'Presumably, you have the cunning device with you.'

'In my bag. Shall we go upstairs?'

'It's either that or coffee. Suddenly, I find that coffee hasn't the appeal it had earlier.'

They stood and kissed before climbing the stairs to Vincent's room.

'I should warn you,' he said, 'I'm terribly out of practice.'

'So am I. I'm also quite inexperienced.'

They lay together, he with his arm around her, and she with her head resting on his shoulder. Vincent had switched off the bedside lamp, so they were in total darkness.

'I told you I was out of practice,' he said.

'No more apologies,' she insisted. 'In my limited experience, it was far from brief, and what's more, it was lovely, so there.'

'All right, I shan't argue with you.'

'You'd better not, and I'll tell you something else.'

'Please do.' If it was at all positive, he needed to hear it.

'You're the gentlest man I've ever known.' She said hurriedly, 'I haven't known all that many, but I'm sure you know what I mean.'

'I have a rough idea.' He was reminded of an observation his father had once made, to the effect that there were difficult foreign languages, impossibly difficult foreign languages, and the utterances of women. 'It may have something to do with being a pianist,' he said, 'or even with my new calling, removing sensitive devices from their high-explosive hiding places.'

She laughed. 'As analogies go, that one is less than flattering. Are you really comparing me with an unexploded mine?'

'I treat you both with respect, don't I?'

'Stop digging, Vincent, and just accept that you're a gentle soul. You're also very good at finding hidden secrets.'

He made no reply. The mine analogy still appealed to him, and her last remark seemed to reinforce it, but he knew better than to argue. Instead, he contented himself by creating a circle of kisses around one nipple before celebrating its arousal in the same way.

'Oh, Vincent….' As a statement, it was incomplete, but it said everything. 'Is it happening to you as well?' She reached downward. 'It is,' she said with great satisfaction. Thereafter, conversation ceased, and she gave only a gasp as she received him.

13

The Führer's Recognition

With the battle still raging overhead, Vincent was nevertheless required to report periodically to Lieutenant Commander Ghyll at *HMS Vernon.*

'Things seem to have quietened down in your neck of the woods, Reid,' remarked Ghyll.

'If you mean that, instead of three incidents per day, two has become the new norm, yes, sir, I agree.'

'Irony is an easy refuge. I've come to expect wit of a subtler kind from you, Reid. In any case, be thankful you weren't here earlier in the month.'

Clearly, Vincent was expected to respond to that hint of more to come, so he asked, 'What happened earlier this month, sir?'

'Six fatalities and a number of injuries. It happened in the mining shed when they were dismantling a Type C at the time, and when they tried to open the back door, there was an explosion, not of the mine itself, but an anti-handling device.'

The 'back door' to which Ghyll referred was the panel that separated the tailfins from the main body of the mine. 'I'm very sorry to hear that, sir.'

'So was I. We lost some good men.'

'Presumably, the scientific chaps were able to piece together the parts and form an idea of how it had happened, sir?'

'Yes, although it was a while before it occurred to anyone to do that. I suppose everyone was in a state of shock.'

Vincent imagined they would be. 'But they got there in the end, sir? One of the few principles I remember learning from physics lessons at school was that matter cannot be destroyed. Those bits and pieces were no doubt bashed out of shape, but they would still tell a story once they were reassembled.'

Ghyll stared at him incredulously. 'Now that I think of it, Reid,' he said, 'it's a pity you weren't here at the time. Not in the mining shed, of course, but on the site. You might have made a useful contribution. Was that an example of the analytical thought processes you told us about when we first met?'

'I suppose so, sir. By the way, did they form any conclusion about the device in question?'

'Yes, it was an anti-handling device triggered electro-mechanically, and its purpose was to conceal a new and deadly feature from our notice.'

'What was that, sir?'

'A clicker.'

Rather than reveal his ignorance, Vincent simply waited to be enlightened.

'Instead of being primed to explode immediately a ship passed over it, the mine had a clicking device that counted the first two ships, and then allowed the mine to explode at the third click, when a third ship came along. You can see the thinking behind it. A minefield could be swept and reported safe, but the mines would be armed and waiting for the next victim to come along, believing naively that all was well.'

'We're dealing with particularly malevolent minds, sir.'

'Don't I know it.' The thought seemed to lead to another, because Ghyll asked, 'By the way, have you seen your cinematic debut?'

'Yes, sir. I didn't recognise myself on the screen.'

'You wouldn't in that diving helmet. I suppose the film served its purpose, and I imagine the enemy have seen it by this time and drawn their conclusions. I wonder if they were taken in by it.'

Vincent had also wondered about that. 'I think it's just possible, sir. Given the paucity of humour in their souls, I imagine they watch everything seriously.'

'Let's hope so, Reid.'

Vincent thought no more about his conversation with Ghyll until almost a week later, when received a telephone call from him.

'Reid,' he said, 'I'd like you to go down to Dorset and assist a group of officers with a mine that, on the face of it, is a Type C, but which has some unusual characteristics.'

'Of course, sir. Whereabouts in Dorset is this mine, sir?'

'A place called Piddletrenthide. Honestly, that really is its name. I'll give you directions and then I want you to go straight there.'

The journey from London to Piddletrenthide was one that Vincent had no wish to repeat, and he was relieved when he reached the Red Lion Inn, where he'd been told to meet Lieutenant Commander Stewart, the officer in charge of the operation.

'You must be Reid,' said Stewart, a huge man with hands to match, that seemed intended for almost any task other than that of rendering mines safe. 'Come into the bar and have a drink.' His invitation was so hearty, it reminded Vincent of The Ghost of Christmas Present welcoming Scrooge into his presence.

'Thank you, sir. I'd like a gin, if that's all right.'

'Pink?'

'Why not, sir?'

Stewart raised his arm to capture the landlord's attention and ordered two pink gins. 'The others will be joining us in the morning, Reid. You and I have had to travel further.'

They talked for some time. In view of the presence of locals in the pub, they avoiding the subject of the mine. Instead, Stewart said, 'I've been waiting to meet you ever since Ghyll told me about you. He says you're a music professor. Is that right?'

'In peacetime, yes, sir.'

'Amazing. You temporary chaps come from so many different backgrounds, it's quite fascinating.' He stared at Vincent for a little longer as he might view a curiosity on display, before changing the subject completely and saying, 'The food here's very basic, but we have to accept what's available, and my room's very adequate. Don't know about yours, of course.'

'I'm sure I'll be all right, sir.'

Vincent spent a comfortable night, When he went down to breakfast in the morning, he found Stewart with another officer at the table, whom he introduced as Lieutenant Commander Byrne. He was also tall, but very slender. He'd driven up from Poole.

'We'll meet the scientific chaps on site,' Stewart told him.

Vincent looked around the room at the other residents and said, 'I'll look forward to that, sir.' He had no idea why the scientists would be there, but he imagined he would find out in due course.

'I believe Reid is a professor of some kind,' said Byrne.

'Yes, Byrne, he's a professor of music.' Stewart made the announcement as if he were unveiling Vincent's most interesting feature.

'Good lord. What will they send us next?'

'Reid comes highly recommended, Byrne,' said Stewart.

'Really? Well, I doubt if there'll be much for him to do.'

Vincent remained silent, as Byrne clearly had no intention of addressing him.

Breakfast continued to be a solemn affair, its main feature being a conversation between Stewart and Byrne that excluded Vincent despite repeated attempts by Stewart to involve him, and it was a relief when they had to leave.

'We could all go in my car,' said Stewart. 'It makes sense.'

'Thank you, sir,' said Vincent, but I'd like to take my own, and then I can leave as soon as our work is done.'

'Very well.'

Byrne seemed almost relieved as he accepted Stewart's offer.

Vincent followed Stewart's Rover for about two miles until they reached the site of the mine. Two civilians were waiting for them.

'We're going to try a new piece of trepanning equipment,' said Stewart. 'It's designed to drill a four-inch diameter hole in the mine's casing. Depending on where we drill the hole, we should be able to dismantle whichever device we choose.'

After checking the mine with a stethoscope, the scientists set up the trepanning drill and connected a bottle of compressed air. The party moved back to a temporary slit trench that the army had dug for them in readiness. The trepanner started up with a high-pitched wail.

After a while, Stewart stopped it, they waited five minutes to be sure it was at least relatively safe, and then he walked over to have a look.

'It still has some way to go,' he reported on his return before restarting the drill.

They waited for what seemed an age, until the note of the drill changed, and they knew it had cut through the iron casing. After another five-minute wait, Stewart inspected the casing again. 'It's most of the way through,' he said. 'There's just a small place where it's not quite cut through.'

'I have a hacksaw,' said Vincent.

'All right, we'll try your hacksaw, but be careful.'

His warning was hardly necessary, because Vincent had no intention of taking risks. Using a hacksaw blade with a makeshift wooden handle, he sawed gently through the thin, remaining scar left by the trepanner and lifted out the four-inch disc of iron casing. Part of the battery and the leads to the primer lay exposed.

'Bugger,' said Stewart. 'Why the thing was designed to cut only a four-inch hole I'll never know, but I can't get my hand in there.'

'Let me try,' said Byrne. He attempted to insert his hand, but had to admit that he, too, was unable to gain access to the wires.

'That leaves me,' said Vincent, patiently reaching into the hole and lifting the wires so that he could cut them. 'I'd be grateful if someone would cut me some insulating tape,' he said.

Surprisingly, it was Byrne who cut the tape and handed the pieces to him.

'Thank you, sir.' Vincent taped off the leads.

'There's another charge near the after part of the mine,' said Vincent. 'I can just see it.'

Byrne asked, 'Can you see how it's fired? It can't be electrical.'

'No, sir, it's mechanically fired, but I've no idea how to tackle it.'

'It'll take far too long to use the trepanner again,' said Stewart. 'We'll have to fall back on plastic explosive.

Painstakingly, he made a circle of the explosive and inserted a fuse.

With that in place, he set the fuse and joined the others in the slit trench. Ten seconds later, the charge went off. They waited and then walked warily towards the mine. When Stewart was within seventy or so yards of it, there was another blast, and he flung himself on to the ground as various items showered the area.

Byrne asked, 'What the devil happened?'

'It was the charge in the tail of the mine,' said Vincent, 'the one I told you about.'

'But why wasn't it fired by the controlled explosion, damn it?'

'For my money, sir, it was triggered by a delayed-action fuse.'

Eventually, Vincent was free to return, not to London, but to Portsmouth, where he was to report to Lieutenant Commander Ghyll.

On his arrival, he was so tired after his journey that, rather than go through the routine of requesting accommodation at *HMS Nelson*, he forsook the barracks in favour of a hotel room, where he slept very soundly until his travelling alarm clock reminded him of his meeting with Ghyll.

He left his car at the hotel and walked to *HMS Vernon*. It allowed him time to think about what he was going to tell his superior about the Type C at Piddletrenthide.

Eventually, he arrived at the gates of *Vernon*, showed his identification to the sentry and made his way to Ghyll's office. A Wren seated at a desk in the passageway asked him to identify himself, and he did.

'I'm sorry, sir. It's an awful nuisance, and officers don't like it, but I have to ask.'

'Yes, you must, and any officer who voices his resentment to you is wrong,' he told her. He knew the kind she was talking about, having spent much of the previous day with Lieutenant Commander Byrne.

'Thank you, sir. I'll tell Lieutenant Commander Ghyll you're here.' She picked up the telephone and rang through to his office. 'Lieutenant Reid is here, sir.' Then, putting down the telephone, she said, 'Lieutenant Commander Ghyll will see you now, sir.'

He walked along the passage until he arrived at Ghyll's office, where he knocked on the door. At the word, 'Come,' he opened the door and saw not just Ghyll, but Commander Todd as well. They were both hatless, so Vincent removed his and came to attention.

'Come in, Reid,' said Commander Todd. 'Take a seat and tell us about Piddletrenthide.'

'Thank you, sir.' Vincent took the nearest chair.

'I gather you made yourself very useful.'

'When I was allowed, sir. Lieutenant Commander Stewart was most accommodating.'

'Quite.' Todd and Ghyll exchanged looks. It seemed that they knew Byrne and his ways.

'You used the trepanning equipment, I gather.'

'Yes, sir, it was largely successful. I had to finish the job with a hacksaw.'

'And when you'd done that?'

It seemed odd that Todd was asking such questions, when presumably, either Stewart or Byrne had already reported to him, but he imagined he wanted to hear about Vincent's part in the investigation from his own lips. Ghyll sat beside Todd, hitherto silent.

'The four-inch hole that had been drilled posed a problem for the senior officers, sir, so I took out the battery leads and cut them.'

'Don't be coy, Reid. Tell us what you discovered.'

'Well, sir, having cut and insulated the wires, I could see inside the mine. In particular, I noticed a separate charge in the tail, with a mechanical trigger. In view of the time constraint, Lieutenant Commander Stewart decided to use plastic explosive on the tail, and he carried that out.'

'Then what, Reid?' Unable to contain himself, Ghyll asked the question.

'We were about to inspect the mine, when there was another explosion, sir. We were all far enough away from it, and we were fortunate enough to escape being hit by flying parts. It seemed that the Nazis had planted two extra booby traps, three in all, and the final explosion was triggered by a delayed-action device.'

Todd asked, 'Have you anything else to report, Reid?'

'Yes, sir. When I examined the interior of the mine, I could find no main charge.'

‘Incredible,’ said Ghyll.

‘That’s what I thought, sir, and then I put two and two, or rather, the three booby traps, together, and suddenly it made sense. That mine was never intended to be a threat to shipping. It was purely an attempt on the part of the Nazis to hinder our work and to kill anyone who tried to render the thing safe.’

‘It was most likely sanctioned by Hitler himself,’ said Todd.

Ghyll smiled and said, ‘Maybe he saw your film, Reid, and took umbrage at the idea that the “cool and competent officers” mentioned in it were being so successful.’

‘I suppose it’s possible, sir. When I put the diving suit on and descended into the dock, I never expected to gain the Führer’s recognition.’

‘Maybe the Ministry of Information has been too successful on this occasion,’ said Commander Todd.

‘Don’t worry, sir. I know just who to complain to.’

14

September

It's My Home

On the 7th of September, London was subjected to the kind of onslaught it had never previously known. Bombs fell like hailstones, causing extensive damage as well as creating many casualties. Parachute mines also continued to fall, and RMS teams were rushed into the capital.

For Vincent and Jimmy, it was business as usual, although they were far from complacent. Hazel was also busy in her own way, and had discovered something of importance.

'Did you know you had an Anderson shelter, Vincent?'

'Have I?'

'Yes, at least, you rent one as part of this property, but the garden's so overgrown, I'm not surprised you haven't noticed it. I didn't see it until yesterday.'

It was the end of a long and stressful day, and Vincent was inclined to be dismissive. 'I've always thought those things looked squalid,' he said.

'It's none too inviting at this stage,' she admitted, 'but with a little attention and perseverance, it could… let's say it could be a welcome alternative to being trapped in a collapsed building.'

'I've seen a few collapsed buildings recently.' Now that Hazel had raised the subject of air-raid safety, he asked, 'What air-raid arrangements have you at your flat?'

'None.'

'None at all?'

'At a pinch, I could crawl under the kitchen table. It's recommended.'

'By whom?' As he spoke, he wished he hadn't asked the question.

'Sir John Anderson, Minister for Air Raid Precautions, Ministry of Information Film 1201. I forget the date.'

'Do you really believe your own propaganda?'

'No, but you asked me a question, and I answered it.'

A mental image of her sheltering beneath a flimsy table caused him to wince in horror.

'What's the matter, Vincent?'

'You can't stay there, Hazel. Move in with me.'

'And live over the brush?'

'What?'

'It's an expression that's used where my family originated. It means "to live in sin".'

'Where did your family originate?' He'd never asked her.

'Cheshire.'

'I didn't know that, but you will consider my offer, won't you.'

'All right. Will you let me tidy up your Anderson shelter?'

'Yes, but please decide quickly.'

'Kiss me, Vincent.'

He kissed her, and she looked thoughtful for a moment, before saying, 'I'm still considering it.'

'Good.'

'By the way, another recommended sheltering place is under the stairs.'

'Don't quote the minister and the film, Hazel. I'll take your word for it.'

They were drinking tea when the air-raid sirens sounded again.

'Not content with what they did earlier,' said Hazel, 'they've come back to do it again.'

'Let's sit here until it becomes personal, and then we can adjourn to the understairs cupboard.'

'You sounded almost seductive when you said that, Vincent.'

For a moment, he seemed to consider the possibility, and then he said, 'I doubt if there's enough floor space under the stairs for that.'

'What about your piano? Could we shelter under that?'

'Absolutely not.'

'I promise I won't play "Chopsticks" or anything silly.'

'No, the space beneath a grand piano is very dangerous.'

'Seriously?'

'Yes, seriously. In fact, fatal injuries have been known.'

She adopted a surprised look and said, 'I can't remember hearing that at the Ministry.'

Vincent inclined his head to listen to the noise outside. 'They're here,' he said. As he spoke, there was a loud explosion, and the building shook. 'Let's withdraw to my alternative drawing room,' he said. 'It's beneath the stairs, and it'll be safer.' He picked up cushions from the sofa, and she did the same.

'I hope there's room for these in your cupboard,' she said.

'I really don't know. I've never looked in there.' He opened the door and found only an ironing board and a brush and dustpan. 'I think there's room,' he said. 'The cleaner brings her own things.'

They arranged themselves inside the cupboard, and he closed the door, imposing pitch darkness.

'What are you doing, Vincent?'

'Finding my way around in the dark.' There was another loud explosion.

'You're doing it very well.'

'Thank you. I need encouragement.'

'You certainly don't.' Even so, she let him kiss her.

There were more explosions that sounded a little further away. He kissed her again and said, 'There's something I need to tell you.'

'You do choose your moments.'

'This won't wait.'

'All right, spill the beans.'

'I love you, Hazel.'

'What a time to tell me that.'

'Do you want me to take it back and tell you when things are quieter?' It was an option, although he couldn't see the point.

'No, I don't.' She sounded emphatic. I want you to tell me again and again and again, every morning and every night. Also, when you're at home during the day, I want you to tell me at various times, even when I least expect it.'

'So you don't mind?'

'No, I can live with it. For what it's worth, I love you, Vincent.'

'That's a relief, and by the way, it's worth everything.'

They kissed in the darkness. Eventually, she said, 'There are one or two things I'd like to bring with me, just so that I feel at home.'

'Are you saying you'll move in with me?'

'Of course. I wouldn't be talking about bringing things with me, otherwise, would I?'

He felt like a child attempting a grown-up crossword. 'I'm a simple soul, Hazel,' he said. 'I need to be fed information in small helpings.'

'You'll soon learn.'

Hazel had left for the office when the telephone rang calling Vincent to a parachute mine in the Isle of Dogs. He called for Jimmy and was relieved to find that his assistant's home was still entire.

As they drove to the site, Jimmy asked, 'Do you know why it's called "The Isle of Dogs", sir?'

'Not really. In fact, I haven't a clue. There was a story that the kings of England used to keep their hunting dogs there, but that's been discredited. I'll tell you what. If you can find out the true story and tell me by the end of the day, I'll recommend you for your hook.' He'd been meaning to request Jimmy's promotion to leading seaman, and it was as good a pretext as any.

'I appreciate that, sir. As a matter of fact, what I really want to do is apply for a commission.'

That was a surprise. 'All right, Jimmy. Find out the truth about the Isle of Dogs, and I'll recommend you for a commission.'

'What if I can't find out, sir?'

'I'll recommend you, anyway. I don't want to be saddled with a rating who can't solve a simple conundrum.'

'Thank you, sir.'

'You're welcome, Jimmy.'

An ARP warden was waiting for them at the end of the road. He directed them to where a solitary policeman stood guarding the area.

'It's outside the rear of one-four-six, sir,' said the policeman. 'You can see the parachute from here.' He pointed, and Vincent saw the expanse of green silk stretched across the roof of the house. When they walked round to the front, they saw that the mine was in a kind of alley, nose-down and leaning against the side of the house where it adjoined an outside lavatory. It seemed that, in its fall, it had damaged both the wall of the house and that of the lavatory. After a careful assessment of the site, Vincent surmised that the parachute, which appeared to be wrapped around the chimney, was playing its part in holding the mine upright. The situation was less than encouraging.

He examined the bomb fuse plate, which was easily accessible, and saw that the car horn and pump were required. The opposite plates were less accessible, but he found that he could reach them via the damaged wall of the lavatory. 'I'll need the car horn, Jimmy.'

'I'll find a bucket of water, sir.'

'Thank you, Jimmy. Leave it across the road and then go back to the safety point.'

'Aye, aye, sir.'

'Very good.' As he spoke, he found himself wondering how a magnetic mine had fallen so close to metal hinges, presumably made of steel, and various other items of ironmongery without being triggered. A closer look at the convenience provided the answer. There was no cistern, but simply a red, glazed earthenware closet with a wooden lever in front of it and a bottle half-filled with, judging by the ambient odour, something like Jeyes Fluid. He could only surmise that it was one of the earth closets he'd heard about, and it made a pitiful kind of sense that the terrace would have no adequate sanitation. Beside the closet, and presumably serving as tissue, was a quantity of newsprint cut into conveniently-sized rectangles. The door hung from a single hinge. The lower hinge was missing along with a section of the door itself. It was a humble and abject excuse for such an essential facility, but if ever a brick privy deserved to survive a visit from a magnetic mine, it was that of number one-four-six, Gladstone Road. Vincent was at a loss, however, to understand why the single hinge had not activated the mine, until he examined it more closely and found that it was made of brass. Someone must have picked up the nearest hinge available, and the house, along with the others in the street, owed its continued existence to the fact that the hinge was non-magnetic.

Jimmy arrived at the house to report that a bucket of water now stood across the road, as promised.

'Thank you, Jimmy. Go back to the safety point.'

'Aye, aye, sir.'

Vincent fitted the bicycle pump to the bulb, and was about to start pumping, when a voice interrupted his concentration.

'Would you mind moving away?' The question came from an elderly woman clad in a woollen coat that covered, as far as he could make out, a flannel nightdress. He also noticed a pair of shabby bedroom slippers. She followed it with another question, 'What yer lookin' at me like that for?'

'I'm trying to check that you're not wearing anything that's likely to set this mine off.' He'd already noted the wooden buttons on her coat.

'Well now you've had a look, will you do as I ask?'

'Are you wearing any zip fasteners or press studs?'

'Who d' yer fink I am? Lady Muck? I'm wearin' me nightie, ain't I?'

'I meant on your coat.'

'No,' she answered impatiently. 'Will you move?'

'Why do you want me to move?'

'So that I can go to the lav.'

It was unbelievable. 'I'm afraid I can't. I have to make this mine safe. How on earth did you get through the cordon?'

'Through the what?'

'The tape that the police put up to close off the area.'

'Oh, that.' She seemed unimpressed, but offered no explanation. Instead, she persisted with her initial request, but with rather more urgency. 'Will you go somewhere else, just for a few minutes?'

'Do you know what this thing is?' He pointed to the mine.

'I know it's made a mess of my house. Now, listen, young fella, will you go for a walk while I do what's necessary?'

'You want to use this lavatory? There are others you could use, some distance from this mine.' The situation was completely surreal.

'This *Levatreh*,' she mimicked. 'I'm not as posh as you, but I certainly don't want to use anybody else's. You don't know what state some of 'em are in. They have 'em at the Salvation Army, but there ain't enough for all them what needs to use 'em. Will you go somewhere else before it's too late?'

Vincent knew when he was beaten. 'All right, but don't on any account touch the mine.'

'I'm not interested in your bloomin' mine,' she said, stepping into the cubicle and closing the ramshackle door as far as she could. 'All I'm interested in is doin' what I 'ave to do. Now, buzz off and leave me in peace.'

Vincent could only walk round to the front of the terrace and wait, wondering if the day could get any sillier. After some time, the woman reappeared.

'There,' she said, 'you can carry on tinkering with that thing out there.'

'Thank you. Will you please go back to the Salvation Army, or wherever you're supposed to be, and stay there while I deal with this mine?'

'Listen, young man. It's my home, an' no warden or bobby or whatever you reckon to be, is going to tell me I can't come to it when I please.'

'All right. Good day to you.'

'Good day to you, young man.'

An obliging constabulary relayed messages calling Vincent to two more incidents that day, both punctuated by air raids. He was weary by the time he and Jimmy set off to Bloomsbury, but he remembered to ask, 'Did you find out about the Isle of Dogs, Jimmy?'

'Yes, sir. You were right about the hunting dogs thing being nonsense.'

'I thought I was.'

'It's actually a corruption of "Isle of Ducks". Long ago, the area was marshland and it was populated by waterfowl. The island-thing is because it's bounded on three sides by the River Thames, sir.'

'How did you find out?'

'One of the policemen on the cordon told me. He's lived here most of his life.'

'Well done, Jimmy.' He remembered their agreement. 'Consider my recommendation written. I'll be sorry to see you go, but I shan't stand in your way.'

'Thank you, sir.'

'Think nothing of it.'

He arrived home during another air raid and, after making tea, he took it to the cupboard, where Hazel was waiting.

She said, 'Bless you, darling, but are we going to drink it in pitch darkness?'

'No, I'll leave the door open until we feel properly threatened.' Two explosions close by seemed to drop a hint to that effect, but he concentrated on his tea.

'Don't you feel threatened yet, Vincent?'

'No, and neither should you.' He put an arm around her to give her what comfort he could. 'I saw something today that was a model of either dogged determination or extreme foolhardiness,' he said. 'At all events, it amounted to putting two-fingers up to Hitler and his Luftwaffe.' He told her about the old woman who'd dodged the police and the ARP wardens just to use her own lavatory.

'I don't believe it,' she said when he'd finished the tale.

'Neither did I. I'm still convincing myself that it happened.'

'At such a time, people must feel particularly strongly about their homes.'

'They must,' he agreed, 'and with good reason.'

'And you lost yours only recently.' She stroked his hand in sympathy.

'But only for the time being. If it's still in one piece when the War Office have finished with it, I intend to move in again.'

'Why shouldn't you?'

'Why indeed? As the old woman said, it's my home, and…'

'What?'

'And, hopefully, it will be yours as well.'

15

October

When I Grow Rich

Towards the end of October, the Nazis changed their tactics. Hitherto, air raids had taken place in daylight, but that came to an end when, mindful of mounting losses, the Luftwaffe took to bombing by night. For day workers, such as Vincent, it was a mixed blessing; daytime disruption was no longer the problem it had been, but the nightly air raids made sleep at first a precious, and often sporadic, luxury.

Soon after night bombing began, Vincent was called to the district of Shoreditch, where a mine had fallen into an alley and become wedged between its opposite walls.

'Of all the places it could have landed,' said Jimmy, 'it managed to slot itself into this alley.'

'It's like one of those stones you suddenly find in your shoe,' said Vincent. 'Somehow, it makes its way between your shoe and your sock, quite by chance. Mind you, I'd rather have that problem than this one.' Taking the stethoscope from his toolkit, he walked carefully along the alley. Any excess vibration could potentially start the clock, so he crept as silently as he could.

He noted the two plates that confronted him. The other two were on the other side of the casing, but he would consider that problem later. For the time being, he simply needed to know if the mine was, at least relatively, safe.

He held the stethoscope against the casing above the clock housing and, as usual, all he could hear was his own excited circulation, so he stepped backward to assess the position of the mine in the alley. It was effectively leaning against the wall on his right, and its nose was a few inches from the wall opposite. For him to crawl either beneath the mine or over it without disturbing the clock was impossible. The other entrance to the alley appeared to be blocked.

Leaving the mine for the moment, he went to the spot where Jimmy was awaiting further orders. 'I'm going to have a look at the other end of the alley,' he told him. 'It's a Type A, and the only way I can get to the main detonator and the priming charge is by gaining access that way.'

'I'll come with you, sir, in case we need to move anything heavy.'

'Good thinking, Jimmy. You're earning that commission already.'

They walked along the row, counting the houses as they went, because there were several alleys, which made the job more complex than ever.

Eventually, they came to the entrance, and Vincent could see at once why it had appeared at first to be blocked. A dustbin had been placed in the opening, and on top of it was a large cardboard box.

'Let's get the box down,' said Vincent, wrinkling his nose at the stench that surrounded them.

'Let me do it, sir. I'm younger than you are.'

'Don't rub it in, Jimmy.'

Jimmy seized the box, almost gagging at the odour that emanated from within. He dropped it on the pavement, causing one corner to split and provide two rats with a convenient exit.

'Bedclothes,' said Vincent. 'Here, I'll give you a hand with the dustbin.'

Together, they manhandled the dustbin on to the pavement beside the box.

'Thank you, Jimmy. I'll have another look at the mine, now.' He made his way along the alley, sickeningly conscious of more rodent activity, until he reached the mine. As he'd suspected, the two plates were accessible, and there appeared to be sufficient light for him to do the job. He hurried back to where Jimmy was waiting. 'Jimmy, will you fetch my seaboots from the car, please?'

'Your seaboots, sir?'

'If I have to work with rats around me, the distraction will be less with a barrier between us.'

'Of course, sir.' Jimmy hurried back to the car.

While he waited, Vincent looked up and down the row of houses. Most of the doors were closed and presumably locked. Typically, however, a few had been left open. Maybe their owners had panicked and run. It was impossible to say, but the house that abutted on to the alley was one such abandoned home. He remembered his conversation with Hazel about people and their homes, and he felt a wave of pity for anyone who'd been evacuated from the place they'd always regarded as their ultimate refuge.

Jimmy returned, carrying Vincent's seaboots and wearing his own. 'I put mine on, sir, in case you needed help again.'

'You're going to make me regret giving you that recommendation, Jimmy.'

'I'm sure you'll find a good man to take my place, sir.'

'Right, Jimmy, go back to the safety point and wait until I give you the signal to join me.'

'Aye, aye, sir.'

Vincent picked up his tools and entered the alley once more. Some time had elapsed since he'd last worked on a Type A. It shouldn't be too difficult, but he was careful not be complacent. Taking the four-pronged wrench, he tackled the plate that covered the anti-handling device. As usual, it was stiff and required some persuasion, but he managed to loosen it and withdraw the device. So far, so good, but when he reached for a roll of insulating tape, something live and furry brushed his hand. With an involuntary shout, he stamped wildly, scoring some kind of hit, because the thing retreated along the alley, squeaking horribly.

Forcing himself to concentrate, he cut the wires and insulated them. It was time, then, to go to the other end of the alley. The thought repelled him, but he had to deal with the detonator and primer, so he picked up his tools and set off.

The dustbin end of the alley was as busy as ever with rats, and he kicked and swiped at them with his feet. It seemed to give him some respite from their attentions, and he continued to the mine.

Out of habit, he listened again with the stethoscope and was rewarded with silence. Exceptionally, he was able to unscrew the peculiar cross-bar device without needing a hammer, and the detonator with its five wires came free. He looked carefully, this time, before reaching for tape. As he crouched to pick it up, he heard another animal noise, this time a friendlier one, and he looked to the source of the miaowing. It was a huge silver tabby that approached him from the front of the terrace, an ally when he sorely needed one.

'That way,' he told the cat, pointing to the dustbin and other detritus.

'Miaow,' it told him companionably.

'Go on, earn your keep.'

'Miaow.'

Their conversation seemed set to go on for some time, but a noise at the far end alerted the cat, and it set off, clearly with business in mind.

Vincent attended to the cutting and taping of the wires, and was turning his attention to the primer when he was distracted again, this time by a loud and frantic squeaking. It went on for some time, and he had to summon his concentration to remove the primer.

The squeaking, which had occupied a good five minutes, had now stopped, and Vincent made for the dustbin end again, expecting anything. It was that kind of day.

When he reached the opening, the reason for the noise became apparent. There in his path lay a huge rat. It was grey, with an open mouth, hideously jagged teeth and long, curled claws, but it was dead, and the noises coming from behind the dustbin suggested that it would soon have company in rat hell. Vincent wasn't a vindictive man, but he was cheering silently for the cat.

He returned to the front of the terrace to work on the hydrostatic valve, confident that, if it had any sense, any rodent life that remained must be keeping its head down.

The hydrostatic valve came out easily. It seemed that, having fallen into a less-than-accessible place, the mine had become the least troublesome element of the whole experience, and he was as grateful for that as he was for the cat.

He carried his tools out and was about to signal Jimmy, but he heard something happening in the house with the open door. He imagined it might be rats again, but then he heard footsteps that were too slow and heavy for any rat. He opened the door to see what was happening and almost walked into a man carrying a woman's handbag.

'Where are you going with that?' It was a ridiculous question, but he asked it purely in response to a reflex.

'Out of my way,' snapped the man, knocking Vincent aside to get to the doorway. Vincent quickly recovered and leapt on him, bringing him down half across the threshold. The bag flew from his hand and he reached for it just as Vincent scrambled to his feet. For want of a better means of restraint, he stepped on to the thief's outstretched fingers.

The man screamed in pain, but Vincent maintained the pressure while he signalled Jimmy to join him.

The miscreant seemed to have a limited vocabulary, and Vincent was surprised when he realised quite how limited it was. Almost every word seemed to begin with 'f'.

Jimmy was about fifty yards away when Vincent shouted, 'The mine's safe. Fetch a policeman, quickly!'

Some people, although Vincent would never claim to be one of them, were able to move very quickly, and he was heartened to learn that Jimmy and one of the policemen on the boundary were in the high velocity category. They joined him in what seemed a mercifully short time, although he was more than ready to be relieved of the bag snatcher's vocal demands, which were restricted to, 'Gerroff, you f…ing bastard! F…ing gerroff me f…ing hand!'

'I caught him stealing a handbag from number ninety-four, Constable. That handbag, actually.' He pointed to the stolen article lying on the pavement.

'Very public-spirited of you, sir, I must say,' said the policeman, handcuffing the felon. 'Oh, I know you, don't I, Spry? I wonder who else you've robbed.'

''E's broken me f…ing fingers,' wailed Spry.

'Well, you should've kept 'em in your pockets instead of thieving other people's property.' Transferring his attention to Vincent, he said, 'We'll need a statement from you, sir, when it's convenient.'

'By all means.' Vincent handed him a card with his new address and telephone number handwritten on it.

'You did well to hold him, sir.'

'It's all down to practice, Constable. He's not the first rat I've trodden on today.'

A hearty 'Miaow' from behind Vincent reminded him that he wasn't the only nemesis of the undeserving. It was a timely reminder of the need for modesty.

'Thank you, sir. Come along, Spry. I have to caution you.'

'Me f…ing fingers!'

'It makes no difference. I'm arresting you for the theft of this handbag….' Their conversation continued into the distance.

Jimmy asked, 'Are you all right, sir?'

'Yes, thanks, Jimmy. Thank you for coming so quickly.'

'It was the least I could do, sir.'

Hazel asked, 'Where have you been today, darling?'

'All over the East End.'

'You must be jaded.' She handed him a cup of tea. 'There was a telephone call for you this afternoon from Old Street Police Station. What have you been up to in Shoreditch?'

'Rodent control.'

She regarded him blankly. 'Please explain.'

'I had to work on a mine, surrounded by rats. It was very difficult, but I wasn't alone.'

'Not poor Jimmy as well?'

'No, a big tabby cat. He was a friendly soul and much better at dealing with rats than I was, but I struck the final blow.'

She screwed up her eyes in distaste. 'I don't think I want to hear this,' she said.

'The furry ones had been dealt with,' he assured her. 'My final victim was a sneak-thief who'd stolen a handbag from one of the abandoned houses.'

'Oh, no. That's despicable.'

' "Despicable" is an understatement. That's why I likened him to a rat. As far as I know, it's one of the few species that prey on their own kind.'

Now satisfied that the story had moved away from rodent vermin, she asked, 'What did you do?'

'I rugby-tackled him and held him until Jimmy arrived with a policeman.'

'How brave.'

'Not really. He couldn't do very much while I was standing on his fingers.'

'Well, I'm still proud of you.'

'Are you, darling?' He put his arm round her and drew her close. 'I'm just glad I did it, because it means that some woman who's existing on very little hasn't lost her handbag. Let me tell you, I've seen a level of poverty in the East End that I never knew existed.' Bringing himself back to the present, he said, 'I suppose I should telephone the police station now.'

'I wonder if it was his first offence. You do wonder about these things, don't you?'

'You can stop wondering, darling. He's known to the local police. The officer who arrested him recognised him immediately. His name is Spry.'

'How very appropriate.' She thought again. 'No, I'm being unfair to Spry products and possibly to synthetic lard itself. At least, it performs a useful function.'

'Whereas he was trying to grow rich at the expense of the needy. Let's take satisfaction in the knowledge that he won't profit where he's going.'

'At least, he won't suffer the penalty that many criminals did after passing through Shoreditch.' She pondered that briefly until another thought occurred to her. 'I suppose you've no idea where you might be going tomorrow. Göring doesn't seem to recognise weekends.'

'Oh yes, I have. Jimmy and I are being rested for forty-eight hours. It's as long as they can give us, but I think you and I will make good use of it.'

16

November

Bedside Manners

Lieutenant Commander Ghyll telephoned from the new temporary headquarters situated between Havant and Rowlands Castle, *HMS Vernon* having suffered recent heavy bomb damage.

'It's a Category "A",' he explained, 'the highest priority, because it's in the London Hospital in Whitechapel.'

'Whereabouts in the hospital, sir?' Vincent needed as much information as he could get.

'It landed on the children's ward in Alexander Wing, just off Whitechapel Road. The whole wing has been evacuated, and the Army are working on a UXB in the adjoining West Wing, so do mind your manners. We'll just have to hope that they mind theirs as well. All right, Reid?'

'Yes, thank you, sir.'

'Good. Carry on.'

'Aye, aye, sir.'

Vincent collected Jimmy and they set off for Whitechapel. The journey took much longer than it would in normal times, because of diversions caused by bomb damage.

Jimmy asked, 'Did you hear Solomon on the wireless last night, sir?'

'Yes, I did. He never lets us down, does he?'

'I should say not, sir. I heard Neville Cardus say that he takes interpretation almost to the point of creativity.'

Vincent smiled. 'Cardus does tend to go overboard sometimes, and not only when he reports on cricket. Even so, Solomon has a rare ability.' He drove a little further, making yet another detour, and said, 'Mind you, Jimmy, it's often occurred to me that it's possible to interpret Classical and Romantic music too much.'

'Really, sir?'

'Oh, yes. You see, they told us so much about tempo, articulation, expression and so forth. Most of the Baroque composers, including J S Bach, told us very little. Instead, they gave us the freedom to explore their music, using our own good sense.' He came to a halt in response to a policeman's signal, although the barrier behind him told its own story.

'Where are you heading, sir?'

'Whitechapel Road. We're on our way to deal with an unexploded parachute mine.'

'Let me lift this barrier, sir, and you can go through.'

'Thank you, Constable.'

'It's no trouble, sir. Good luck.'

'Thanks again.'

Ten or so minutes later, they were outside the London Hospital, where they parked in front of a Royal Engineers Bomb Disposal lorry. 'We're the senior service, after all,' said Vincent, getting out of the car.

They tried the nearest entrance, where a stolid-looking sentry barred their path. 'Sorry, sir,' he said, 'I've orders to see that no one passes this point.'

'I appreciate that, Sapper, but we're here to deal with the parachute mine in the children's ward.'

'I don't know nothin' about that, sir.'

Vincent summoned his patience. 'Is there a corporal, a sergeant or someone else you can refer to? I assure you it's extremely urgent that we get to that mine.'

The man's features reflected the thought going on laboriously behind them. Eventually, he said, 'Excuse me a minute, sir.' He disappeared for a short time and returned with a corporal, who saluted Vincent and said, 'I imagine you're here about the parachute mine next door, sir.'

'That's the idea, Corporal.'

'Please carry on, sir. The Children's Ward is right off the corridor.'

'Thank you, Corporal.' As they continued, Vincent heard the corporal say to the sentry, 'Jackson, you're a good looking lad. If you were a bit more intelligent, you could train to be a hyacinth or a geranium, but you're bloody useless as a sentry.'

Vincent and Jimmy followed the corporal's directions, followed the sign marked *Children's Ward*, and went through the swing doors. The mine was impossible to miss. It had entered the ward via the roof and ceiling, and had come to rest leaning against the windowsill of a small office, possibly the ward sister's, having broken the window itself. Thankfully, it was at a safe distance from the nearest iron bedstead. It seemed quite secure, unlikely to move, which was a good thing, but it had landed with two of its plates uppermost, which meant that the other two were on the underside of the casing. There was, however, room for him to wriggle underneath when the time came. It was far from satisfactory, but there was nothing he could do to change it.

'It's a "Type B", Jimmy, with a blue polarity fuse.' He stood up and walked over to a far window from which he could see his car quite easily. 'When it's safe, I'll signal you from this window. Meanwhile, go back to the car and wait.'

'Aye, aye, sir, but in case you haven't noticed, we're not alone.' He was looking down the ward to where an attractive, dark-haired nurse sat beside a patient who was lying very still, possibly unconscious.

'Hello, Nurse,' said Vincent in as calm a tone as he could muster, 'I'm afraid I have to ask you to leave the ward. We'll give you a hand to move your patient, of course.'

'Thank you, Lieutenant, but this patient mustn't be moved. She's recovering from a serious and delicate operation, and she must keep perfectly still. I'm here to see that she does.'

'In that case, if I tell you to run, you must run, literally for your life. Is that clear?'

'Perfectly, Lieutenant. Let's just hope it doesn't happen, because I'd hate to disobey what would possibly be your last order on earth. I'm here to care for my patient, and that's the order I'll follow.' She gave an uncomfortable look and said, 'I have to say, though, I've been on duty all night, and I'm in need of relief, in more senses than one.'

'If you need to go to the heads,' said Jimmy, 'I'll watch your patient for you.'

'The heads?'

'Sorry, the lavatory.'

'Will you really?' She looked relieved already. 'How very kind. I'll be back in two shakes.' She turned to say, 'If she regains consciousness, just tell her very gently that she's all right, but she must keep perfectly still.'

'All right. Off you go.'

As the nurse left the ward, Vincent said, 'She'll remember you for that, Jimmy. You may be on to a good thing, but if you are going to try your luck, be quick about it.'

'Aye, aye, sir.' Jimmy had taken the nurse's chair and was watching the patient minutely. Meanwhile, Vincent took out the stethoscope and held it to the mine.

He was about to tackle the bomb fuse, when the nurse returned, looking much more comfortable. Jimmy vacated her chair, and there was a whispered conversation between them. Out of the corner of his eye, Vincent saw Jimmy leave the ward, smiling happily. 'Good luck, sir.'

'Thank you, Jimmy.' He attended to the bomb fuse, giving silent thanks that it was one of the two that were uppermost. The primer, underneath, would be a challenge, but he would take one step at a time.

He'd unscrewed the locking plate that covered the bomb fuse. The next stage was the critical one, drawing the fuse without letting it touch the casing. He could hear the nurse speaking to her patient, who must have regained consciousness. She was saying, 'Everything's all right, Irene. Just keep still.' Vincent made himself concentrate on the blue fuse, easing it in stages, a fraction of an inch at a time, with perspiration running down his face and into his eyes, so that he had to blink repeatedly before he could see what he was doing.

Eventually, he drew it clear of the casing and, breathing more easily, he removed his sweat-smeared glasses before unscrewing the gaine. Before tackling the main detonator, he removed his jacket and used his handkerchief to mop the perspiration from his face. The nurse was still speaking softly to her patient.

He had to put his weight behind the four-pronged spanner, but he managed to remove the plate. Again, the plug with the crossed-bars arrangement proved very tight, and he had no alternative but to use the four-ounce hammer and a brass rod. A gentle tap was all it needed, but he listened again with the stethoscope before unscrewing the plug. The detonator came out, trailing its five wires, which he cut and taped prior to removing the gaine. He could hear the patient crying and the nurse talking to her soothingly, repeating that everything was all right. Vincent hoped it was.

It was time to deal with the primer and the hydrostatic clock, and that meant crawling beneath the casing. Happily, neither of those instruments presented a challenge, other than by being where they were, and he was able to remove both.

In a relieved state of mind, he picked up his jacket and walked over to the window, waving to Jimmy, who responded immediately. Next, he spoke to the nurse. 'The mine's quite safe now,' he told her. 'A team will come to remove it, but it won't hurt anyone.' He saw the relief in her face.

'Thank you,' she said. 'That's a wonderful thing you've just done.'

'I was just doing my job, but let me tell you that you're a very remarkable young woman and you have my heartfelt admiration.'

'Thank you, Lieutenant, but if you were only doing your job, that's all I was doing.'

'Goodbye, Nurse and patient.' He picked up his toolkit as Jimmy appeared in the doorway. 'I'll take these down to the car, Jimmy. I have a feeling we'll be required again, so don't be too long, will you?' He walked down the corridor and learned that the bomb had been made safe, and the section, as they called themselves, were about to load it into the lorry. The lone sapper was still at his post, and he saluted Vincent, viewing him uneasily.

Vincent patted his shoulder. 'Don't worry, Sapper,' he said. 'You were only carrying out orders.'

He was waiting for Jimmy when a policeman stopped his bicycle beside the car to ask, 'Are you Lieutenant Reid, sir?'

'Yes.'

'I have a message for you, sir. I don't know who sent it, but the message is for you to go to a parachute mine in Albert Road, Poplar.'

'Thank you very much, Constable. I'll go there straightaway.' The passenger door opened, and Jimmy got in. 'You're just in time, Jimmy. I was about to leave you here, but I don't suppose you'd have minded that.'

'No, sir.'

'When are you going to see her?' He started the car and moved off.

'We've left it that I'll get in touch the next time we're rested, sir. Daisy's on nights this month, so it's not easy, but we'll find a way.'

'Daisy, eh? It's a nice, fresh, outdoor name.'

'She's a nice girl, sir.'

'Oh, she's much more than that, Jimmy, as well you know.'

As usual, Hazel dispensed tea, comfort and her complete attention, but Vincent wanted to know about her day at the Ministry.

'Why do you want to know about the boring old Ministry?'

'Because it's commonplace, as you said, and because sometimes, after a day of excitement, it's good to hear about something that's not so exciting.'

'Of course it is. Now, where shall I start? There was the hunt for the missing treasury tags, the two-inch ones, naturally.'

'Naturally.'

'Then, a shortage of bank was reported.'

'A shortage of what?'

' "Bank" is the flimsy paper that's used for carbon copies.'

He affected a look of concern. 'That's absolutely vital,' he said. 'How can a ministry worthy of its name function without copy paper? What price reports in triplicate, then?'

'They discovered some in the basement, so the war can continue uninterrupted.' She stroked his hand. 'Are you going to tell me about your day, or is it all a big secret?'

'Much of it is,' he confirmed, 'but I can tell you something that should be made known to the whole population. I saw a glorious example of genuine, unconditional care and cold courage, and I saw those things embodied in a girl of, maybe, twenty. I'll know her age soon enough, because Jimmy's going to start seeing her.' He told her about Daisy, the nurse at the London Hospital, and her insistence that she was only doing her job.

'What a wonderful story, darling, and you're right. The population should hear about those things.'

'I'm not exactly inarticulate, but I must say it's difficult to put my admiration for her into words. Under stress, even her manners were faultless.'

‘But I know what you’re feeling. I see cold courage every day.’

‘Do you?’

‘Yes, every time I look at you,’ she said, adding, ‘and you have lovely bedside manners, too.’

17

Hydrophones and Hand-Blown Goblets

At the end of the month, Vincent was called to a conference at West Leigh House. All he knew was that a cottage in the grounds had become the new base of the Mine Design Department, so he was curious, but orders were orders, so he contained his curiosity and reported at the stated time to be enlightened.

Within a very short time, Lieutenant Commander Ghyll took him into a room where several senior naval officers as well as a number of civilians were grouped around a table. At the head of the table sat Commander Todd.

'Hello again, Reid,' he said.

'Good morning, sir.'

Todd spoke to the others. 'When Lieutenant Reid applied to join RMS,' he told them, 'I was on the point of sending him away, but he told me something I didn't quite understand at the time, and I confess I still find it challenging, but I was sufficiently impressed to take him on board, as it were.' Turning to Vincent, he said, 'Tell everyone what you told me, Reid. They know about your diving experience and your success as an RMS officer, but they need to hear the rest.'

It wasn't at all what Vincent had expected, and he felt as vulnerable as he had that day in Portsmouth. Nevertheless, he was under Commander Todd's orders, so he did his best to oblige. 'I believe Commander Todd is referring to the fact that, in peacetime, I am Professor of Music History at the London Institute.' He was immediately conscious of the disbelieving looks of the gathering. Nevertheless, he went on to say, 'RMS were looking for officers with analytical minds, and that was partly what I had to offer. As Commander Todd has said, you know about my diving and RMS record.'

'They do, Reid,' said Todd, and the time has come for me to tell you why I've brought you here, but first, gentlemen, is there a chair for Lieutenant Reid?'

'I see one, sir.' Vincent picked up what looked like a Sheraton dining chair in a corner of the room and placed it nearer the table.

'Good,' said Todd. 'Now for the important part, which concerns the acoustic mine, or mines, as we have no idea of the full picture. Do you know what I'm talking about, Reid?'

'Presumably, a mine that is detonated by soundwaves, sir? I imagine a ship's propellors would perform that function.'

'You imagine correctly. The mine is equipped with hydrophones that pick up the acoustic signature of a ship's propellors. So far, mines have been detonated at some distance by a destroyer at speed, and more locally by slower craft. They were less fortunate than the destroyer.' Turning to one of the civilians, he said, 'Doctor Stevenson, perhaps you would care to explain the principle to Lieutenant Reid.'

'I'm happy to, Commander.' Stevenson launched into a scientific discourse that, far from elucidating, left Vincent clueless.

'Thank you, Doctor Stevenson,' said Todd. 'And now the problem, which is that, whilst we know that the mine can be triggered by ships' engines, our knowledge is very approximate. We know nothing definite about the range of frequencies to which the mine is sensitive.' He gave a gesture of hopelessness, and the civilians around the table looked suitably embarrassed. 'After this brief introduction to the subject, have you any suggestion to make, Reid?'

'Yes, sir, I have.' He also had everyone's attention, which surprised him, because he would have expected the scientists to have arrived at the same conclusion. 'I think we need to find an acoustic mine and strip it of its detonator, primer, etcetera, so that the acoustic receptor can be examined in the laboratory. It can also be bombarded with sound at infinitely variable frequencies.'

Dr Stevenson gave him a sharp look and asked, 'Just what piece of apparatus do you propose to use, Lieutenant?'

'The human voice, Doctor Stevenson.'

Stevenson shook his head dismissively. 'I don't believe this,' he said.

Vincent was determined to convince him. 'I remember a time during my childhood, Doctor Stevenson,' he said, 'when my father arrived home with a record of Dame Nellie Melba. It caused great excitement, and we could barely wait for him to lower the needle. There was more excitement, however, when Dame Nellie reached one of her celebrated high notes and, with no warning at all, it caused one of our antique, hand-blown wine goblets to shatter. She had unknowingly produced the exact frequency required to make that happen. Fortunately, we never discovered the frequencies to which the other goblets were vulnerable. One accident was enough, but isn't it also enough to demonstrate the feasibility of my suggestion?'

'A soprano voice?'

'Also a bass, a baritone, a tenor and the rest. My guess is that the male voices will bring forth a result because their frequencies will be most closely related to those of a ship's propellors.'

The scientists looked thoughtful.

'There is a mine lurking beneath the surface in Pegwell Bay in Kent,' said Commander Todd, 'and we're quite certain it's acoustic. Will you go down there and render it safe, Reid?'

'With pleasure, sir. I take it a mobile diving unit from Chatham will be made available?'

'No, you're going to need the services of a diving tender. It's been out there keeping an eye on the mine ever since it was discovered. We were alerted to it when the other mine that was sown there was detonated by a fishing boat. Anyway, Reid, I look forward to hearing about the results of your experiment.'

'By the way, Jimmy,' said Vincent, 'you can tell the fair Daisy that they're resting us for seventy-two hours after this operation.'

'Oh, good. Thank you for telling me that, sir.'

Vincent pulled in beside a small van marked *RN*, and was pleased as well as surprised to see the petty officer who'd officiated on the occasion when a police launch had come close to detonating a mine.

'Good morning, PO. Have you been here long?'

'Only half-an-hour, sir. We haven't as far to come as you have, you see.'

'Quite. Do you know where the mine is?'

'Yes, sir. It's flagged.' The petty officer pointed to a red flag that appeared to be some distance from the beach.

'How on earth am I going to get to the diving tender?'

'We have the means, sir. A dinghy will take you out, if you care to follow me.' The petty officer led him and Jimmy to a small wooden jetty, where a dinghy was waiting. 'For obvious reasons, we couldn't use a launch, sir. Instead, we have to rely on the gentlest of manpower.'

Vincent found himself staring up at a colossal able seaman.

'Able Seaman North, sir,' said the man, introducing himself. 'Let me help you aboard, sir.' He held out a great ham of a left arm and steadied Vincent and then Jimmy as they stepped aboard the dinghy.

'Thank you, North.'

'It's my pleasure, sir.' North pushed against the jetty with one oar and gave way towards the tender, dipping the oars into the sea with the delicacy of a watchmaker. 'I have to row quietly, you see, sir,' he explained.

'You're doing an excellent job, North.'

He took them to the diving ladder on the side of the tender's hull and hung on to it while Vincent and Jimmy climbed aboard.

'Thank you, North.'

'It's my pleasure, sir.' North demonstrated the fact with a huge smile as he tied up the dinghy.

'Welcome aboard,' said a new voice. 'I take it you're Reid. I'm Wilkinson.' He, also, was a lieutenant in the RNVR.

'How d' you do.' Vincent took his hand.

'I see you have your own attendant.'

'Able Seaman Riddle, yes.'

'Good. I'll show you to the changing compartment and leave you to it.'

Vincent and Jimmy went through the familiar routine as meticulously as ever, after which Vincent walked ponderously towards the stool beside the ladder. Jimmy fixed the helmet to the corselet and waited for the signal from Vincent. When he was sure the air supply was working correctly, Vincent gave the 'thumbs-up' sign and went to the ladder, steadied by Jimmy and another rating. He quickly reached the bottom of the ladder, but the shot rope was there, as reassuring as ever.

When his feet touched the bottom, he adjusted his air intake until he could move without difficulty, and looked around for the mine, which was easy enough to identify, being almost spherical, unlike the magnetic mines with their sausage-like shape. He examined it carefully and began work on what he imagined was the bomb fuse.

At this stage, he became aware that something wasn't right. The plug had turned easily when he put gentle pressure on the spanner, but then he'd come up against resistance. It was more than a warning sign. It was a full stop. He made his way back to the tender and increased the air flow into his suit, so that the extra buoyancy bore him to the surface. As he climbed the ladder, waiting hands helped him over the side.

Lieutenant Wilkinson was there, and his surprise was evident. He voiced it when Jimmy released the helmet. 'That was quick,' he said.

'I've left it for the time being. I think it's booby-trapped.'

'Hell.'

'Have you got on board about a hundred-and-fifty yards of towing line?'

'We should have. In any case, we can splice it. What do you have in mind?'

'I'd like to go down again with a long line made fast onshore or at least tied to a buoy, and secure the mine so that it can be hauled inshore for easier dismantling.'

'If that's what you recommend, it shall be done. We'll find the rope, and I'll get North to take one end inshore and secure it.'

In the end, the crew found nearer two hundred yards of rope, which Able Seaman North took inshore and attached to the jetty. Vincent prepared again to dive with the other end of the rope.

He had a nasty feeling about it now, and he worked as quickly as he could to make the mine secure. It was with a huge feeling of relief that he returned to the tender and allowed himself to be helped back on board.

'I'll have to report to RMS,' he said as soon as he was free of his helmet. 'They'll probably send a trepanning device, but we'll have to wait and see.'

Wilkinson asked, 'What's a trepanning device?'
'A drill that cuts a large, circular hole in the casing.'
'Won't that trigger the mine?'
'That's what we'll find out soon enough.'

Vincent sent Jimmy back to Chatham with the petty officer, so that he could catch a train to London. Meanwhile, he drove to West Leigh House.

Commander Todd was occupied, but Lieutenant Commander Ghyll took Vincent into his office.

'I gather it didn't go quite as planned, Reid,' he said.

'It didn't happen at all, sir.' He described his experience with the bomb fuse. 'I have a bad feeling about it, sir. I'm fairly certain it's booby-trapped. I've secured the mine with a line attached to the jetty, so it should be possible to haul it safely ashore. Then, I think we'll need to fall back on the trepanning device.'

Ghyll considered the possibility and said, 'But that could trigger the detonator, surely.'

'I don't think so, sir. The trepanning drill makes a high-pitched noise very different from a ship's propellors.'

'Very well, I'll report your findings to the team and let you know their decision.'

'I'd be grateful if I could be allowed to take part in the operation, sir.'

'After your experience, you should be. I'll put the matter to Commander Todd.' Ghyll knew as well as anyone the psychological importance of allowing an RMS officer to see the task through.

'What a long day you've had,' said Hazel. 'Are you sure you don't want anything to eat?'

'Absolutely, thank you. I had something at West Leigh House. In any case, I'm too tired to eat.'

'Would you like a hot water bottle?'

He smiled mischievously. 'I'd rather have you.'

'How can I refuse you after what was obviously a gruelling day?'

' "Tell me not in mournful numbers, Life is but an empty dream!" '

'What's that?'

'I'm just saying let's forget about my long, hard day, which I'm not at liberty to discuss, anyway. Tell me instead about your day.' He filled two glasses and waited for the welcome distraction.

'All right.' Hazel was accustomed, by this time, to his insistence on hearing about her work at the Ministry, rather than pondering the frustrations of the day. 'I've given a lot of thought to the story you told me about the nurse and the patient who couldn't be moved, and I agree that heroism of that order should be made known.'

'Good, but is anything likely to happen?'

'Well, I've spoken with my boss, and he's in total agreement, subject to the usual safeguard.'

'What's that?' Tiredness was invading his memory.

As if in quotation, she asserted, 'The morale of the people must not be undermined by references to fear, weakness or unreliability.'

'Heaven forbid that we should be seen as less than perfect.'

He sipped appreciatively and then looked thoughtfully at his glass. 'I think we should use the antique goblets more often,' he said.

'Do you really think so? They look very fragile.'

'They're very old, but surprisingly robust. We had them for years, and they're likely to last a few more years,' he said, smiling to himself, 'now that Dame Nellie is no longer with us.'

18

Though Every Prospect Pleases

Jimmy was allowed to enjoy his seventy-two-hour rest period and to become better acquainted with Daisy, but a telephone call from West Leigh House curtailed Vincent's recuperation.

'It's all set for tomorrow,' said Lieutenant Commander Ghyll, speaking cryptically, as usual. 'The drill will be available, and we'd like you to be there by oh-nine-thirty.'

'Who else will be there, sir?'

'An army of us, if you'll forgive my choice of metaphor. There'll be a party from Chatham, some of our people and the… drilling team. You, however, will be chief surgeon.'

'Excellent, sir. Thank you.'

'Good. I'll see you down there. Carry on, Reid.'

'Aye, aye, sir.'

Vincent enjoyed his day of rest, largely at the piano, where he could dispel, at least for the time being, thoughts of the next day, which, he was soberly aware, would be more than challenging.

Getting out of London was the hardest part of the journey. Thereafter, the road through Dover and that to Pegwell Bay presented no difficulty, and he parked again beside the Chatham vehicle, which, on this occasion, was the familiar lorry.

'We'll need the lorry's winch,' Ghyll told him. 'I just hope the line on the mine is long enough.'

Vincent thought of the diving equipment in the lorry, and said, 'I'm sure we could extend it, sir.'

The team from Chatham were hard at work, fixing a pulley block whereby the lorry could remain on the metalled road whilst hauling the mine up the beach.

In the event, the line proved too short to reach the lorry, and it was necessary to attach an extension, but it was eventually hitched to the winch, and the first part of the operation could begin.

'We'll make the other side of the road the safety point,' said Ghyll, observing the natural hollow that would afford protection from any blast. 'I'll leave it to you to communicate with the driver, Reid.'

'Aye, aye, sir.' Vincent waited until everyone was behind the safety point, before speaking to the driver, an earnest-looking able seaman. 'Now, Cartwright, as slowly as the winch will turn. We don't want to give the mine a bumpy ride.'

'No, sir.'

'All right, take it away.'

'Aye, aye, sir.' Cartwright engaged the lever and started the winch. The line gradually became taut, and Vincent saw part of it rise from the water.

'Keep going.' He was mindful of the elasticity of the rope. He wasn't sure how far it would stretch, but he knew the difference would be considerable.

Suddenly, he saw movement in the water. 'It's coming, Cartwright. Keep it dead slow.'

'Aye, aye, sir.' Serious as ever, Cartwright kept the winch turning so that the line remained taut without jerking.

It was now visible above the surface, eventually clearing the water and inching up the beach. Vincent waited until it reached a hollow in the sand, and said, 'Stop there, Cartwright. You can go behind the safety point now, and thank you for doing an excellent job.'

'Thank you, sir.' Cartwright headed for the safety point as Ghyll emerged to greet Vincent.

'Well done, Reid.'

'Thank you, sir.'

'We may as well leave the line attached. We'll need it to haul the mine on board.'

'Yes, sir.' Vincent hoped quite fervently that they would.

'I'll get the trepanning crew on the job.'

It was a great relief to everyone that the trepanning device did not trigger the detonator, and they settled down for a long wait. At a little before noon, an examination revealed that the cutter was almost through, so everyone retired again to the safety point while the trepanning device was restarted.

Half-an-hour later, the high-pitched note changed, and they knew it had cut through the casing. The device was stopped. The time had come for Vincent to make his examination.

He peered into the four-inch hole made by the cutter. He could hear the clock quite clearly now. It could tick for several days or it could be near the end of its setting, in which case it would detonate the mine. He reached inside and hooked his fingers around the detonator to the auxiliary charge. Conscious of the sharp edge left by the cutter, he withdrew it carefully. The next job was to disconnect the battery, which was tantalisingly out of his reach, so he returned to the safety point to speak to Ghyll.

'I can't reach the clock, sir. It calls for another hole next to the first one.'

'All right, Reid. Show the trepanners where you want it. It's going to be a long day, but it should be worth the wait.'

Two hours later, they knew that the cutter was through again. Vincent was able to reach through the hole and retrieve the battery leads, which he cut and insulated.

The third hole over the clock had to be cut in the rear door of the mine, a process that offered quite a challenge, but the team eventually fixed the cutter between the fins, and the process began again.

The familiar whirr of the cutter told them that it was through, and Vincent returned to the mine to examine it. He found more batteries than he'd expected, and he disconnected the leads to all of them. In theory, the mine was now incapable of electrical detonation, but as Vincent straightened up to report back, the clock suddenly stopped, and he sprinted up the beach. Logic had nothing to do with it. He was simply reacting.

He crossed the road and hurled himself into the hollow. 'The clock's stopped,' he told Ghyll. They waited until they knew they were safe, and then Vincent took a length of rope back to the mine. Carefully, he unfastened the screws that held the back door on, propping it temporarily with a wooden case from the lorry. In the event of an explosion, its disappearance would have to be explained, but that held no worries for Vincent. With the rope attached to all four fins, he walked up the beach, paying it out as he went. When he reached the safety point, he gave it a sharp jerk and waited. Nothing happened, so he peered over the edge of the hollow and saw that the after part of the mine had come away. It was now safe.

He returned to his car and sat for a while, reluctant to drive back to London until his wits were once more together.

Lieutenant Commander Ghyll came to him as the team were winching the mine into the lorry. 'A magnificent job, Reid,' he said. 'Well done indeed.'

'Thank you, sir. I suppose the next stage is to dismantle the mine and recover the hydrophones and other bits of devilry.'

'That's right, and then we'll bombard them, as you said earlier, with the best efforts of Covent Garden or wherever, and find out the optimum frequency required to detonate such a mine. When we've done that, we have to work out a way of sweeping the abominable things, but be assured, Reid, you played your part to the full today.'

'Thank you, sir.'

'And to think we almost let you go. It's a reminder that we have to keep our minds open to new ideas.'

Rain began to fall, spotting the windscreen. 'Would you care to shelter, sir, while they're putting the baby to bed?'

'Thank you, Reid. That's most considerate of you.' Ghyll opened the passenger door and got in. 'Are you settled at your new address, now?'

'For the time being, sir, although I'll be happier when my house is returned to me.'

'Quite, but I think you'll be in for a long wait. At least, I hope you will.'

'So do I, sir. After the lesson we taught the Kriegsmarine in the

Norway Campaign and the one the RAF have just delivered, Hitler might well have second thoughts about planning an invasion.'

'You're right, Reid. He would do well to think again.'

'Meanwhile,' said Vincent in a more confident tone, 'we're still at the crease, and the umpire is yet to raise his finger.'

Ghyll laughed. 'Well said, Reid.' Looking at his watch, he made a decision. 'It's time I left you.' He opened the car door to leave, and offered his hand. 'Congratulations again.'

'Thank you, sir.'

Living at home was an unusual luxury for a serviceman, and Vincent appreciated it all the more for having Hazel there. They'd settled, as usual, on the sofa, just until the bombing persuaded them to take refuge in the cupboard.

'I know you can't tell me what you've been up to, apart from what I already know, that your job is to make mines safe, but I wish I could do more for you when you come home weary and preoccupied.'

'You do plenty for me, darling, and I'm not really preoccupied, although, to be honest, when I arrived home, I thought you might be.'

'You're very perceptive.'

'So you are preoccupied?'

She didn't respond immediately, and it was clear that something was troubling her deeply. 'Do you remember my telling you about Lily at work?'

'With the two boys who ran away from their evacuation home? Yes, I remember.'

'You always do. It was a silly question.'

'Isn't the legal guardian application going according to plan?'

'Oh, she should hear about that soon. Her solicitor's confident that it'll go through. No, it's not that.'

Vincent put his arm round her and drew her close. He said nothing, but waited for her to speak again.

Hazel took a breath and said, 'Lily's already had a breast removed, and it seems, now, that the other will have to go.'

'Oh, no. The poor woman.'

'The thing is, Vincent, would you mind terribly if I brought the boys to stay here while Lily's in hospital?'

'The patter of tiny footsteps? Of course I don't mind.'

Despite her obvious relief, she had to warn him. 'They're ten and eight years old, Vincent, hardly tiny.'

'That's all right. We can send them out to clean chimneys and sell matches. That way, they can earn their keep.'

'You are awful.' Even so, she kissed him. Then, as the thought occurred to her, she said, 'I don't know what we'll do about sheltering them from the bombing. It's far too cold to use the Anderson shelter.'

'They can use the understairs cupboard. They'll like that.'

'All right, but what about us?'

He thought about something he'd seen at *Vernon*, the place where those not involved in critical examinations took shelter. Scaled down, it would do the trick. He asked, 'Can I ask you to find a carpenter?'

'Are you being serious?'

'Very serious. I'm going to draw something, and I want a carpenter to make it happen. It'll resemble a cage with a very strong vertical structure, rather like the dining table idea, and it needs to be the size of a double bed.'

'Are you still being serious?'

'Of course I am. I'll have you know I take double beds very seriously.'

'I've noticed.' She was quiet for a short spell, and then she said, 'It sounds like an excellent idea. If it's successful, I may even ask my superiors to suggest it to the government. You know how they're always asking for ideas.'

'I don't like it when politicians get ideas.'

'If they were to adopt it, they might even name it after you. "The Reid Shelter".'

'Or "The Air Reid Shelter". No, I'm sorry, that was awful. In any case, the politicians would take all the credit for themselves, as usual.'

She snuggled more closely and said, 'You're a lovely man to say you'll take the boys in, and after a tiring, and no doubt trying, day.'

He'd been thinking about that. 'Shall I tell you what was the worst thing about today?'

'Please do.'

'We went to Pegwell Bay, near Ramsgate.'

'I've heard of it. What's it like?'

'It's more of an inlet than a grown-up bay, but it's a beautiful place, and we went there to deal with a fiendish device that only the depraved mind of a Nazi could conceive. That was the worst part.'

'I'm sorry, darling.'

'I was reminded of a hymn we used to sing at the end of the Michaelmas Term.'

She looked at him oddly. 'You'll have to translate, darling. My school wasn't as posh as yours.'

'I'm sorry. It was just before we went home for Christmas.'

'Now I understand. What was the hymn? Maybe I know it.'

' "From Greenland's Icy Mountains".'

'Very Christmassy, I'm sure.' She still looked lost.

'Singing that hymn was an annual tradition.'

'And what reminded you of it?'

'Finding that evil contrivance in a place of such innocent beauty.' He quoted the hymn:

"What though the spicy breezes,
Blow soft o'er Ceylon's isle;
Though ev'ry prospect pleases,
And only man is vile:" '

19

December

Terror Packs

Lily's operation was deemed sufficiently urgent that it was brought forward to the twentieth of December, and the boys arrived with their luggage at Vincent's house. They were understandably shy. Even Reggie, with his reputation for pluckiness, was uncertain. The boys had met Hazel, and they seemed at ease with her, but Vincent was a different proposition.

'Reggie and Eric,' said Hazel, 'this is Uncle Vincent. It's his house, and he's very kindly invited you to stay here while your mum's in hospital.'

'Hello,' said Vincent, 'I'm not all that frightening, really. I'm good at frightening spiders away, but that's all.'

Reggie asked, 'Can you really scare spiders?'

'I can terrify the wits out of them. You should see how they shake when I'm around.'

Disbelief or the possibility of a demonstration prompted Reggie to look around for a convenient spider. 'I can't see one,' he said finally.

'That's because I've scared them all away.' He turned to Eric, who was standing silently by, and asked, 'What do you want to do when you're older, Eric?' It was as good a question as any for breaking the ice.

Eric looked more uncertain than ever and mumbled, 'I don't know.'

'Well, don't worry. You're only like lots of other boys.' He could tell Eric was unconvinced, so he said, 'Most boys don't know what they want to do until they're much older than you. Girls decide a lot sooner, but they're impatient.'

'I want to be a deep-sea diver,' said Reggie. 'I want to fight a giant octopus.'

'I don't know where you'd find one of them,' said Vincent.

'In the sea,' said Reggie confidently.

'I wouldn't bank on it. I went diving last month, and I didn't see a single giant octopus, as hard as I looked.'

'Go on.' Clearly, Reggie wasn't easily taken in.

'It's true.'

Hazel was leafing through a file. 'Just a minute,' she said. 'I've got something to show you.' She took out a still photograph from the Ministry's RMS filming and showed it to Reggie. 'That's Uncle Vincent going into the water in his diving suit.'

'Is that really you?'

'Yes, it is. If you look carefully,' he said, pointing to the tiny print on the back of the diving suit, 'you'll see that it says, *Lieutenant Vincent Reid. This way up*.'

'I can't read it. It's too little.'

Eric looked as if he might be about to speak, but his nerve failed him at the last minute, and he whispered something to Hazel.

'Eric wants to know what the big black thing is in the drawing room, Vincent.'

'Ah, the big black thing in the drawing room,' he repeated mysteriously. 'Come along, and I'll show you.'

Emboldened by curiosity, Eric followed him, while Reggie asked, 'Have you got any more photos of deep-sea divers?'

Vincent checked that the black-out was in place in the drawing room and switched on the light. 'There's no mystery,' he said, lifting the fall to reveal the keyboard. 'It's a piano.'

'It's not like the piano at school.'

'No? Well, they come in all shapes and sizes. This is a grand piano. Do you want to hear it?'

Eric stared with open-mouthed fascination, but it was clear that he did, so Vincent played him some of Chopin's Black Key Study. The fascination remained and, finding his nerve once more, Eric asked, 'Did you get it for Christmas?'

'Yes, I did, now I think of it. My father bought it just before Christmas nineteen-twelve. He said it was for the next twenty Christmases because it was so expensive.'

'Did he?'

'Yes, but he didn't mean it. He was only joking.'

Eric was already thinking about something else. He asked, 'Do you know "Winter Wonderland"?'

'Yes, do you want to hear it?'

Eric nodded excitedly, so Vincent began. It was the kind of thing he'd used occasionally to surprise his more seriously-inclined students, but he played it now because a shy, ten-year-old boy had asked him for it, and that was a much better reason.

When he came to the end, he saw Eric's rapt expression and went on to play 'Away in a Manger'. Suddenly, he was aware that Hazel and Reggie were in the room and they were singing. Before long, Eric was singing, too, softly and not exactly keen to be heard, but he was joining in all the same. They sang several carols, only calling a halt when Reggie insisted on singing his own versions: 'Good King Wenceslas knocked a bobby senses-less on the floor of Marks and Spence-eses' and 'We three kings of Orient are, one in a bus and one in a car, one on a bicycle sucking an icicle, piddling into a jar.' At that point, the air-raid siren sounded, and it was time for the boys to go to bed in the Wellington bomber under the stairs. Vincent and Hazel retired with a bottle of wine to their bedroom to listen to the wireless and congratulate each other on having settled the boys into their home.

Vincent was called briefly to West Leigh House to be appraised of the latest from the laboratory. It transpired that the sound receptors in the acoustic mine could be set to react to a broad spectrum sound signature, which would presumably target various sizes of ship, or a narrow spectrum, which would only be triggered by a large ship. Experiments were now taking place to find a means of detonating acoustic mines at a safe distance. Vincent found the news very satisfying.

Then, it was time for him to return to routine RMS work, largely in

London, but occasionally in Essex or Kent. He could now identify an acoustic mine, but he was thankful that he'd not so far come across one.

Another task he'd taken on was that of preparing Jimmy for his interview. He was a bright lad, and he could probably think on his feet, but a little extra help was never a bad thing.

As they drove home from the Essex Marshes, he asked Jimmy, 'Why do you want a commission?'

'Because I want to fulfil my potential, sir.'

'How would you describe your potential?'

That caught him out. 'I don't know, sir.'

'You see, they're likely to seize on an answer and pursue it in that way. You could say that, having worked in RMS from the beginning, you feel that you have an appreciation of the trials that beset an RMS officer, and that you believe you can manage your responses and concentrate on the task in hand.'

'That's good, sir.'

'Keep thinking about it, Jimmy. They'll try to wrong-foot you, but you must be ready for that, and never tell them you don't know.' He smiled at the memory of his interview and said, 'You could always go out on a limb as I did at my board. That was before the war, of course.'

'What did you say, sir?'

'When they asked me why I wanted to be an officer, I told them that without wishing to sound trite, I believed that it would enable me to engage the potential enemy more closely. It made them chuckle, but they couldn't fault my aim to follow one of Lord Nelson's hallowed precepts.'

'Oh, well done, sir. I'd never have thought of that.'

Reacting to Jimmy's obvious disquiet, he said, 'You have to remember that I've been able to observe officers and sometimes inadvertently overhear their conversations since the last war, and memories become embedded. Now, let's try another question. What do you consider to be the requirements of leadership?'

'Oh, example, fairness, the ability to earn respect, clear thinking, decisiveness….'

'All right. How would you set about earning the respect of the ratings under you?'

'By being scrupulously fair and by keeping my word, sir.'

'Full marks, Jimmy. You're in with a chance.'

'It's just as well, sir. I have to wear my white cap tally from tomorrow, to show that I'm a candidate for a commission.'

That evening, Hazel said, 'I went shopping today, Vincent.'

'Good for you. When you need money from me, just say the magic words.' They were speaking softly in the kitchen, where the boys were unlikely to hear them.

'What are the magic words?'

' "Hand over your money. This gun is loaded." '

She gave him a playful dig in the ribs. 'Seriously,' she prompted.

'Seriously, let me know.'

'Thank you. I went to Hamleys at lunchtime.'

'What do they do?'

'It's the oldest toyshop in the world, known to everyone but you, it seems. I went there to find something for Eric and Reggie from us. Their mum's left them presents, but I thought I should make an effort.'

He was glad Hazel had thought of that. He'd been far too busy. 'Did you have any luck?'

'Yes, I found a miniature air force for Reggie and a small fleet of battleships, destroyers or whatever for Eric. It's what they wanted.'

'Well done, darling. It's a shame Churchill hasn't got someone like you. He'd welcome a few more aircraft and warships.'

Hazel was thinking about something else. 'I hope you'll get some time off over Christmas,' she said, 'because I've bought four tickets for the pantomime at the London Palladium on Boxing Day.' She looked round the doorway to check that they were still alone. 'The boys don't know yet,' she said.

'You're a marvel. What's the pantomime?'

'Babes in the Wood.'

'Excellent. I wonder if Robin Hood and his Merry Men will be played by girls. I hope so.'

She sighed. 'Don't tell me I've taken up with a shameless *roué*, she said.

'No, I just like to see girls in tights.'

'That's shameless enough.'

'Oh no, it isn't.'

'Oh yes, it is.'

They gave way to gentle laughter in each other's arms, after which Hazel recovered to say, 'The other thing I have to tell you is that I'm going to the boys' school tomorrow afternoon for the carol service and nativity play.'

'Are they both involved?'

'Yes, Eric's in the choir, and Reggie's in the nativity play. It'll be a convenient distraction from their mum's operation.' Remembering something about the play, she said, 'Reggie's playing the innkeeper who offers Mary and Joseph the stable. Maybe they've cast him in a supporting role because of his history of ad-libbing. I imagine it should limit any potential damage.'

'At all events, it should be entertaining.'

Vincent was called to a mine in Bromley. It had fallen into a large vegetable garden, which made digging an access path to two of the plates relatively easy, but he was still unable to get to the school in time for the play. Instead, he arrived as the carol service was about to begin. Hazel saw him and Jimmy, and pointed to a row of empty seats, where she joined them.

The parents sang with enthusiasm, having recovered from the play, and the choir items were quite well performed. In any case, Vincent wasn't inclined to be too critical of a junior school performance. He did wonder a little about the inclusion of a choral item sung in Latin by young children untutored in the language, but he imagined the teachers knew what they were doing, and the number came over quite well, so he accepted it for what it was: a cheerful song at the festive season.

After the service, Jimmy went to the nurses' home to meet Daisy, and Hazel and Vincent took the boys home. Eric and Reggie were already excited after the afternoon's activities, and a ride in a motorcar put the finishing touch to the day. When they arrived home, Hazel related the events that had taken place before Vincent's arrival at the school.

'If Reggie is ever in any doubt regarding his future career,' she said, 'he could do worse than tread the boards, ideally in farce or comedy of some kind.'

'Was it terribly embarrassing?'

'For the teachers, quite possibly. In fact, they must have been cringing.'

'Go on,' he said, 'spill the beans.'

Hazel poured hot water into the teapot, still struggling to control her laughter. 'To begin with, he delivered the lines he'd been given, plus a few of his own, in a northern accent. Lily told me once that he likes to listen to Robb Wilton on the wireless, and he does a passable imitation of him.'

'Wonderful. I'm sorry I missed it.'

'I'm glad I was there.' She stirred the tea and put the lid on the teapot. 'Mary and Joseph turned up at the inn and asked very seriously if a room was available, whereupon Reggie clapped his hand to his face *alla* Robb Wilton, and said, "I don't know. We've been rushed off our feet ever since war broke out. I'll have look for you, though." While he was leafing through his register, Joseph made the point that it was quite urgent, as his wife was expecting a baby. "I see," said Reggie. "You'll be wanting a room for three, then." That brought the house down, I can tell you. Anyway, it soon transpired that no room was available. If, however, he told them, they weren't too proud, there was the stable round the back. "You'll just have to take it as you find it," he said.'

'Oh, glorious.'

'That's not all, Vincent. Having played his scene, Reggie couldn't remain off-stage for long. He just had to keep asking if the baby had arrived yet, and when the shepherds came to the stable, he welcomed them and ushered them in, all in what I imagine was a Liverpool accent.' She poured the tea and handed a cup to Vincent.

'The wonderful thing is that, all the time he was doing that, he wasn't worrying about his mother, so I think we can forgive him for a great deal.'

'That's right, darling.' The sound of footsteps made her turn to the doorway. It was Eric, and he was looking as serious as usual. 'Hello, Eric. Are you all right?'

'Yes, thank you.'

'You're looking lost,' said Vincent.

'I'm just wondering about something. What's a terror pack?'

'A terror pack?' It was a mystery. 'It sounds rather like the things I deal with on a daily basis, but I confess I've no idea. Where did you hear about that, Eric?'

'In choir, that song we sang at the carol service.'

Vincent thought hard. The choir had sung two songs.

'One of them was about terror packs,' Eric prompted.

Suddenly realisation came to Vincent. 'Are you talking about *Et in terra, pax hominibus*?'

'Yes.' Eric sounded unusually pleased at being understood, for once.

' "*Terra*" means "earth", and "*pax*" means "peace",' he explained. 'I don't imagine for one moment that the angels delivered their message in Latin, but "*Gloria in excelsis Deo, et in terra, pax hominibus*" means "Glory to God in the highest, and on earth, peace to all people." Let's just hope and pray that the Luftwaffe still have some respect for Christmas and the message of peace, and they refrain, even for a day or so, from dropping the other kind of "terror packs".'

20

January 1941

A Demon and Denial

The pantomime was a huge success, although the boys, unlike Vincent, were a little disappointed to discover that Robin Hood and his Merry Men were all played by girls. Everyone was delighted, however, that Lily had recovered from her operation and was due to come home, and Hazel felt that the event called for some preparation.

'Eric and Reggie,' she said, wrapping her arms around both of them, 'it's been lovely having you here with us, and we're going to miss you. I know you're very happy that your mum's coming home, but it's very important to remember that, much as she would like to hold you close like this, she won't be able to for a while, and you'll have to be very gentle with her.'

Reggie asked, 'Why can't she do that?' He'd been very young at the time of Lily's first operation.

'Because she's had an operation on her chest, and she'll have lots of stitches and be very sore at first. You will remember that, won't you?'

They assured her that they would, and she kissed them both, after which Eric asked, 'Aren't we going to see you again?'

'Yes, Uncle Vincent and I will still be here.'

'Good. I like it when he plays the piano.'

'So do I, Eric, and you'll hear him again. Just for now, though, let's pack your things and get you ready to go home so that you can see your mum again.'

In the short time they'd all been together, Hazel had grown very fond of them both. Strangely, they'd quickly become part of her life, and she was going to miss them terribly, but they belonged with their mother, and that was that. She kept repeating that fact to herself throughout the day, because it mattered.

When Vincent arrived at the address in Barking, firemen were still damping down the fires that the incendiaries had started during the night. There was nothing unusual about that; it was a nightly occurrence, but what was less usual was that the mine had been discovered by one of those firemen when he was eighty feet high on a turntable ladder, fighting a fire in a warehouse.

'It won't be easy to reach it,' he told Vincent. 'Half the floor's missing, the mine's on the river side of the building, and you'll have to crawl along maybe ten or fifteen feet of steel girder to get to the bit of floor it's resting on. That's unless you want to walk across.'

Vincent was already overtaken by the horror the fireman described. 'Are you sure it's a parachute mine and not a bomb?' There was always the chance that it had been wrongly identified, in which case it would be the Army's responsibility.

'It's a mine, all right,' said the fireman. 'When I saw it, the ropes from the parachute were still attached.'

He had to stop thinking about the girder. 'Can you remember how the mine was presented?'

'Presented? I don't follow you.'

'Whether it was on its side or leaning against something, or maybe just suspended by its ropes?'

'I'm with you now, sir. It certainly won't be hanging from its ropes by now. The fire took care of them while I was up there. No, as far as I can remember, it was wedged in a hole in the floor, sort of slanted. Does that help?'

'Yes, thank you.' He forced himself to return to the part that terrified him. 'How wide are the girders?'

'Oh, they're big buggers, sir, fourteen or fifteen inches wide. You should be all right as long as you don't look down.'

Vincent's stomach heaved at the thought, but he managed to ask, 'How do you suggest I get up there?'

'I'd take you up on the ladder,' he said, inclining his head towards one of the fire engines, where the turntable ladder was being retracted, but they're putting it to bed. The interior staircase will be unserviceable by now, so your best bet's the fire escape. I'll pull the bottom flight down for you. It'll fold up again when you go on to the next flight, because it's counter-balanced. When you come down again, tread carefully, and the bottom flight will fold down for you.'

'Will the door be open at the top?'

'Yes, I can tell you that for certain.' With an encouraging smile, he asked, 'Is there anything else I can help you with, sir?'

'No, thank you. I have an admission to make, though.'

'You're not good with heights, sir, I know.'

'How did you know?'

'It's written all over your face. Just remember not to look down.' He offered his hand and Vincent shook it.

The fireman placed a hook over the bottom flight of the fire escape ladder and pulled it down so that Vincent could mount the bottom step.

'Thank you.' He picked up his bag and ascended the steel ladder. When he hadn't been completely preoccupied with the prospect of crawling along a steel girder eighty feet high and with nothing beneath him, he'd been intrigued by the fact that, although in close proximity to several steel girders, the mine's magnetic pistol had not been triggered. It made no sense at all.

He continued to the top of the fire escape, all the time taking great care not to look down. The door, as the fireman had promised, was ajar, and he stepped carefully inside on to what seemed to be secure floorboards.

It had seemed a nonsense at first that the mine was listed as Category 'A' and therefore of prime importance, until he learned that the telephone exchange was almost next door. There was no ducking the responsibility, no matter how much he would have preferred it. It had to be rendered safe.

It was positioned as the fireman had described it, wedged slantwise in a jagged hole, and incredibly, between two steel girders, which, by the laws of magnetism, should have detonated the charge several hours earlier. Also faithful to the fireman's helpful description, was the abyss between the two sections of flooring. The nearest girder was probably fourteen inches wide but, in terms of safety, it might as well have been six inches or less.

He picked up his bag of tools and heaved it across, where it landed safely. If he could only do the same, everything would be fine. Breathing deeply, he lowered himself on to the floor and approached the girder. At close quarters, it looked almost reassuringly wide, and he knew that if it were laid across a floor, he would be able to walk across quite easily. Unfortunately, it was stretched over nothing but fresh, cold air.

He inched forward, concentrating on nothing but the need to reach the place where the mine lay waiting for him. Not surprisingly in January, the girder was cold to the touch, and his hands were becoming numb, but he continued to move inch by inch. It was taking forever, and he was gripped all the time by the worst kind of fear. On he crawled, resisting the urge to make a grab for the floorboards that were now tantalisingly close. Still inching forward, he grasped the wooden boards, but he knew that if he slipped at that stage, the weight of his body would tear his fingers from their puny purchase.

He was now able to place his forearms on the nearest floorboard, and he wormed his way forward, using his elbows as levers. In a few moments, he was lying on the boards, gasping with relief.

Some time elapsed before he could bring himself to tackle the mine; in fact, it was difficult at first to remind himself of his primary function. Eventually, however, he examined the mine and found that the bomb fuse was the blue polarity type. A fraction of an inch either way, and he would have no need to worry about the girder. It was almost tempting, but he applied himself to the task and withdrew it safely.

When he came to the main detonator, he found it surprisingly easy to turn, and he wondered at first if he might have stumbled on a new booby-trap device, but the plug came out cleanly, in fact, a little too cleanly, because none of the wires was connected to it. He peered inside the housing and saw the neatly-bared ends. No attempt had been made to connect them. It was clearly a six o' clock job. Home had beckoned, and the factory worker had either forgotten, or neglected for whatever reason, to connect the detonator to the battery. That was why the magnetic pistol hadn't operated. He closed his eyes to gather his wits. After all the drama of crossing the missing floor, he'd come to a mine that had never posed a threat.

He removed the primer and the hydrostatic valve, so that the mine was completely safe. After all that, he needed rather urgently to relieve himself, and he searched the floor for a place where he could do so discreetly. He had no wish to leave a wet patch where it might be discovered. A small cubicle in one corner caught his eye, and he opened the door to find that he'd located the lavatory.

Now relieved, he left the cubicle and was about to return to the dreaded girder, when he noticed a door behind the cubicle. A quick look told him that at least one flight of the internal staircase was intact. There was just a chance he might be able to return in reasonable safety. Picking up his bag, he ventured down the staircase to the floor below. The staircase was blocked with fallen wreckage beyond that point, so he peered into the floor itself, and his heart danced a little jig, because a stretch of intact flooring led to the fire escape, his route to safety.

Descending from the third storey didn't seem quite so forbidding, although he clung to the handrail and proceeded backwards until he came to the bottom flight. Recalling the fireman's instructions, he trod carefully and felt the counter-balance mechanism take over until the feet of the ladder touched the ground.

He reported to the warden that the mine was now safe, and joined Jimmy in the car.

'Hello, sir. How was it? I was bored mindless, so I spent the time thinking up questions I might be asked.'

'You were bored, Jimmy?'

'Yes, sir.' His expression changed to puzzlement when Vincent began to laugh uncontrollably.

Not surprisingly, the remainder of the day was comparatively uneventful, and Vincent drove home, dropping Jimmy and then driving the final stretch with the window down in spite of the cold. It was a glorious feeling to have defied his personal demon and discharged his duty in spite of it. The fact that the mine was relatively harmless was immaterial.

He found Hazel in a subdued frame of mind, so having made a cryptic report to *Vernon* and sat down with a cup of tea, he asked her to pour forth her troubles.

'I took the boys home this morning,' she said. 'I'd never realised how attached to them I'd become.'

'It can't have been easy for you,' he said, drawing her closer. 'How's Lily?'

'Sore and unsettled, but happy to see her children again.'

'The house is certainly quiet without them,' he remarked. 'Maybe it was too quiet before they came. Maybe a house should resound to children's excited voices and those of their unfortunate parents.'

'Don't, Vincent.'

'Have I touched a raw nerve?'

'I suppose so, but it's not your fault. You weren't to know.'

'On the contrary,' he said, giving her a squeeze, 'it's my business to be aware of your frailties, to make allowances and, whenever possible, lighten your load.'

She laughed gently. 'You make me sound feeble.'

'You're anything but feeble, but you know what I mean.'

'I just have to keep reminding myself that….'

'That what?'

'That someone else's children are just that.'

'Huggle up closer,' he suggested.

'*Huggle*?' She looked at him strangely but obviously got the idea, because she did as he asked.

'It's a portmanteau of "hug", "snuggle" and "cuddle". It's very straightforward when you think about it, and it's always a good thing to do in a crisis.'

'It is, she agreed, kissing him. 'I love you, Vincent.'

'Maybe that's the answer.'

'What? Loving you?'

'Yes, we could make a baby ourselves. I vaguely remember how to go about it, and when I look at some of the people who've done it, I'm convinced that it can't be all that difficult.'

'You know how it's done,' she said, laughing, but with tears not far away. 'Vincent, I'm thirty-three now. Having children becomes more difficult after thirty, and the risk of a first baby being born with problems is much higher than it is for younger women.'

'So it's not the first option.'

'No.'

'But it's not the only option.'

'A city at war isn't the best place for children. For the time being, darling, let's just practice self-denial.' Seeing his crestfallen look, she clarified her suggestion by saying, 'I'm talking about denying ourselves children, not the other thing.'

'Phew.'

'Honestly, Vincent, you're a child yourself, sometimes.'

He had to agree, albeit to himself. A proper grown-up might have come home still affected by the girder incident, and been unable to cope with frustrated parenthood. He was glad he'd been able to shrug that off and make himself useful.

21

February

A Combined Operation

After all his preparation and Vincent's coaching, Jimmy was not required to appear before an interview board. The enemy were sowing mines in such profusion, and RMS was so dangerously undermanned, that his advancement to midshipman, supported by Vincent's recommendation, had gone through unchallenged. Consequently, he reported to HMS Vernon on Monday, the third of February, as ordered, for instruction in RMS procedure, and Vincent was left temporarily without an assistant.

It was unfortunate, because he was called four days later to a parachute mine that had landed in an exposed field near Sidcup in Kent, and it was clear from the outset that it was a job for more than one man. Mr Butcher, the farmer on whose land the mine had fallen regarded it simply as 'a bloody nuisance.'

'I'll have to roll it, somehow,' Vincent told him. 'Two of the bits I need to get to are underneath the damned thing, and I have to have all four of them exposed.' It was almost a repeat of the Hornsea mine, but with the difference that he could no longer call on the services of an able seaman and a local policeman. In addition, a heavy week had left him tired and less resilient than he might otherwise have been.

'How are you going to do that, then?'

'That's just the question I'm asking myself. I need manpower.'

Mr Butcher looked very doubtful. 'I've got lumbago,' he said, 'an' my men have all gone off to the war, 'cept old Henry, an' he wouldn't be much use to you at his age.'

'How old is he?'

'He owns up to seventy-five, but I reckon he's in his eighties.' He looked sourly over his shoulder and said, 'All my men are girls now, the Women's bloody Land Army. Worse than bloody useless, they are.'

Vincent took the non-magnetic spade from his car and answered the farmer's enquiring look by saying, 'I'll have to dig a trench at one side of it, and I'll just have to see if I can roll it myself.'

Perhaps feeling that he'd been less than helpful, Mr Butcher said, 'You could maybe hitch a horse to it. I wouldn't want to use the tractor in case it got damaged.' With a nod in the direction of the mine, he said, 'It could go off, couldn't it?'

'It could, and you're right about the risk. It could damage a tractor, but it could kill a horse and the person leading it.'

'Either way, it's an expensive risk.'

Vincent didn't trust himself to comment further. Instead, he said, 'Tell those land girls to stay on the other side of the line. You'd better do the same yourself.'

'You're bloody right, I will.'

Vincent started digging. The trench only needed to be about a foot deep to expose the plates, but the soil was frozen hard and heavy, and he was moving snow as well, so that simply digging the trench took him almost an hour, and he was exhausted by the time he was finished.

He trudged back to the car to get some rope, and he was taking it out of the boot when he heard a female voice calling, 'Hello.' He turned and searched the snowy landscape for its owner, but there was no sign of her. As he closed the boot lid, he heard it again, and it seemed to be coming from a different direction.

'Wherever you are,' he called, 'I can't see you.'

'We're here.' The voice was much closer, and he looked up from the boot to see three land girls, all looking appealing in their distinctive hats and breeches. They wore coats, but their hands were uncovered and they looked raw in the cold wind.

'Don't go past the line, whatever you do,' he warned them.

'We're not daft,' said one of them, a tall, dark-haired girl. 'We just wondered if you needed any help.'

He thought about the trench he'd just dug. He would have welcomed some help with that, but not from land girls. 'It's kind of you to offer,' he said, 'but mines are dangerous things.'

One of them asked, 'Why are you doing it, and not the Army?'

'Because it's a mine, not a bomb. The Army only work on bombs.'

'Well, what do you have to do, exactly?'

It was a ridiculous situation. The mine lay almost in the middle of a field, at a safe distance but still very threatening, and he was about to explain his task to three young women who seemed to have no fear at all. 'I have to remove four devices from the mine to render it harmless. Unfortunately, two of them are underneath, where I can't get to them, so I have to roll it a quarter of a turn into the trench I've dug, and then I can make a start.'

'We saw you digging that trench,' said the girl who'd spoken to him first. 'We'd have offered to help you then, but old "Touch-up" Butcher was watching us. We'd have dug it in less than half the time, as well.'

'I've no doubt you would, girls, but I wouldn't have allowed it.'

'All right,' said the same girl, looking genuinely interested, 'how are you going to move it?'

'I'll attach ropes to it and haul on them from a safe distance.'

One of them appeared to be studying the mine, and she asked, 'What do you think it weighs?'

'One like that weighs five hundred kilogrammes,' he told her wistfully. 'That's nearly half a ton. It's only a small one, but it's heavy enough.'

'Could you hitch it to your car?'

'Good thinking, but no. It's a sensitive business, and hauling by hand is safer.'

'You do need our help,' said the girl who'd done most of the talking. 'I'm Josie and these two are Mollie and Steph. Fix up your ropes and we'll give you a hand to roll it over.'

In normal circumstances, Vincent would never have dreamt of asking girls to do hard, manual labour, but they were employed as manual workers, they were keen to help, and he needed their help, just as Josie had said. 'Thank you,' he said, 'that's a very kind offer. I'll take you up on it.' He picked up the two coils of rope and said, 'Stay here and wait for me.' The stretch of road where he'd parked the car was set down five feet or so from the field, and it was an excellent safety point. He clambered up the track and approached the mine again. The wind was bitterly cold, and the air was filled with snowflakes again, but he pressed on and tied a loop over each end of the mine, as he had at Hornsea. That done, he walked slowly back to the safety point, paying out the rope meticulously so as not to jolt the mine, even minutely.

Back at the safety point, he joined the two ropes to form a bight, and then addressed the girls. 'I want you each to take hold of this rope, and when I give you the word, I want you to haul on it until the mine rolls over. When that happens, keep your heads down and wait until I've counted at least seventeen seconds.'

Mollie asked, 'Why seventeen seconds?'

'Because that's how long the clock runs before it detonates the mine. I should add that while we're counting the seconds it's a good idea to put your fingers in your ears, just in case it does go bang, or you'll be hearing it for the rest of the day, if you can still hear anything at all.'

They grasped the bight and took up the slack.

'On my three. One, two… three!'

They all hauled as hard as they could, until Vincent felt a slackening on the rope. 'Hold it there.' He counted seventeen seconds and a little more to be on the safe side, and then peered over the mound. At that distance, it was difficult to see very much.

'It moved all right,' said Josie. 'That was an uneven trench you dug, and the mine's no longer level.'

She was right, it had rolled. 'Wait here a minute,' he told them. He walked over to the mine and saw immediately that the plates were visible on both sides. Returning to the safety point, he said, 'Thank you all, girls. I couldn't have done it without your help, but I have to ask you to go back to wherever you should be, while I make the mine safe.'

'You're not getting rid of us so easily,' said Josie. 'We're going to stay to the end. This kind of thing doesn't happen every day, you know.'

'Won't you be in trouble with Mr Butcher, taking time off like this?'

'No, old Touch-up's gone on his travels this morning. He won't know a thing.'

'I'll probably wish I hadn't asked, but why do you give him that name?'

There was general laughter, and then Steph said, 'You only got here this morning, but if you'd been a girl, you wouldn't have needed to ask that question, because he'd have touched you up in the first five minutes.'

He was appalled. 'Is there no one you can turn to?'

'No one who could do anything about it, and we wouldn't say anything to Mrs Butcher. She's a nice, harmless old girl, and we don't want to upset her. No, we have our own way of dealing with him. He's a simple soul, and he hasn't yet worked out the connection between him trying it on, and one of us accidentally treading on his toes or even being a bit clumsy with spade handle.'

'All right,' he said, laughing, 'you can stay here. If you want to get out of this biting wind, sit in the car, by all means.'

'Thanks.... What's your name?'

'Lieutenant Reid.' Then he thought again. They were an informal trio, so he took their example and said, ' "Vincent" to my friends.'

'Thank you, Vincent. Good luck.'

They'd demonstrated that could take care of themselves, and he left them with the car while he attended to the job he'd been sent to do.

He took out the stethoscope and ascertained that the clock hadn't grown impatient in the last hour or so. The iron casing felt incredibly cold, and he reflected that nothing felt quite as cold as iron or steel. Even so, he had a job to do, and he rubbed his hands to improve the circulation. Every so often, he stopped to wipe his glasses as well, because snowflakes seemed particularly attracted to them.

The sub-zero temperature had affected the locking ring on the bomb fuse, so that it took a great deal of effort to dislodge it, but he eventually succeeded and went on to pump air into the car horn. With no water handy, he was unable to test it for leaks, and he held it for several minutes to ascertain that it was holding its pressure, before gently screwing it on to the fuse and opening the valve.

Thereafter, the operation went smoothly and, with the mine now safe, he returned to the safety point, where the girls were waiting for him at the gate.

'Oh, Vincent,' said Mollie, the redhead, 'that was really exciting!'

'It usually is, but it's safe now. When I report back, they'll send a team with a lorry to take the mine away and destroy it.'

'Where do they do that?' It was as if, in their fascination, they had to find out every detail of the procedure.

'They'll take it to the Essex marshes and carry out a controlled explosion.'

Steph was eyeing the wet, but no less desirable, silk parachute. She asked, 'What happens to the parachute?'

'It's government property,' he told her, 'but they do disappear quite mysteriously from time to time.' He looked unnecessarily around him and said, 'I'm going to release it from the mine, but with all this snow in the air, I shouldn't be surprised if this one were to vanish while my back's turned. Come and give me a hand, anyway.'

There was a chorus of, 'Thanks, Vincent,' and they followed him eagerly across the field.

'Vincent,' said Josie, when the parachute was folded ready for concealment, 'come back to the farmhouse with us and we'll give you a cup of tea and a bacon sandwich. How does that sound?'

Shivering inside his duffel coat, he said, 'It sounds like champagne and caviar.'

'It won't taste like it,' she assured him, 'but it'll make a better job of warming you up.'

'All right, get in the car and I'll drive you all back to the farmhouse.'

By the time they arrived, Mr Butcher had returned, and Vincent was able to report to him and his wife that the mine was now safe.

'An' what 'ave you lot been up to?' He eyed the land girls truculently.

'We've been helping to make your top field safe instead of a hundred feet in the air,' said Josie, 'and now we've brought Vincent back for a brew and a bacon sandwich,' she said, filling the kettle and taking bacon from the larder.

'You lot think I'm made of bacon.'

'That's right,' they agreed.

Vincent drove back to London through the ever-falling snow and telephoned *Vernon* from home.

'The Sidcup mine is safe, sir,' he told Lieutenant Commander Ghyll.

'Excellent, but you're needed now at West India Docks.' He gave him the address. 'Your new assistant should be there by now.'

'Oh, that's a relief, sir. I had to enlist the help of the Women's Land Army this morning.'

'Reid, I may become more accustomed in time to your unique brand of humour, but I doubt that I shall ever subscribe to it.'

Vincent followed Ghyll's directions to the site in West India Docks, where a policeman was waiting to direct him to the mine.

'There's a sailor here to see you, sir. He says he's your new assistant.'

'Oh, good.'

The rating who approached him was tall and smartly turned out. He saluted and asked, 'Are you Lieutenant Reid, sir?'

'That's right.'

'P-nine-eight-four-two-seven-four Able Seaman Barber, S. M. reporting, sir.'

'Known as "Ali", I suppose?'

'Yes, sir.'

Vincent offered his hand. 'How d' you do, Barber.' He would keep things formal until he knew Barber a little better. 'You're a welcome sight,' he said.

'I have a new assistant,' he told Hazel. He was waiting for me at West India Docks. He's quite meticulous in carrying out his duties, and he doesn't appear to have any uncouth habits, so I'll see how he develops.'

'It must be a relief for you. What's his name?'

'Barber. I don't know his Christian name, except that it begins with "S". He lives in Camden Town, by the way, which is quite convenient for me.'

She stirred the tea and replaced the teapot lid. 'I imagine you'll miss Jimmy.'

'Yes, but I'm hoping our paths will cross again. I've asked him to keep in touch. I may be able to help him with his student career after the war.' He was uncomfortably aware that any help he could give depended on either or both of them surviving the war, and Jimmy's promotion had just shortened the odds against that, but it was better to be optimistic.

Possibly to steer his thoughts away from the long term and its uncertainty, Hazel said, 'You said you were in the countryside this morning. That must have been a welcome change.'

'It was pleasant at times,' he agreed, 'but beastly cold, and not only that. The mine was laid badly, and I had to roll it until I could get to all the things I needed to work on.' He took a cup of tea from her.

'You had to *roll* it?'

'Yes, all five hundred kilogrammes, but I didn't do it alone,' he told her reassuringly.

'But you'd no assistant. Who did you rope in?'

'The Women's Land Army. I suppose you could describe it as a combined operation.'

22

March

Two's Company

Lieutenant Commander Ghyll sounded unusually agitated when he said, 'We've got a Category "A" for you, Reid, right next to Poplar Gasworks, and it's particularly urgent, because ours isn't the only Category "A" in the vicinity. The Army have been digging for two days, trying to find a bomb that was reported on the fourteenth, and now, to upset the apple cart, a parachute mine joined the party last night.'

'I take it they want ours dealt with first, sir?'

'Correct, Reid. They don't want a potential explosion while they're trying to locate their bomb, and I'm equally unhappy about a squad of pongoes digging with steel picks and shovels near our mine. On top of everything else, of course, the Gaslight and Coke company and countless customers, not to mention the householders who've been turfed out of their homes, will all be drumming their fingers.'

'I'll deal with it, sir.'

'I'm sure you will, Reid, but you'll need to be diplomatic in this case, as well as bloody quick.'

'Aye, aye, sir.'

Vincent picked up Barber and briefed him as they drove to Poplar. 'We're eagerly awaited,' he told him. 'The Royal Engineers, the Gaslight and Coke Company, lots of evacuated civilians and, not surprisingly, people whose gas has been turned off are all expecting us to work frantically for their benefit. Needless to say, the job will take just as long as it needs.'

'Are we likely to get any argy-bargy from the Army, sir?'

'I doubt it, as we're all in this thing together, but the fact is that we didn't drop the bloody thing. They have to blame Hitler and Göring for that.'

Barber appeared to ponder that thought. Eventually, he said, 'The longer this war goes on, sir, the more I find that people just lash out at the nearest convenient person.'

'You're probably right about that, Barber.' He drove on for several minutes before remembering a question he'd been meaning to ask. 'Barber?'

'Yes, sir?'

'What did you do for a living before you enlisted?'

Barber hesitated, and then said, 'Believe it or not, sir, I was a hairdresser.'

'Really? Men's or ladies?'

'Strictly speaking, sir, ladies, but gentlemen's requirements pose no problem.'

Vincent fingered the ends of his overgrown locks and asked, 'Do you think you could bring your scissors tomorrow? I never have time to get a haircut, and I'll pay you for it fair and square.'

'It'll be a pleasure, sir.'

They came to a road block, where a policeman stopped them. 'What's your business here, sir?'

'We've come to deal with a parachute mine that I believe is quite close to the gasworks.'

'That'll be a relief for somebody, sir.' He lifted the barrier. 'Good luck, sir.'

'Thank you.'

As they drove along the deserted road, Barber said, 'I can see the top of the gasholder, red one-zero, sir.' He added apologetically, 'I spoke in a hurry, sir, and it came out as a bearing.'

'Don't apologise, Barber. We both represent the Senior Service, after all, and yes, I can see it too, thanks to your timely sighting.'

They passed another road block, and an air-raid warden addressed Vincent.

'You'd best leave your car here, sir. The mine's on the other side of the gasholder, before you get to the street, if you get my meaning.'

'Thank you, Warden, I'll find it.'

'Look out for the big hole, sir. That's where the Army have been digging.'

'They're not there now, are they?' He had visions of soldiers wielding picks and shovels. It was just what he wanted to avoid.

'No, sir. They're giving it a wide berth for now. I can't say as I blame 'em.'

'Good. I'll go and have a look.' He took the stethoscope from the bag and put it in his pocket. 'Stay here for now, Barber,' he said.

'Aye, aye, sir.'

Vincent made his way into the gasworks and around the huge gasholder, only to find his progress curtailed by an enormous hole. From that point, however, he could see where the parachute was caught on the framework of the gasholder. The mine couldn't be far away, so he retraced his route and tried the other side of the gigantic cylinder, where he found the mine half-embedded in a pile of building sand. Taking the stethoscope from his pocket and listening to it, he assured himself that all was well. The mine was a Type 'B', and two of its plates were angled down at four o' clock. Sand was a different medium from solid earth, however, and he was fairly confident that he could gain better access to what appeared to be the bomb fuse and the main detonator.

The sound of footsteps behind him made him turn quickly and say, 'Stay there! Don't come any closer!' The recipient of that warning was a second lieutenant in the Royal Engineers.

'I just came to find out how long you think you'll be.'

'Did you? Well, I haven't started on it yet, so you'll just have to go on wondering and let events occur in their own good time. Meanwhile, if you have anything about your person that's remotely ferrous, you could easily eliminate the need for waiting, by blowing us both to Kingdom Come, which is why I told you to stay there.'

Clearly, the subaltern was nettled, an impression that he confirmed with his next remark. 'I think you're attitude's a little high-handed, sir,' he said. 'All I'm doing—'

'All you're doing is being a bloody nuisance. When I've dealt with this mine, I'll inform the authorities, and then I've no doubt they'll pass the word to one of the grown-ups at your establishment, who will, if you're lucky, pass the information down to you. In the meantime, will you please bugger off and leave me to concentrate?'

'If that's your attitude, sir, there's no more to be said.'

'On that we can agree.' Vincent folded the stethoscope and placed it in his pocket. As he stood on one side of the gasholder, he could see Barber faithfully awaiting orders, so he took off his cap and used it to beckon him. The subaltern watched him sourly, and Vincent felt his patience drain away. 'Are you still here? I told you to leave!'

With unconcealed resentment, he saluted Vincent and returned Barber's salute as he went.

'Thank you, Barber. In case I don't live to tell the tale, the mine is a Type "B" with a blue polarity fuse.'

'I've got that, sir. Good luck, sir.'

'Thank you, Barber. Go back to the safety point and wait for my signal.'

'Aye, aye, sir.'

Vincent waited for a while, breathing deeply, before starting work. In a few minutes, he would be handling the most dangerous fuse so far encountered, and he had no intention of doing so in an unsettled frame of mind. Gradually, he let his annoyance recede until the offending juvenile was banished at least from conscious thought. Only then, did he take the four-pronged spanner from the bag.

It was a simple matter to brush the sand away from the plate, and he was able to apply force from above to loosen the obstinate plate before lifting the device, as painstakingly as ever, and a fraction of an inch at a time, from its housing.

He realised that his mouth and tongue felt like yesterday's ashes. He kept meaning to bring water, but other considerations usually took precedence. He made himself concentrate again, unscrewing the gaine and removing it carefully from the fuse.

The 'cage' that led to the main detonator was proving unresponsive, a state of affairs that led to a secondary concern. He was naturally reluctant to use a hammer, but there was regrettably no other way. He took a brass rod and a four-ounce hammer and tapped against the crossed bars. After one tap, he took out the stethoscope and listened. As usual, he could only hear the blood pounding in his ears. He was about to pick up the rod and hammer again, when he thought he heard a whirring sound. He replaced the ear pieces and pushed the stethoscope against the casing again. The whirring had stopped. Then, he realised with an overwhelming sense of relief that it had nothing to do with the mine. The whirring sound was coming intermittently from him. As usual, his digestive system was making its feelings known about the situation in which it found itself. He tapped the rod again and listened. He could hear nothing, but the cage was now loose. In a more positive frame of mind, he withdrew the detonator and cut and taped the wires.

The primer and hydrostatic valve offered no resistance, and he was able to transfer his attention to the parachute. One of its suspension lines was just within his reach, so he pulled on it, causing the silk canopy to tear where it was caught on one of the cast-iron columns. Having freed it, he hauled the whole thing down and folded it as tidily as he could. The government would have no use for a parachute with a torn canopy, and Vincent had other ideas for it.

With everything packed, he picked up his bag and the parachute and headed for the safety point.

As he handed the bag to Barber, a captain in the Royal Engineers approached him.

'I say, old chap,' he said, returning Vincent's salute, 'have you a moment?'

'I have now, sir, and I can report that the mine is safe. Your men can continue digging without the threat of danger from above.'

'My dear chap, I am so grateful, and I'll pass the information on in a minute, but first, I have to address the subject of the unfortunate exchange that took place this morning between you and one of my rookies.'

Once again, Vincent summoned his patience. 'He was about to come dangerously close to a magnetic mine, sir. I had to warn him. That was one thing—'

'I know, old man. That's why I want to apologise on the silly bugger's behalf. Not only did he come close to triggering the mine, he also ruffled the feathers of the unfortunate officer who was about to defuse it. I refer to your goodself, in fact. I'm most awfully sorry, Lieutenant. If it's any consolation, I gave him an almighty bollocking.'

Vincent smiled, more in friendly agreement than at the thought of the second lieutenant receiving a reprimand. 'There's no harm done, sir. The main thing, as I'm sure you'll agree, is that he learns something from this episode.'

'I'm glad you're taking it like this, Lieutenant. I'll go and tell my chaps that it's business as usual. Thank you again.'

'Not at all, sir. I think the press are waiting for something. Perhaps we should shake hands for their benefit.'

'Of course, old man. Inter-service co-operation and all that sort of thing.' He extended his hand and Vincent shook it warmly while the cameras clicked and flashed.

When Vincent found a telephone kiosk, he reported his success to Lieutenant Commander Ghyll, who was quick to enquire about relations with the Royal Engineers.

'They've never been better, sir. In fact, you may possibly see evidence of that in tomorrow's newspapers.'

Ghyll's response was wary. 'Have you been speaking to the press, Reid? You surely know better than that.'

'I haven't spoken a word to them, sir.'

'In that case, what do you mean about evidence?'

'All I did, sir, was to shake hands in the friendliest manner with a captain in the Royal Engineers. That the gesture caused excitement among the press was a matter for which only they can answer.'

In the event, one such picture appeared in the *Evening News*, a fact that wasn't lost on Hazel in spite of the obvious fact that something was troubling her.

'What on earth have you been up to, darling?' She showed him a copy of the newspaper.

He laughed. 'It was an example of inter-service co-operation. I'd just roasted a second-lieutenant who was full of himself, even though he's wet behind the ears, and his senior officer agreed with me.'

'Good heavens.'

'Yes, I defused a mine that was possibly only yards away from one of their bombs. It was a close thing in more senses than one. Whoever said, "two's company" clearly wasn't referring to a pair of explosive devices.'

He'd just brewed tea, having arrived home before Hazel, and he carried it into the sitting room. 'Now,' he said, sitting beside her, 'are you going to end the suspense?'

'The suspense?'

'Are you going to tell me what's churning around inside you?'

'Oh, Vincent,' she said, 'you're uncanny. How did you know?'

'It's my analytical mind. I see the signs, and it helps as well that I care about you.'

'I know you do.' She leaned forward so that he could put his arm round her.

'Talk to me, Hazel.'

'All right. Lily's been given the results of her quarterly examination, and the X-rays have shown that the second operation failed to eradicate the tumour completely.' She sighed wretchedly. 'It's up to its old tricks again.'

'Oh, the poor woman. It just rains down on her, doesn't it?'

'She has to go in for treatment, but there's no guarantee it'll be successful. Meanwhile, I've offered on our joint behalf to have the boys again while she's in hospital. I hope that's all right.'

'Of course it is. After all the effort we put in getting to know one another, it would be awful for them if they went anywhere else.'

'Thank you, Vincent.' She kissed him with much feeling.

'Well, you know, two's company, as I said earlier, but so is four, and whether it's in the short or long term, those boys are going to need not just our company, but much more from us besides.'

'Meanwhile, there's still a chance that the tumour will respond to radiotherapy.'

'Yes, we must stay positive.' He was also trying, with some difficulty, to stay awake. It was important that Hazel knew she had his support, but a heavy workload and the resulting shortage of sleep were exacting their toll. He almost forgot his surprise for her, but he managed to stay conscious long enough to ask her, 'Could you use a quantity of silk?'

She had to repeat her reply when he was once again able to hear it, but her pleasure was undiminished.

23

April

A Sensitive Charge

Vincent was constantly aware that familiarity had a way of begetting contempt, and, familiar though he was with the blue polarity fuse, he reserved his contempt for those who had devised it. For the fuse itself, he felt only unremitting respect. He had no idea how many he'd drawn; he felt that to keep a tally would be to tempt providence, but he approached each of them with the same, intense concentration, finally taking a minute or more to regain his mental equilibrium before going on to the main detonator.

The feeling of relief was always the same. It began with a breathless and heady thankfulness that he was still alive, giving way, then, to a sense of satisfaction at having succeeded in the face of such malevolence, because that was the only way to describe the thinking behind it. The main detonator was there to force the explosion when it was triggered by a ship's magnetic field, but the blue polarity fuse could have only one purpose, and that was to kill anyone who tried to render the mine safe.

And now, as he removed the plate to reveal yet another fuse of the same type, he felt his hands shaking uncontrollably. The shaking was normal; he'd experienced it at his first incident, and he knew he would be abnormal if he weren't affected by the threat of imminent and violent death. It was quite normal, except that it was becoming worse with each incident.

He laid the four-pronged spanner and the plate on the ground and waited for the shaking to ease. Curiously, he wasn't afraid of death itself. If the fuse exploded beneath his nose, he would know nothing about it. No, his fear was for Hazel, who would be left alone to care for the boys. He had no illusions about Lily's situation. Like Hazel, he desperately wanted her to recover, but he knew it would take a miracle, and a big one at that.

At length, the shaking grew less, and he commenced the gut-churning task of drawing the fuse.

With the heels of both hands in contact with the casing, he gradually eased the fuse towards him, concentrating on maintaining the gap between the two. A fraction either way, and he would leave the site in a body bag, like the tragic sub-lieutenant who'd attended a Type 'C' in Chatham only two days earlier.

He forced himself to banish the incident from his mind and concentrate only on the present.

With just an inch or so to go, incredibly, his hands began trembling again. Anchored as they were to the iron casing, they should have been rock-steady, but not today, it seemed. Cold sweat was coursing from his brow, and he blinked to clear his eyes as he gripped the fuse with his thumbs and two fingers of each hand. If he gripped hard, until his fingertips were white, he thought he could control the shaking. No more than an eighth of an inch at a time, he drew the fuse towards him. Only when he could see daylight beneath it, he snatched it away and, in the same moment, rose to his feet to vomit over the pile of rubble created by the mine's impact.

It was fear, or blue funk, as they'd called it in the previous war, and it worried him. He could, of course, request a medical examination, which would probably result in his being classified as 'lacking moral fibre'. It was no option. Somehow, he had to control his fear.

In a very sober frame of mind, he withdrew the detonator, the primer and the hydrostatic valve.

Hazel waved a buff envelope and said, 'It's come. My guardianship has been approved.'

'I'm delighted to hear it, darling.' He kissed and hugged her in celebration.

'I'm sure you are,' she said, 'but you're also exhausted. Have a cup of tea and then you can have a nap before dinner.'

He sank into an armchair in the sitting room, and his eyelids began to droop. A noise in the doorway roused him temporarily to say, 'Hello, Eric and Reggie. Is everything all right?' He didn't hear their reply, but he did hear Hazel say to them, 'Don't bother Uncle Vincent. He's very tired.'

He knew it was wrong; the children needed to know that Hazel and he were available at any time. His exhausted mind tried briefly to extend that thought into something that made complete sense, but the flesh proved weaker than the spirit, and sleep claimed him.

They discussed the matter in their patent shelter after the boys had gone to bed.

'I think you're wrong, Hazel told him. 'It goes without saying that they're at a particularly vulnerable time in their lives, but they still have to learn that adults are human, too. They know you do a very demanding job, and they need to bear that in mind.'

In his fragile state, he still found it hard to agree. 'They don't need rejection,' he protested.

'There's rejection and there's asking for consideration. One is unpleasant, and the other is part of growing up.'

'You don't fight fair,' he said.

Half-amused, she asked, 'What are you accusing me of, darling?'

'Being too good at arguing.'

'If you were in charge of your faculties,' she pointed out, 'I wouldn't stand a chance, arguing with you.'

He tried to muster a reply, but sleep overpowered him again.

The next morning, Hazel tapped on the door of Eric Tyndall's glass cubicle and waited. She had quite a lot to do, but a summons to her sub-editor's office wasn't to be ignored, and so, with a rough idea of what to expect, she prepared herself.

'Come in.' It was the peremptory command of an important man, at least in his own estimation.

Hazel opened the door and walked in. 'You demanded my presence,' she reminded him in a tone that warned him that if he intended to deliver a browbeating, he should expect a return of fire. The last phrase was a delightful expression that she'd learned from Vincent.

'Yes, Miss Wythenshawe, you were late again this morning, and after I spoke to you about it on Wednesday.'

'If you remember, I told you on Wednesday that I'm responsible for two children, and one of those responsibilities is that of ensuring that they arrive at school on time.'

'Your sole responsibility is to this department!' He was a slightly-built man, whose round, tortoiseshell-framed glasses contributed to his uncanny resemblance to Arthur Askey. It did nothing for his presence.

'Oh well, there, your information fails you,' she said, taking the official letter from her bag and showing it to him. 'As you'll see, I am the children's legal guardian, appointed by the court. They are very much my responsibility.'

'But you're employed by the Ministry, and it doesn't employ you to take children to school when you should be working in this office.' He made a visible attempt to calm down, and said, 'I know you made a private arrangement with Lily Lawrence, and that's quite possibly to your credit, but the fact remains that you can't expect to do this job and care for those children at the same time.'

'In that case, I'll just have to give up my job.'

His attempt to calm himself failed completely. 'Don't be ridiculous!' His voice had risen to the extent that the attention of everyone in the outer office was now centred on his glass tank. 'You know perfectly well that you can't leave a job to which you've been directed in wartime without the approval of the Ministry of Employment.'

'They'll let me go soon enough when they learn that I'm responsible for two children. Lily won't recover overnight, and the children will still need a home.'

'But *we* need you, for goodness' sake.' He accompanied his assertion by beating his desk with his fists.

'Why, when you have so many other people you can shout at?' She inclined her head towards the outer office. 'And most of them won't answer you back, either.'

'Miss Wythenshawe, be reasonable.'

'I am being reasonable, Mr Tyndall. You're being most unreasonable. Now, listen to me—'

'This is impossible!'

'Listening? For you, probably, but do make an effort. If I arrive at work fifteen minutes late during term time, and leave half-an-hour early, why can't you just dock the time off my salary? I'll still do the work in the time that's left, and you'll have to manage without me next week and the week after it, anyway.'

'That's another thing. Taking annual leave in April.'

'Is that against the Ministry's rules as well? I'm doing it because of the school's Easter holiday.'

'It's damned inconvenient!'

'Not unlike Lily Lawrence's predicament. I expect she finds that damned inconvenient, too.'

'You're evading the issue!' He thumped his desk again, causing a box of paperclips to jump sideways. 'What are you going to do about the school summer holidays when you've no more leave entitlement?'

'Oh, I'll have left by then.'

He lowered his head, cradling it with his hands. With heavy patience, he asked, 'And just what will you do for employment, then?'

'Either, I'll go back to one of the papers I was on before I came here, or I'll work freelance.' She glanced at her watch. 'I was writing a piece when you called me. May I go, now, or have you something else you wish to shout?'

'I think you'd better go.' To say that his calling was one of words, they had clearly failed him on this occasion.

'I think so, too,' she agreed, leaving his office and smiling at the inquisitive stares of those outside it.

An explosion somewhere quite near had roused Vincent, and he lay still, waiting patiently for sleep to return. The luminous face of the alarm clock told him it was five-and-twenty past two, so there was still some of the night remaining. Hazel lay sleeping beside him, apparently unaware of the ferocity of the raid. She was probably in a very relaxed state, having given her resignation to the Editor-in-Chief. It was a rash move, but one that made Vincent prouder of her than he'd ever been. He closed his eyes and tried to clear his mind of all activity.

Other than a few desultory bombs, the raid was effectively over, and he felt himself drifting off to sleep again, when he heard the door latch click, and feet padded across the room. It was too much. 'What the hell…?' He stopped himself.

'Uncle Vincent.' The voice was Reggie's.

He whispered, 'What's the matter, Reggie?'

'I'm scared.' His voice was shaking as he said it.

'Just a minute.' He opened the side of the shelter and slipped out, careful not to waken Hazel. 'Come with me.' He took his dressing gown from the chair, ushering Reggie out of the room before switching on the electric torch he kept in his pocket. In its beam, he saw Eric's frightened face in the stair cupboard doorway. 'Right, you two,' he said, 'have you room for one more in your Wellington bomber?'

He settled again, with Eric on one side and Reggie on the other, as the sounds of distant explosions gradually receded. He never heard the 'All Clear', because he was once more fast asleep.

When Hazel woke him at six-thirty, the boys were already up. 'She said, 'You should have woken me.'

'No,' he said, 'you need your sleep as well.' He also had an admission to make. 'There was another reason,' he said.

'Go on.'

'When Reggie came in, I caught myself letting him know just how I felt, but I stopped myself. Then, to make up for it and show him I wasn't really cross, I joined them in the stair cupboard, as you can see.'

'I love you, Vincent,' she said, kissing him, 'but they really have to learn that grown-ups also have their needs, and we're none of us perfect.'

'I know, but they shouldn't have to learn that lesson when they're terrified.'

'No,' she agreed, 'not when they're terrified.

Vincent went to an incident in Wapping that day. Mercifully, the bomb fuse only called for the car horn and pump. He was just as careful, but very relieved.

On the way home, he asked, 'Have you ever attended a diver, Barber?'

'No, sir, it's not one of my skills, I have to admit.'

'There's no shame in it,' Vincent assured him, 'and the mobile units always send an attendant, just in case.

'Even so, sir, I'd like to learn how to do it.'

'Good. I'll dig out the Diving Manual for you.'

'Thank you, sir. I feel that I'd like to do the job properly. The rating you had before me used to do it, didn't he?'

'That's right.' Vincent had been wondering how Jimmy was faring.

'Well, I need to learn the ropes if I'm to take over from him properly, don't I, sir?'

'If you say so, Ali. I must say I commend your attitude.'

Hearing Vincent address him that way, Barber grinned. 'Well, sir,' he said, 'considering all that you and the other RMS officers do, it'd be a shame if I couldn't make a bit of an effort.'

'How very laudable,' said Hazel. 'I'm glad they found you a good man.'

'Ali's shaping up nicely, and he always makes a first-class job of trimming my hair.'

'He spoils you.'

Suddenly, the quietness around them prompted him to ask, 'Where are the boys?'

'They're playing in the Anderson shelter. It's a submarine, now.'

'So they've forsaken the RAF, and not before time.' He smiled at the thought, just as the telephone rang.

'Reid.'

'Oh, is that the number for Miss Hazel Wythenshawe?' It was a woman's voice.

'Yes, I'll get her for you. Who shall I say is asking for her?'

'It's St Thomas's Hospital.'

'One moment, please.' Hazel was now by his side. 'It's the hospital, darling,' he said.

Hazel took the telephone from him. 'Hello,' she said, 'Hazel Wythenshawe here.' After a few seconds, she said, 'Thank you. Yes, I'll make all arrangements.' She replaced the receiver and stood in silence for what seemed a long time before she let Vincent take her into his arms. 'She died at ten-past six,' she said, almost in a whisper.

Vincent looked up at the wall clock. It was twenty-past.

24

May

A Mixed Blessing

With the facts before them, the tribunal set up by the Ministry of Employment had been happy to release Hazel from her post, and she was able to devote her time to caring for the two boys.

Occupied though he was with the relentless profusion of parachute mines, Vincent had nevertheless given her the benefit of his experience, guiding her through the arrangement of Lily's funeral and providing reassurance for her when she'd lavished what comfort she could on the children.

The most demanding and sensitive task was that of coping with the boys' grief. To have lost their father must have been heart-breaking enough, but to lose their mother as well was a tragedy no child should have to bear, and Hazel and Vincent could only take their task a day at a time. For Hazel, it was simply heartrending to see how Lily's death was affecting the boys. For Vincent, it was all of that as well as presenting a huge emotional distraction when he was least prepared for it. Rendering mines safe demanded total concentration, and that was best achieved with a quiet mind. In the absence of that luxury, Vincent was obliged to call on a level of application he'd never previously recognised as his own. At other times, however, he was naggingly conscious that the odds against his survival were shortening all the time.

In the second week in May, he was called to an incident on the Essex marshes, and was surprised on his arrival to find another naval officer, a commander, RNVR, waiting for him.

‘Reid? I’m Cawood, DTMI,’ he said, offering his hand.

‘How do you do, sir. I confess I’m not acquainted with your department.’

‘Directorate of Torpedo and Mine Investigation,’ he translated. ‘We do the detective work.’

Recalling his interview at *Vernon*, Vincent asked, ‘Are you a lawyer in gentler times, sir?’

‘Yes, I am.’ Cawood seemed surprised by Vincent’s insight. ‘I’m a criminal barrister, actually.’

‘Your secret is safe with me, sir.’

‘What? Oh yes, very good. What led you to that conclusion?’

‘When I joined RMS, sir, there was a possibility that I might become involved in your line of work. However, urgency took the upper hand, and I was directed to routine RMS work.’

‘Well, you’ve evidently been doing a fine job.’ Curiosity intervened, and he asked, ‘Are you a lawyer, by the way?’

‘No, sir, I’m a professor of music history.’ He left Cawood to make of that what he would, while he retrieved his tools from the car.

‘Now,’ said Cawood, ‘this mine is unusual, which explains my presence.’

‘In what way is it unusual, sir?’

‘No parachute. In this case, only a drogue, the inference being that Nazi High Command are tired of seeing their best efforts being blown too far inland to do much damage. Also, the likelihood is that this is a bomb mine, a device that’s capable of performing either function.’

‘So you’ve encountered this type already, sir?’

‘Not exactly.’ Cawood hesitated, perhaps wondering how much he could tell a mere RMS officer, and then he said, ‘All we know has come from Intelligence, from the interrogation of prisoners of war, so we’re keen to find out more, as you can no doubt imagine.’ He indicated the site with a gesture and said, ‘Because of its bomb-like design and the absence of a parachute, it’s rather burrowed its way into the earth, but a party of seamen have dug down to it, using non-magnetic tools, and it’s now laid bare for us to tackle.’ He pointed to Vincent’s tool kit and said, ‘By all means bring those things. We may need some of them, but the loosening of bolts, nuts and screws must be carried out using special instruments.’ He explained as they walked to the site. ‘In case the mine is acoustic, we're using stainless steel instruments that will emit frequencies that are unlikely to trouble the microphones inside. I believe you were involved in retrieving the first acoustic mine, Reid?'

'That's right, sir.' It seemed an age ago.

'A ship's engines and propellors give off a sound in the region of two-hundred-and-fifty cycles, quite low, so the trick is to make sure our noise is always too high for the mine's microphones to detect, as I said earlier.'

They approached the excavated site, which was now deserted, and began work on the mine. Vincent was conscious of his role as assistant, and he was content with it. Cawood was an easy companion and colleague, and was clearly competent.

'Right,' he said eventually, 'it's time, now, to loosen the screws on the rear casing, but to leave it in *situ* until we're at a safe distance. I believe you did that with the acoustic at Pegwell Bay.'

'That's right, sir.'

'Good. Let's get to work.'

Together, they removed the machine screws that secured the rear casing, propping it against the mine with stones from the excavation. Then, with a line attached to the rear casing, they retired, carefully paying out the line, to their safety point, where Cawood gave it a sharp tug. The dome came away, and they waited until they were reasonably sure it wasn't going to explode, before approaching it again.

'I wouldn't mind betting,' said Cawood, 'that this crack in the casing has caused internal damage.' He examined the fracture more closely and said, 'It's all been too easy. I wonder if this is what stopped the mechanism.'

'There's something else here, sir,' reported Vincent, 'the very latest in booby-traps.'

'What have you found?'

'Why would they put tiny glass windows into a mine, unless it's to protect light-sensitive something-or-other?'

'Let me look.' Cawood moved into the place Vincent had just vacated, and examined the windows. 'You're right,' he said. 'Behind each of those things is a photo-electric cell, no doubt wired to a hefty charge, possibly the main charge, which I estimate to be about a thousand kilogrammes.'

'More than enough to kill the poor devil who innocently removes the rear casing.'

'And that was no doubt their intention. Listen, Reid, would you be interested in joining us in DTMI? Yours is the sort of enquiring mind we need.'

'I don't know, sir.'

'Most of the job is brain work. You wouldn't spend as much time in the field as you're used to.'

Suddenly, it sounded much more attractive. 'You know, sir, I'm tempted.'

'I'll speak to Commander Todd. There shouldn't be a problem.'

'Thank you, sir.'

That night saw one of the heaviest raids since the Blitz began. When Vincent, in his pyjamas and dressing gown, looked outside the front door and to the east, London appeared to be on fire from one end to the other. Wearily, he returned to the sitting room prior to turning in. When he reached the doorway, he saw Hazel sandwiched between two terrified faces. He asked, 'What's the crew of a Wellington bomber? Five?'

Unable to speak, Reggie nodded.

'In that case, it'll take four of us. Come on, Skipper, lead the way.'

They took their places in the cupboard and prepared themselves for a long and noisy operation.

The explosions continued until after two-thirty, but Vincent knew the truth about them, that it was the incendiaries that were the greater threat, and likely to create a recurrence of the Great Fire of London.

With Eric and Reggie between them, he and Hazel did what they could to calm them, until the 'All Clear' sounded, and tiredness asserted itself.

The telephone roused Vincent the next morning, and he emerged, stiff and half-asleep, to answer it.

'Reid.'

'Good heavens, Reid,' said Lieutenant Commander Ghyll, 'you sound awful. Are you sickening for something? It's a bad time for you to go sick on shore.'

'No, I'm all right, thank you, sir. It was a hectic night in London.'

'It wasn't all that peaceful in leafy Hampshire. Still, I'm glad you're all right, because we have business for you, believe it or not, in the East End. It's at, or rather in, West India Docks.'

'My car knows its way there, sir.'

'Good. There'll be a mobile unit from Chatham. Is your assistant experienced in attending a diver? I forget his name.'

'Barber, and he'll be fine, sir.'

'Take him along, then.'

'I shall, sir.' He fingered the locks above his ears and said, 'I'm due for a haircut.'

'When you get into the dock, try to drown that sense of humour of yours, Reid.'

'I'll do my best, sir.'

'Good, We'll be calling you to West Leigh fairly soon, I imagine, when the chaps at Vernon have examined the thing you and Commander Cawood found.'

'Oh, good.'

'Right, carry on, Reid.'

'Aye, aye, sir.'

'Are you ready to help me into that diving suit, Ali?'

Ali closed the car door and said, 'I'm game if you are, sir. Where are we going?'

'West India Docks.'

'Again? If we're not careful, we're going to be popular there, sir.'

'Let's hope so.' As he drove towards the East End, he asked, 'What do you do when you're off-watch, Ali?'

'I read a lot, sir. When I grew up and realised that reading was for enjoyment and not just something we had to do at school, I started re-reading the stuff I'd rebelled against as a kid.'

'That doesn't say much for your teachers.'

'No, they were a miserable lot, sir. At the same time, though, how do you teach kids to use their imagination when they're reading?'

'You've got me there, Ali.' In Vincent's experience, it was something that had just happened.

'You see, sir, I live in Camden Town, as you know. I've always lived there, and when I read about Bob Cratchit and his family, I tried to see it as it was a hundred years ago. That's what I like to do, sir, to visualise what the author's trying to say. They didn't teach us to do that at school.'

'It sounds as if you're making a fair job of teaching yourself.' He slowed down and stopped at a road block where yet more of the East End had been reduced to rubble. 'I'm trying to get to West India Docks, to an unexploded mine,' he explained to the policeman on duty.

'Right you are, sir, but you'll have to pick your way through the rubble.'

'I spend my life doing that. Thank you, Constable.' He waited for the policeman to raise the barricade, and drove along a street where weary firemen were rolling up hoses and stowing them in the compartments of a large fire engine, knowing as they did that they would no doubt be required again in a matter of hours.

At West India Docks, a rating from Chatham directed him to the site, where he and Ali climbed into the lorry.

Vincent was safe, letting Ali use his new-found skills as a diver's attendant. He knew the procedure so well himself that he could always prompt his new assistant. In the event, however, he found it unnecessary, because Ali had read the manual meticulously and he knew his job.

When he reached the mine, he decided that Dame Fortune was smiling on him. The bomb fuse called for the car horn only. Moreover, all four plates were accessible.

He removed the bomb fuse plate and screwed in the car horn, opening the valve to equalise the water pressure. The bomb fuse came out without undue persuasion, and he went on to the main detonator, which came away with a little persuasion, and then almost fell into his hands, like the one he'd encountered on the fourth floor of the warehouse. Again, some German worker had failed to connect the wires. The only difference was that Vincent hadn't needed to crawl along a steel girder to discover the anomaly.

He completed the task and made his way to the surface, where the ever-watchful Ali was waiting to help him on to the dock side.

He sat for a while in the lorry, examining his feelings. He was ridiculously relieved that the job had been so easy. How would he feel when he tackled his next blue fuse, or even the kind he'd just dealt with, but with its wires connected? It was intensely worrying.

Another relief occurred that night, although the nation seemed to be holding its breath. For the first time in ages, the Luftwaffe gave London a miss, and it repeated the omission on the following night, so that, when Commander Todd sent for Vincent, he was reasonably alert, having slept properly for two nights.

'Commander Cawood has spoken to me about the possibility of having you transferred, Reid, and the matter is receiving attention. It appears that my initial fears about you were groundless.'

'You weren't to know, sir.'

'That's true.' He rose to his feet and said, 'That wasn't the only reason I asked you to come, Reid. In a moment, we're going to join Lieutenant Commander Ghyll and some of your other colleagues. As you're still officially with us, you need to hear about the new mine.' With an odd smile, he said, 'It seems only right, as you and Commander Cawood recovered it.'

They went to Ghyll's office, where Vincent saw several officers he'd known in the past, including Jack Andrews, the Australian who'd stayed at his house. They greeted each other enthusiastically, and Vincent was about to ask after Stan, the other Australian, when Jack said, 'Before you ask, mate, Stan didn't stay the course, poor bugger.'

'I'm sorry, Jack.'

'It's the luck of the bloody draw, isn't it, Vince? But you're still here, and that's good.'

Ghyll called the meeting to order. 'The latest excitement,' he said, 'is a bomb mine, the BM 1000, a device that can behave as either one or the other, and it's different from anything you've met so far. To begin with, it has no parachute, only a drogue or a cardboard tail, which, for some reason, is usually painted light blue. It will detonate instantly when it hits a hard surface; if it falls into less than four fathoms of water, the clock will run for ninety seconds, and if it finds its way into deeper water, it behaves as a mine.'

'Someone asked, 'What about booby-traps, sir? Surely they haven't let us off the hook so lightly.'

'Nor have they. Inside the rear casing is a fiendish array of photo-electric cells, each with a tiny glass window, and they're wired to the main charge, which is one thousand kilogrammes of high explosive. The only stimulus they need is light. It seems, however, that the cells are not susceptible to faint, blue light, and so, gentlemen, when you set out to deal with one of these things, *you must do it at night*.'

'Did you see anyone you knew?' Hazel poured him a glass of wine. The boys were in bed, and it was time for grown-up relaxation.

'Quite a few, actually, including Jack Andrews, the Australian who stayed at my house.'

'He and a Wren officer, if my memory serves me correctly.'

'Well, you know, darling, these things happen in wartime.'

'Don't they just. Do you remember when you and I happened?'

He pretended to search his memory, and when she gave him a poke in the ribs, he said, 'Of course I do. I'd just had the most exciting time of my life with a mine in several fathoms of water, and you arrived with your pen and notebook at the ready.'

'You called me "madam".'

'You were lucky I didn't call you something worse. I was very angry.'

'Was it really the most exciting time of your life?'

He recalled the incident and the cold fear associated with it. It could certainly compete with a few other instances. 'No,' he said, 'the most exciting time of my life was the moment when I realised that your feelings for me matched those I felt for you.'

She kissed him in celebration. 'You do all the right things and you say all the right things.'

'Let's hope I continue to do that,' he said. 'How have the boys been today?'

'Very steady. It's going to take time, obviously, but I think we're beginning to see a glimmer of daylight.'

'Good.' Unbidden, his mind returned to the new bomb mines and the prospect of having to work on them. Finally, he said, 'Daylight can be a mixed blessing.'

25

From Dross to Gold

It seemed that, for once, the enemy had done themselves a disfavour. In calling a halt, however temporary, to the nightly air raids, they were making it easier for RMS to deal with the BM 1000, and Vincent was now required to deal with a number of them. His proposed transfer to DTMI was still under consideration, but, for the time being, the nightly RMS work continued, because the new threat demanded darkness. Fortunately, the incidence of parachute mines seemed to have dwindled, and Vincent found himself working at night and sleeping by day.

Leaving nothing to chance, he always insisted on removing the rear section remotely, as he and Commander Cawood had. There were degrees of darkness, and Vincent had no way of ascertaining that the photo-electric cells were completely blind. In the first week, the booby-trap had already killed two RMS officers.

The new instruments, too, presented a challenge at first, but only because familiarity carried with it a curious sense of security. Vincent worked as he always had, with total concentration, taking absolutely no chances.

Neither was the novelty of the BM 1000 lost on Vincent's assistant. On the way to an incident, he asked, 'Why do you think they paint the tail blue, sir?'

'Search me, Ali. Maybe it's Göring's favourite colour.'

Ali considered the possibility and said, 'It seems strange to me.'

'What does?'

'That they might have their favourite things, sir, just like normal people.'

Vincent hadn't given that aspect of the Nazi mentality much thought. 'I suppose we do tend to think of them as a separate species, but they're bound to have their foibles. They say that, although Genghis Khan was a tyrant and mass murderer, he respected people's beliefs. He even made religious toleration compulsory.' The thought made him smile.

'What's funny, sir?'

'It's not really funny, Ali. It's just the irony of imposing toleration. In fact, it's possibly the ultimate oxymoron.'

'Oxy-what, sir?'

'Oxymoron. It's a contradiction in terms, like "frightfully good", or "a small crowd", words that are at odds with each other. In this case, the dictator was enforcing tolerance by being *in*tolerant, which is what enforcement means.'

'I see, sir.' Ali appeared to give the matter further thought before saying, 'You know, sir, I learn something every time I go to an incident with you.'

'Ah, well, Ali, it's possibly a bad habit of mine, because you're not the only one who's mentioned my need to enlighten the company I'm in. It's a legacy of my civilian job.'

'What's that, sir, if you don't mind me asking.'

'I taught at the London Institute of Music and Theatre.'

'Really, sir?' Ali sounded surprised.

'Yes, but beneath my learned exterior, I'm actually quite human.'

'I won't argue with that, sir. Anyway, music is another thing I've come to enjoy since I left school. At least, I enjoy listening to it. I just wish I knew more about it.'

Vincent laughed shortly. 'Stop there, Ali, before I give you a reading list.'

'I wish you would, sir.'

'All right, when we're not so busy, I'll give you some titles to look for. I believe I can identify books that explain music to readers who are not trained musicians.'

'That's very kind of you, sir.'

'Not at all. As I told you earlier, I just like to enlighten people.' Ali's interest and gratitude were a bonus.

'What instrument do you play, sir?'

'Mainly the piano. I wanted to make a career as a pianist, but the Kaiser put paid to that.'

With unconcealed surprise, Ali asked, 'Were you in the last war, sir?'

'Yes, although I'm not so much an Old Contemptible as simply an old minesweeping hand who felt the urge to return.'

'It's good that you did that, sir.'

'Well, I had my reasons.'

They drove on in silence, for which Vincent was grateful. His brief conversation with Ali had given him cause for thought.

Presently, they came to the place where the mine was reported to have landed. Navigation was always difficult with road signs either removed or painted out to deny information to the potential invader, but a road block and the sign *Danger UXB* provided a useful hint.

After Vincent had identified the crater, the chief warden asked, 'Will you need light, sir?'

'No, that's the last thing I need. There must be no light anywhere near this mine, but thank you for the thought. The first job is to create a safety point.' He looked around him and made a decision. 'The only possibility hereabouts is this side of the road, where the land falls away.' He pointed to the side furthest from the mine. 'Everyone must retreat to the safety point when I'm working on the mine.' He peered again through the darkness, and said, 'I was wondering why this was a Category "A", and now I see the answer.'

'The cottage hospital, sir,' confirmed the warden.

'Has everyone been evacuated?'

'Yes, sir.'

'Good. If you'll organise the safety point and get everyone behind it, we'll start digging.'

He and Ali changed into their seaboots, picked up non-magnetic spades, and approached the crater.

Ali asked, 'How deep do you reckon it'll be, sir?'

'Not very deep. The Army sometimes have to dig down thirty feet, but the speed of our mine's descent is governed by a drogue or a flimsy tail, as you've seen. It's unlikely to burrow as deep as a bomb.'

They set to and, after twenty minutes or so, uncovered the tail. The main part of the mine couldn't be far away.

'Gently, now,' warned Vincent.

Eventually, they located the mine and created a space around it where Vincent could work. They also laid a number of clods beside it that he could use to keep the rear casing closed. 'Right,' said Vincent, 'go back to the safety point and wait until I call you or until I… join you.' He disliked the word 'return' and any other word that was likely to tempt fate. He'd never been at all fanciful, but suddenly, he was superstitious about all kinds of things.

With Ali safe, he set about unfastening the rear casing. It was the worst part of the job, because he had to keep the casing absolutely light-tight throughout the operation. When he'd removed the last screw, he took the clods of what seemed to be peat and packed them against the rear section. When he was satisfied that it was secure, he attached a length of the cord that the Navy called 'small stuff', and walked slowly back to the safety point, paying it out very carefully, conscious that if the rear casing and the rest parted company, he could only rely on darkness for his life and for the continued existence of the cottage hospital.

Ali was waiting for him. 'Are you going to pull it, sir, or shall I?'

'Go on, you can do it.'

'Thank you, sir. I like to feel that I'm doing something useful.' Ali took the cord and gave it a sharp tug.

'Keep hauling, Ali.' It was important that he could see the disconnected rear section. 'That's fine. It's come away, and so far, nothing's gone bang.'

He set off again to complete the defusing, which was largely straightforward. Even so, he found himself shaking afterwards, quite manifestly, and he waited until it had subsided, before walking back to the safety point. It was important that no one, especially Ali, saw his weakness.

Ali fell asleep on the way home, and Vincent was left to his thoughts, which were particularly disturbing. He'd been working for RMS since the previous winter, and with little respite. It was no wonder he was getting the shakes, and the fear was no figment of his imagination, either. Every time he went to an incident, he was dealing from the same pack. Statistically, his chances were dwindling, as the recent increase in the number of RMS fatalities seemed to demonstrate. He tried to dismiss the matter and concentrate on his driving, because brooding was unhealthy at the best of times, and downright dangerous in the current situation.

He delivered Ali to his door at a little after five-thirty and proceeded to his own address, still conscious of the unreality of a night without bombing.

Everyone was in bed when he arrived, but he wasn't ready to turn in, jaded though he was. He needed soothing, and for that, he turned to his piano.

He was playing softly and with the door closed, so he was surprised when Hazel appeared at his side.

'You were concentrating so hard, you didn't hear me open the door,' she said. 'Would you like some tea?'

'Not yet, thank you. I'm just relaxing.'

'Good. What are you playing? It's beautiful.'

He stopped playing for a moment. 'It depends on your point of view,' he said. 'Most people would say that it's the most romantic piece of music they'd ever heard, whilst a hard-headed academic might dismiss it as a stock gimmick used by composers of variations. That's if the academic could be bothered to analyse it, the intellectual trend being as it is. I can be bothered, though, and I see it as both. It's an example of how the composer can take base metal and transmute it into pure gold.'

'You still haven't told me what it's called.' Her impatience was nonetheless good-natured.

'Very well. It's the Eighteenth Variation from Rachmaninov's "Rhapsody on a Theme of Paganini".'

'And what is the gimmick you mentioned?'

'Listen to this.' He played a germ of a phrase from the original theme. 'Now,' he said, inverting an imaginary sheet of music, 'I'll turn it upside down.' He played the five notes as they would be seen on an inverted score. 'If I change the C to C sharp, playing the phrase in the major, rather than the original minor, I get this.' He played it again, adding harmony and a little embellishment, and the theme was instantly recognisable.

'Wonderful. Is that what he intended?'

'It certainly is. Composers don't do things by accident. What Rachmaninov did here was to take a commonplace phrase, he inverted it, made a tiny alteration, and produced an unforgettable romantic theme.'

'How marvellous.'

'It is,' he agreed.

'I'm going to bring you down to earth and ask you again if you'd like tea, and then I have to get the boys up and give them breakfast.'

'Yes, please.' He played for a little longer, and then joined her in the kitchen.

She asked, 'Was last night so awful?'

'Does it show?'

She kissed him gently and said, 'When you need to play the piano to make yourself relax before you can face a cup of tea, something is very wrong.'

He thought for a spell before saying, 'Last night, I dealt with the worst abomination mankind can produce. When I came home, I needed to remind myself that, at its best, the human race is also an agent of that which is good, worthy and, in the case of the music I was playing just now, beautiful.' He left his current demon unmentioned.

26

June

Simple Future

Vincent emerged from the shower a little before four o' clock after a welcome day of oblivion. Then, shaved and dressed, he found Hazel ready, as ever, with a cup of tea.

'You spoil me,' he told her. 'Thank you.'

'Did you sleep well?'

'I think so. I don't remember waking up at all, so I suppose I must have.'

'You had a busy day.'

He gave her his full attention and said, 'That was somewhat cryptic. What do you mean?'

'When I passed the room, you were giving orders to Ali and fretting quite a lot. I couldn't make sense of most of it, but you did it more than once.'

'I'm sorry. I try not to bring my work home, but it sometimes follows me uninvited.'

Half-amused, she said, 'There was something about a reading list. I don't know what that has to do with mines.'

'Oh, that.' He laughed. 'Ali enjoys listening to music, but he'd like to learn more about it. The trouble is, there's so little literature for the uninformed.'

'Do you think there's a market for such a book?'

'Absolutely.' He put his cup down to make his point. 'Sir Thomas Beecham said, "It is quite untrue that the British people don't appreciate music. They may not understand it, but they absolutely love the noise it makes." What's more, I agree with him.'

'It's probably as well not to disagree with him. He always looks very fearsome.'

'But he's not,' he assured her. 'He's the musicians' favourite conductor. They regard him as their champion.' He stroked her hand and said, 'And now, before the boys arrive home, will you tell me what's on your mind?'

She closed her eyes, now conscious that her secret was out. 'Oh, Vincent,' she said, 'you've been reading the signs again.'

'I have, but I can't identify the problem without a little help.'

'All right.' She seemed to have some difficulty in approaching the subject, but she made the effort. 'The children need a proper family. It's one thing to have a guardian and an honorary uncle, wonderful though he may be, but the poor little scraps need the basic things other children have.'

Intrigued, he waited for her to continue.

'I'm not allowed, as a single woman, to adopt them.'

'And you feel that you might be if you were married?'

She said quietly, 'Yes.' Then, taking his hands in hers, she said, 'I know it sounds as if I'm backing you into a corner, but I'm not. You asked me what was troubling me, and I'm telling you, that's all.'

'All right,' he said, slipping his arm round her shoulders, 'let's have an arms-round talk.'

'What's that?'

'No daylight between us. I find it makes it easier to wax deep and meaningful. You see, the reason I've held off asking you is the same as that which led me to make my will in your favour. Mine, if you'll excuse the unintentional pun, isn't the safest of occupations; I could, quite literally, be here today and gone tomorrow, and I wanted to ensure that, in the event of my sudden demise, you'd be secure.' He held up a hand to prevent her from interrupting, 'You will be financially secure, but if I married you tomorrow, you might be a widow on Thursday.'

'What a horrible thought.' She clung to him, as if in doing so she could prevent him from being snatched away.

'I've thought about it quite a lot, lately. It tends to go with the job.'

'That's awful.' She continued to hold him tightly, and when she looked up, her eyes were wet. 'Does it sound awful if I say I'd rather be married to you for a day than not at all, but I really want you to be with me for a very long time?'

'No, I think I've broken the cipher.'

'I've really put you on the spot, haven't I? I'm sorry, and you mustn't think it's just because of the children.'

'I don't, and there's nothing to apologise for.' He thought momentarily and said, 'Nineteen forty-one can't be a leap year, but I'll accept your proposal. Of course, if you'd rather I went down on one knee, I could possibly oblige.'

'No,' she said happily, 'it's enough for me that we're going to be married.'

They kissed, breaking apart when the front door opened.

'I must tidy myself up and put a new face on,' she said.

'I'll keep them talking,' he promised.

Eric and Reggie appeared in the sitting room doorway.

'Come in, boys,' said Vincent. 'Tell me what you've been doing today.'

'The usual things,' said Eric with little enthusiasm.

'They always start the day with sums,' complained Reggie. 'Who needs sums?'

'The sad truth,' Vincent told them, 'is that we all do, sooner or later, and they say it's better to make friends with them than have them as enemies, but I confess I always found them difficult characters to get on with.'

Continuing his tirade, Reggie said, 'We have to do mental arithmetic straight after prayers, and then swap with our neighbours for marking. Then, Miss Brown asks, "Who got twenty out of twenty? Oh, good girl. Now, who got nineteen out of twenty?" When she gets down to asking who got nothing out of twenty, and I put my hand up, she says, "Worst in the class", and she spits all over me when she says it. She's a spitting cobra and I hate her.'

'I've got English homework,' announced Eric, not wishing to be left out.

'We don't get homework in Standard One,' said Reggie.

'Well, there's something to be thankful for. What have you to do for English homework, Eric?'

'Parsing. I don't understand it. They started it while we were in Tewkesbury.'

'Don't worry. Either Auntie Hazel or I will help you later.'

'Help him with what?' Hazel joined them in the sitting room, freshened up and only showing the merest traces of her earlier upset.

'Eric has some parsing exercises to do for homework. It seems the rest of the class stole a march on him when he was in Tewkesbury.'

'Oh, we'll soon get on top of that.'

Reggie was eyeing Hazel curiously. He asked, 'Are you all right, Auntie Hazel?'

'I couldn't be better. Shall we tell them our news, darling?'

'Now you've hinted at it, I think we should.'

'Uncle Vincent and I are going to be married.'

For Reggie, it seemed an anti-climax. 'I thought you were married,' he said. 'You sleep in the same bed.'

'Ah well,' said Vincent, 'we have to practise for the real thing.'

Eric's reaction was less assured and not at all judgemental. He asked, 'Will you go away?'

'No, of course not.' Hazel crouched to gather them up. 'You have a home with us for… ever and ever.'

'Amen,' said Reggie.

'Amen indeed,' echoed Vincent thoughtfully.

There was no telephone call from West Leigh, which was a relief for Vincent as well as an opportunity to help Eric with his homework.

'I can't see why we have to do it,' he said.

'It's important that you know about the various jobs that words do, so that you can use them properly. Now, what's the first exercise?' He looked at the bookmarked page and read, "Tomorrow, I shall ride a horse in a field." Right,' he said, we have to parse "Tomorrow, I shall ride a horse in a field".

When the boys were in bed, Hazel said, 'Poor little thing. First he loses his dad, then his mum, and now he has to contend with personal pronouns, future tenses, a case with a silly name, and a spare object. It was easier for us. For one thing, we stayed at the same school; at least, I did.'

‘So did I. I think we learned Latin grammar first, so English grammar seemed easy by comparison.’

‘At all events, you were very patient with him. You’re going to be a lovely dad.’

‘I hope so.’

On the following night, Vincent and Ali drove to Westcliff Beach, Shoeburyness, to attend to another of the new bomb mines. It had apparently, buried itself in sand, but had been spotted after being partially uncovered by the outgoing tide. It was sufficiently close to habitation to warrant defusing.

‘It’s the same drill, Ali. We take no chances, and then, with any luck, it will repay that respect.’

They arrived to find the usual kind of reception party, and it seemed to Vincent that when Milton wrote, ‘They also serve who only stand and wait’, he could have had no idea that his words would be so relevant three hundred years later. Certainly, they applied to the police force, ARP, and anyone else involved in ensuring that the British public kept its distance from something so fascinating but so deadly.

Setting up a safety point was quite difficult, but they managed with what they had, and Vincent and Ali dug a crater carefully around the mine. The only ballast they could find came from the shoreline above the beach. They chose the rocks with great care, knowing how important they would be.

Finally, Vincent said, ‘Thank you, Ali. Off you go.’

When Ali was back at the safety point, Vincent started on the screws that held the rear casing in place. They were quite ungiving at first, and he wasn’t altogether impressed by the way the new tools were coping, but he managed to remove the last one and piled rocks against the rear casing. As he was about to attach the cord, one of the rocks slipped, catching another as it fell, and suddenly the casing was wide open. For a second, Vincent expected to be blasted sky-high, but nothing happened. It seemed that the photo-electric cells were unimpressed with the light as it was, and he replaced the dome, wedging it again with rocks and refusing to take any chances. He knelt beside it for a while, regaining his composure, before walking back to the safety point, paying out the cord more carefully than ever.

The planned exposure of the photo cells was uneventful, and Vincent carried out the defusing.

He told Ali on the way home, 'The thing didn't go bang, but I wasn't going to take chances. I'm going to ask if there's any chance of the technical chaps making a fool-proof wedge for us to use, rather than depending on local facilities.'

'That's a good idea, sir.'

'Thank you, Ali.' Suddenly reminded of a previous conversation, he said, 'I'm working on that idea, by the way, the introduction to music.'

'Just as long as it's not a lot of trouble, sir.'

'Hardly that. Funnily enough, I find it relaxing.' In truth, it was as relaxing as any distraction could be.

Ali made no comment, and Vincent wondered if he'd fallen asleep, but then he asked a question that was quite apropos of nothing.

'Can you tell me, sir, what the difference is between "shall" and "will"?'

'What brought that up, Ali?'

'Well, sir, I was listening to Mr Churchill on the wireless, and he says, "shall" quite a lot, where most of us would say, "will".'

'You're absolutely right, but you have to remember that, whilst Mr Churchill is undeniably a superb orator, his English is of a bygone age, and that he was at school, I imagine, before your parents were born.'

'I can see that, sir, but it's confusing all the same.'

Vincent could appreciate that. 'To begin with,' he said, 'it depends on the person. "I shall" sounds perfectly all right, but not "you shall"; at least, not nowadays. "Cinderella, you shall go to the ball" was coined a long time ago. Also, "he shall", "we shall" and "they shall" belong in the past.'

'But "I will" sounds just as right as "I shall", sir.'

'Well observed, Ali. In that case, "will" denotes intention, often in the face of defiance. "I *will* be heard". It's a little old-fashioned, but there are those in the House of Commons who would say it readily. Generally speaking, though, "shall" and "will" are modal verbs that assist a main verb in forming the simple future tense. A hundred years from now, no one will know the difference.'

'Thank you, sir. You've simplified that for me.'

If only the future were really so simple, mused Vincent as he drove through the blackout.

27

A Straightforward Job

Vincent had been home for less than half-an-hour when the telephone rang. He waited, because the call could easily be for Hazel now that she was beginning to get freelance work, but the bedroom door opened, and Hazel said, 'I'm sorry, darling. It's Lieutenant Commander Ghyll for you. He says it's very important.'

Vincent went to the telephone. 'Reid here, sir.'

'Listen, Reid, I know you've just got in, but there's a Category "A" in the river at Stepney. It's the first magnetic mine we've had for a while; in fact, it may well have lain dormant for some time until it was fished up by accident. It's holding everything up, and you're nearest, so I'm asking you to deal with it, after which you and Able Seaman Barber can take seventy-two hours' rest.'

'Whereabouts in Stepney, sir?'

Ghyll gave him the address. 'I wouldn't normally ask you to do this, but it really is urgent, Reid. Do your best.'

'Aye, aye, sir.' He replaced the receiver.

Hazel asked, 'Where is it?'

'Stepney.'

'Not far, then.'

'No, not far. He's giving us seventy-two hours after this.'

'Oh, good. You need it.'

He kissed her and left the house.

'It's a magnetic,' he told Ali on the way, 'so we can expect anything. The only good thing is that, after this one, you and I will be rested.'

'How long, sir?'

'Seventy-two hours.'

A sideways glance told Vincent how Ali felt about that. 'It's very important that we do this,' he said. 'Traffic on the river has been brought to a standstill.'

'Nobody said the job would be cushy,' said Ali.

'No, we both know the score.' He was thankful for Ali's down-to-earth attitude. He and Jimmy had that in common.

The route to Stepney was tortuous, as usual; temporary repair work was going on all the time, but eventually, a policeman directed them to the site. Vincent surveyed the low-tide riverscape and said, 'Seaboots, I think, Ali. I'll let you know if you're likely to need yours.'

He changed into his seaboots for the trek across the mud and silt to where the mine lay minus its parachute, which must have become detached when it hit the river. For all he knew, it could have been transformed into a cornucopia of female underwear since its emancipation. The mine, however, was no less threatening than when it left the aircraft.

It seemed that Ghyll's assessment had been correct, that the mine had been there for some time, because it was, incredibly, a Type 'A', similar to the first Vincent had defused, and a relatively straightforward job. He remembered the occasion, how he'd joked with Jimmy about the Sword of Damocles. That it was a Type 'A' was quite simply a stroke of luck. What was more, all four plates were exposed and easily accessible, making digging unnecessary. It seemed that, on this occasion, Dame Fortune was smiling on him. It was a welcome change.

He trudged back to the bank, where Ali had set up his safety point. 'It's a Type "A" ', he reported, 'nothing comical about it. I should have it fixed in the next twenty minutes or so.'

'Is there any digging to be done, sir?'

'No, you can sit here and wait for me.'

'Aye, aye, sir.'

Vincent returned to the mine, still incredulous that it had remained submerged for so long and then survived being trawled to the surface by whatever craft had happened across it. For a moment, he wondered if it might be another six o' clock job, but then he dismissed the thought. He could take absolutely no chances.

He opened his toolkit and checked that he had everything he needed: the four-pronged spanner, his new bronze cutting pliers, the big screwdriver, the brass rods and the hammer, which he hoped he wouldn't need, and above all, the stethoscope. A moment later, he realised that one essential item was missing. He couldn't find the roll of insulating tape. He searched again but without success. It must have fallen into the boot of the car. Annoyed with himself, he walked back to the safety point, where Ali was waiting, watchful as ever.

'I must have left the tape in the car,' he said. 'I shan't be a minute.' With the word, 'shan't', he winked and said, 'I'm an old-fashioned soul.' Ali responded with a knowing smile.

Back at the car, he searched the boot to no avail, and the rest of the car yielded nothing. He must have mislaid the tape inadvertently at his last incident. Working in darkness, he could easily have missed the bag altogether when he dropped the tape to concentrate on insulating the bared wires.

He made his way back to the safety point and said, 'Ali, will you find a garage or somewhere where you can cadge or buy some insulating tape? Failing that, sticking plaster will do the job, at a pinch.' In the absence of change, he handed him a ten shilling note.

'Aye, aye, sir. I'll be as quick as I can.'

Cursing himself for his carelessness, he stood at the safety point, waiting. He couldn't even make a start. The anti-handling device had to be dealt with first, and that meant taping off the wires.

As he stood there, the policeman guarding the nearest part of the barrier came over to ask, 'Is everything all right, sir?'

Vincent laughed shortly. 'No, it's not. I'm a bloody fool. I've found myself without something I need, and my assistant's gone to get it.' Surely, he thought, Ali must be able to find some kind of tape.

'We all make mistakes, sir,' said the policeman. 'We're none of us perfect.'

'I'm certainly not.'

No doubt gauging Vincent's mood, the policeman gave him a sympathetic smile, saluted and said, 'I'll leave you in peace, sir.' He returned to the barrier.

Fifteen minutes later, Ali returned, breathless but triumphant. 'I had to go to the tube station, sir. An electrician and his mate were working there and they let me have a roll of tape, as it was in the national interest.' He took out Vincent's ten shilling note. 'I had to take some ribbing about it, but I don't care.'

'Keep it and buy yourself a drink tonight, Ali. You've earned it.' He took the insulating tape from him and returned to the mine.

After listening through the stethoscope, he decided to save time and awkward fumbling by cutting several pieces of tape and sticking them to the casing, ready for use.

It was necessary to clean out the holes in the first plate before inserting the four-pronged spanner, as the dirt from the riverbed had inevitably found a home there, but he managed it and he was able to get a proper purchase on the plate. It was very tight, so that, even with the weight of his body behind the spanner, he could make no headway. Most reluctantly, he took out the four-ounce hammer and gave the spanner a tap. A second tap moved it, but before continuing, he listened again. There was only the familiar symphony of blood pounding in his ears. He put down the stethoscope and turned the spanner. To his relief, it went the whole way, exposing the fuse, which he withdrew without further difficulty.

The new side-cutter pliers were a great improvement on the bronze knife when it came to severing the wires, and with the tape already cut into convenient pieces, he was able to make the anti-handling device safe.

Next was the main detonator, with its familiar arrangement of crossed bars. Again, it proved resistant to hand pressure, but Vincent was reluctant to use the hammer again. He decided to move on to the primer and return to it later.

The primer plate took all his strength. It seemed that the time spent beneath the Thames had caused everything to seize up, but he eventually persuaded it to turn, and the primer came out with surprisingly little persuasion.

Rather than return immediately to the main detonator, he went on to the hydrostatic valve, which was also difficult to shift, but it moved eventually, and the valve came tumbling out.

Now, he had to tackle the detonator. He could delay it no longer.

After some thought, he tried again to turn the crossed bars by hand, but they still refused to budge. He tried using a longer rod as a lever, but that also failed. There was only one thing for it. He checked, first, with the stethoscope and satisfied himself that all was well. Then, he took the brass rod and the hammer. An aircraft flew low overhead, and he waited until he was certain that it was alone. Aircraft presented the worst kind of distraction when he had to keep listening. He lined up the rod with one of the crossbars and gave it a tap. It was difficult to say whether or not it had done any good, but he picked up the stethoscope and listened. Again, it was silent. He wiped the cold perspiration from his eyes and face, and gave the rod a slightly heavier tap. He listened again. Happy that the clock wasn't running, he tried turning the bars again by hand, but without success. Reluctantly, he picked up the hammer and gave the rod one sharp rap. It moved, but before he dared do anything else, he put the stethoscope to the casing. As he did so, his heart seemed to stop, because he could hear the sound he'd dreaded ever since his first incident. Reacting immediately, he dropped everything and ran as fast as his heavy seaboots and the soggy riverbed would allow. It was as if the mud and silt were reaching out to claim him, sucking and clinging like some malevolent creature, and he had to wrench his feet free with every step, frantic in his bid to get to the safety point. He could see Ali and the policeman watching him. He was almost at the steps. If he could reach the top in time, he could shelter.

He never heard the explosion. He was only fleetingly aware of the blast that struck him from behind.

28

A Good Hand

Hazel was working on a piece about the Morrison Shelter, which was becoming increasingly popular with people who lacked the necessary garden for an Anderson shelter. The current easing of the Blitz seemed too good to be true, and many people were dreading the Luftwaffe's return.

Referring to Vincent as her 'husband' to avoid alienating the morally upright, she was describing his hastily-designed shelter, and making the point that there really was nothing new under the sun. It was a light-hearted piece, and she was quite pleased with it. She was reading it when the telephone rang. Ever hopeful for more work, she picked it up and said, 'Hazel Wythenshawe.'

'Ah, Miss Wythenshawe. Lieutenant Commander Ghyll speaking.' He sounded apologetic, and rightly so after sending Vincent to an incident after no sleep.

'Lieutenant Reid is not here, Commander,' she said coldly. She glanced at the mantlepiece clock. It was ten thirty-five. 'It's possible that he's still in Stepney. Shall I ask him to telephone you when he returns?'

'Thank you, Miss Wythenshawe, but that won't be necessary. I'm afraid I'm calling with rather unpleasant news. You see, there was an explosion this morning—'

'Oh, no!'

'He's alive, but he was rushed to hospital. The rating who was assisting him showed great presence of mind and rode with him in the ambulance.'

She sank into a chair, unable to trust her legs to support her. 'Which hospital?'

'Able Seaman Barber telephoned from the London Hospital in Whitechapel. That's where the ambulance took your… where they took Lieutenant Reid. At this stage, I'm afraid I can tell you no more than that. As you're his next of kin, if you telephone them, or even call on them, they'll be able to tell you much more, I'm sure.'

'Thank you, Commander. I'll go there now. Goodbye.'

'Goodbye, Miss Wythenshawe. I do hope you'll hear better news from the hospital.'

In a torment of helpless fear, Hazel left the house and made for the Holborn Underground Station, where she found a taxi.

'The London Hospital, please, as quickly as you can.'

'I do everything as quick as I can, lady. I pick up more fares that way. The London Hospital it is.' He pulled out and joined a line of traffic. 'Have you got somebody in there, then?'

'Yes. Look, I really don't want to talk. I'd much rather you just took me there.'

'Right you are, lady.' He continued in silence whilst, for her part, Hazel fretted throughout the twenty-five minute journey as the driver picked his way around road closures and detours.

After an agony of frustration, they reached the hospital, where she paid the driver, apologised to him briefly for her rudeness, and made for the main entrance. A stern-looking woman sat at a desk.

'Good morning,' said Hazel. 'I've come to enquire about a patient who was brought in earlier, a naval officer called Lieutenant Vincent Reid.'

'Was his admission planned, or was he a casualty?'

Hazel found the nurse's routine calmness irritating. She was being unfair, but so were the circumstances of her visit. 'He was a casualty, injured in an explosion.'

'Are you his next-of-kin?'

'Yes, his fiancée.'

The nurse picked up the internal telephone and dialled a number. After a few seconds, she said, 'Reception here. I have a next-of-kin enquiring about….' She paused and looked questioningly at Hazel.

'Lieutenant Vincent Reid,' she prompted.

'She's enquiring about a naval officer, a Lieutenant Vincent Reid. He was injured in an explosion earlier this morning.' She waited and listened. Finally, she said, 'Thank you,' and replaced the receiver. 'If you follow the signs to "Casualty",' she said, 'you'll be able to speak to someone there who can tell you more.'

'Thank you.' Hazel looked up at the board with its destinations and arrows, and found 'Casualty Department' near the bottom. She followed the arrow.

It was like walking through a maze, except that her destination was clearly marked throughout the route. She'd never realised, though, how huge the London Hospital was, although, at that moment, she saw its sheer size as an impediment. All she wanted was to be with Vincent.

After what seemed a mile-long journey, she reached a large doorway beneath a sign that read, *Casualty Reception.* Several people sat in chairs that lined the walls, but there was no one at the desk except for the official behind it.

'I'm enquiring about Lieutenant Vincent Reid, who was brought in this morning,' she said.

'Reid,' said the official, running her eye systematically down a list of names. 'Are you his next-of-kin?'

'Yes, Hazel Wythenshawe.' She spelt it for her, wanting to snatch the list from her, but she managed to control herself, and was rewarded when the receptionist found Vincent's name.

'He's being examined and assessed. You can't see him yet, but if you take a seat, someone will speak to you as soon as they can. Will you tell me your name again?'

'Hazel Wythenshawe.'

'Thank you.'

Hazel looked around the room and saw a naval rating among those seated. 'Hello,' she said, 'are you Ali?' Remembering her manners, she said, 'I'm sorry. I shouldn't call you that.' Suddenly, she was embarrassed by her tearful appearance.

He rose to his feet to speak to her. 'That's all right, ma'am. It's what everybody else calls me. You must be Mrs Reid.'

'Not yet, but I hope to be.'

'Shall we sit over there, ma'am, where it's more private?' He inclined his head towards the end of the row, where several chairs were vacant.

'That's a good idea.' She followed him readily.

Ali waited for her to take her seat, before joining her, and it occurred to her that he was remarkably well-mannered. It must have something to do with being a hairdresser, she decided.

'What actually happened, Ali?'

'Well, ma'am, Mr Reid was working on the mine. I remember him listening through a stethoscope, and its clock must have started, because he dropped the stethoscope and ran towards the safety point, where I was waiting.' He screwed up his eyes for a moment, no doubt re-living the experience, and then he went on. 'He was wearing seaboots and running through thick mud, so he was never going to break any records, if you don't mind me saying so, ma'am, and he was within feet of the stone steps up to the bank when the mine exploded.' He stopped, clearly affected by the recollection.

'Are you all right?'

'Yes, ma'am, thank you.' He took a breath and continued. 'The blast lifted him off the ground and threw him forward, ma'am, so that he landed on the bottom of the steps. It almost stripped the clothes off him.'

Hazel realised that, quite without thinking, she'd taken Ali's hand between hers. It was as if they were supporting each other.

'The policeman on the barrier called the ambulance. He knew where the nearest telephone was, you see, and I went down the steps…. I don't know why, because you mustn't move anyone if there's even a chance of spinal injury – it's the first thing they tell you on the first-aid course – I just wanted to stay with him in case….' He ended lamely, 'I don't know.'

Hazel squeezed his hand and said, 'Thank you for telling me that, Ali.'

'I can tell you something else, ma'am.'

'Go on.'

'Well, I don't know if it helps at all. You see, when Mr Reid fell on the steps, he fell with his head on his arm, if you see what I mean. I'm trying to say that his arm shielded his head from hitting a stone step. I noticed that particularly, and the only blood I could see was coming from his arm. If it hadn't got in the way of his head, we wouldn't have been having this conversation now, ma'am.'

'Thank you, Ali. You've been a great help.'

'It's no trouble, ma'am. Mr Reid's the best kind of officer.' He looked at his watch and said, 'I've been waiting here since they brought him in. I spoke to *HMS Vernon* on the telephone. I expect they notified you, because I couldn't tell the hospital who his next-of-kin was. He'd left his diary at home, of course.'

She was puzzled. 'Why "of course"?'

'The little pencil that fits inside it, it's the kind with a rubber on the end, and the ferrule that holds it on is made of steel. When we go to a mine, we have to leave behind anything that a magnet can detect.' He shrugged. 'I shouldn't really have told you that, but I don't think the information's all that sensitive.'

'I shan't tell a soul, Ali.' Concern for him made her ask, 'What do you have to do next?'

'I can go home today, ma'am – I live not far away, in Camden Town – but I have to report to *HMS Vincent* when my seventy-two hours' rest is up.'

'Have you got the train fare to Portsmouth?'

'Yes, ma'am. Mr Reid gave me ten bob this morning. He told me to have a drink on him, but drinking's the last thing on my mind in the present circumstances.'

'Don't spend it on train fare, Ali.' She opened her purse and took out another ten shillings.

'It's all right, ma'am, I'll be able to claim it back.'

'Even so, take this and have a meal or something.'

'That's very kind of you, ma'am. Thank you.'

'What's more, when I speak to Lieutenant Commander Ghyll at *HMS Vernon*, I'm going to tell him just how helpful you've been.'

'Thank you, ma'am, but I'm only doing my duty as I see it.'

'By keeping me company all this time, and by talking to me, you've done much more than your duty, believe me.'

They continued to talk until a nurse came into the waiting room and asked, 'Is Miss Wythen…? She looked at the note again.

'Wythenshawe,' prompted Hazel, 'yes.'

'Ah. Can we speak in private?'

'Yes, but Able Seaman Barber needs to know what the situation is, and I'm happy for him to know.'

'Very well.' The nurse beckoned them over. Speaking quietly, she said, 'Lieutenant Reid has regained consciousness, but he's under heavy sedation. He has several cracked ribs, a broken collar bone, and a compound fracture of the two bones in his right forearm. The elbow is also badly damaged. You can come in and see him briefly before he goes up to the ward.'

'I'll leave you to do that, ma'am,' said Ali.

'Ali, you've been a wonderful help.' She looked in her bag again and took out a business card. 'If you call me on that number, I should be able to tell you more.'

'Thank you, ma'am.'

'No, Ali, thank *you.*' She followed the nurse into the examination room, where Vincent lay on a plinth. Most of his clothes had been removed, and his arm was heavily bandaged. Oddly, his face was only slightly bruised, and Hazel remembered what Ali had said about him falling on his arm. His features were quite relaxed, no doubt because of the sedative.

'Don't touch his chest or his arm,' the nurse warned her.

Hazel bent and kissed him, causing him to open his eyes and recognise her. 'Don't try to speak, darling,' she whispered. 'I'll come later, when they've put you to bed. Just rest and get well. I love you.' She kissed him again, and then let the nurse lead her away.

'You'll get no sense out of him while he's sedated,' she said. 'If you telephone, this afternoon, we may be able to tell you more.'

Hazel waited until she was back at home before giving way to her feelings of horror mixed with relief, sobbing until she felt she was empty of tears.

When she'd freshened herself up and was feeling more collected, she telephoned the number Vincent kept for Lieutenant Commander Ghyll. The telephonist answered, and Hazel said, 'I'd like to speak to Lieutenant Commander Ghyll, if I may, please.'

'Who is calling?'

'It's Hazel Wythenshawe, in connection with Lieutenant Reid's accident.'

'I see. Please hold the line.'

Hazel waited patiently until the receptionist said, 'I'm afraid Lieutenant Commander Ghyll isn't available.'

'In that case, I'd like you to try Commander Todd, please.'

'Commander Todd? Is it important?'

Hazel's patience was ebbing rapidly. 'It's in connection with one of his officers, who's just been blown almost into the next world, so yes, I'd say it's very important.'

'Please wait while I try his office.'

Half a minute later, Commander Todd came on the line. He seemed preoccupied when he asked, 'Who is this?'

'*This*, Commander Todd, is Hazel Wythenshawe, Lieutenant Reid's fiancée and next-of-kin.' Vincent might bow down before these tin gods, but she wasn't prepared to be intimidated by them.

His tone changed completely. 'I'm so sorry, my dear. I didn't realise. How is Lieutenant Reid?'

'He's under heavy sedation, with a number of cracked ribs and a badly-damaged arm, which is worrying.'

'Of course it is.'

'I say that, Commander, because when he's not being blown up by a mine, he makes his living as a musician, and one of his duties involves playing the piano.'

'Of course. I remember that from his interview. Yes, I can see why you're so worried about his arm.'

'I thought you should know how things stand, Commander, but my main reason for telephoning you is to tell you that Able Seaman Barber is, in Vincent's words, a good hand. In fact, he's much more than that. He has acquitted himself throughout this horrendous time with loyalty, clear thinking, responsible behaviour and, above all, great sensitivity. Moreover, I am enormously grateful to him for his support and co-operation this morning at the hospital.'

'I'm delighted to hear it, Miss Wythenshawe.'

'Good. Well, I hope that will go down on his service record.'

'Not only that, but either Lieutenant Commander Ghyll or I will speak to him personally.'

'Thank you, Commander. Goodbye.'

That was all she could do before telephoning the hospital. The rest would depend on the grace of God and the skill of the hospital staff.

29

'Plight' is a Funny Word

The benefit of the morphia injection had worn off, and the pain in Vincent's arm and chest was almost unbearable, and now he found a doctor beside him, who seemed keen to question him about his medical history.

'My medical history began this morning,' he said, hesitating for a moment. 'Was it this morning?'

'The accident? Yes, so you've no history of operations, serious illness or allergies?'

'That's what I said.'

'You're obviously not haemophilic.' He said to himself as he made a note, 'Not haemophilic.'

'No, not a bleeder,' agreed Vincent, 'but I can be an utter bastard when I'm in acute pain, and someone insists on asking me silly questions.'

'We need to know these things, Lieutenant Reid, to avoid possible complications. Mr Goodwin is coming later to see you.'

'Let joy be unconfined. Who is Mr Goodwin?'

'He's the chief orthopaedic surgeon. He's interested in your arm.'

'Good. I'll look forward to discussing it with him.'

'Actually,' said the doctor, looking towards the entrance to the ward, 'I think he's here now.'

'Stand by your beds.'

Incredibly, at least from Vincent's perspective, the doctor did rise to his feet, and all-but came to attention.

The sister, whom Vincent had already met arrived at his bedside with a lean, angular man wearing a white coat and carrying a manila folder.

'Good afternoon, Lieutenant Reid.'

'Good afternoon, Doctor.'

'Mr Goodwin is an orthopaedic surgeon,' said Sister, 'and surgeons are addressed as "Mister", rather than "Doctor".'

'A thousand apologies, Mr Goodwin. Blame it on the pain and an unending list of seemingly pointless questions.'

Goodwin opened the folder and took out several X-ray photographs, handing the folder to Sister, who passed it to a convenient nurse. 'I've been looking at your X-rays, Lieutenant, and they tell a most regrettable story.'

'It wasn't one of my favourite experiences,' agreed Vincent.

'Your ribs and collar bone will heal in time. All we can do is protect them from external contact. Your arm, I'm afraid, is another matter. You have extensive damage to your right elbow, compound fractures to the ulna and the radius. Those are the bones of the forearm,' he explained. 'In addition, your wrist, I'm sorry to say, is quite shattered. On the other side of the coin and according to information supplied by the naval rating who was with you at the time of the accident, your arm appears to have saved your head from direct contact with surrounding surfaces, and that, without doubt, is the reason why you are still alive.'

It was a great deal to take in. 'What's the prognosis, Mr Goodwin?'

'I'm sorry, old chap. I have absolutely no alternative but to amputate your arm above the elbow.'

'So, no happy, eleventh-hour alternative springs to mind?'

'None whatsoever, I'm afraid. I must ask you to give your consent to the operation.'

It was like a switchback ride. First, he was told that his life had been spared, but now, he had to lose his arm.

Sister asked, 'When did you last eat, Lieutenant?'

'Last evening, at about seven. I had a cup of tea this morning at between seven and eight.'

'I shall operate tonight,' said Mr Goodwin.

'Have you any more nasty shocks for me?'

'No, I'm sure the news is bad enough, and I'm truly sorry.'

Sister was hovering with a clipboard and pen. She asked, 'Are you able to sign the consent form, Lieutenant?'

'Yes, I'm left-handed, as it happens.'

'In the circumstances, it's perhaps as well.'

'Even so, Sister, I'm not in a mood to celebrate. In civilian life, I'm a musician. I play…. I should say, I *used to play* the piano.'

Hazel sat between Eric and Reggie with an arm around each of them, reluctant to send them to bed in a worried state of mind. Fortunately, the next day was Saturday, so school didn't present a problem. All the same, though, she felt guilty about allowing them to stay up. She'd been advised not to telephone the hospital before ten, and that was very late indeed for two children. Eric seemed about to fall asleep, but Reggie's mind was still active.

He asked, 'Why can't we go to see him?'

'Hospital rules, darling. They don't allow children to visit. I don't really understand it, but it has something to do with infection.'

'What about children having operations? They don't tell them to stay away.'

'That's true. As I said, I don't understand it, but please remember that I didn't write the rules.'

Eric roused himself sufficiently to say, 'They wouldn't let us see our mum before she died.'

'I know, darling. That was awful for you, but Uncle Vincent's not going to die.' She hoped quite fervently that she was right.

'My dad did,' said Eric.

'I know.' There was little else she could say.

Reggie said, 'He's the best uncle we've ever had, so he'd better not die.'

Curiosity made her ask, 'How many uncles have you?' She knew that Lily had a divided family. It was why she'd asked Hazel to become the children's guardian.

After some thought, Reggie said, 'Uncle Vincent's the first.'

'Good. Who needs competition at a time like this?'

The boys were asleep by the time Hazel dialled the hospital's number, but they woke up quickly when they heard her voice.

'Good evening. I want to enquire about a patient who had an

operation this evening.' She gave Vincent's details and identified herself as his next-of-kin.

After some time, the senior nurse on Vincent's ward came to the telephone, and Hazel repeated her request.

'Lieutenant Reid underwent surgery this evening. It was successful, and he is now coming round from the anaesthetic. He is as well as can be expected.'

'Is that all you can tell me?'

'At this stage, I'm afraid so.'

'When can I see him?'

'Visiting is from two-thirty pm to three-thirty pm, but we may be able to tell you more if you telephone after eleven, tomorrow morning.'

'Thank you.' She rang off and returned to the sofa, where Eric and Reggie were avid for information. 'All they could tell me is that Uncle Vincent had his operation, that it went very well, and that he's still sleeping off the anaesthetic.'

After some thought, Reggie asked, 'What will they do with his arm, now they've cut it off?'

'I suppose they'll cremate it.' As the words left her mouth, she regretted saying them.

Eric said, 'They cremated our mum.'

Hazel did some quick thinking. 'Not really, Eric. She had no further use for her body, and it was full of that horrible thing that killed her. That was what they cremated – her useless body and that awful disease. Your mum lives on in a different form, no longer ill, just happy to keep an eye on her two boys.'

'In Heaven?'

'Yes, Reggie.' Hazel was determined not to send them to bed with thoughts of the parents they'd lost and the possibility, as they saw it, of losing their uncle as well. 'I'll tell you what, you two. As a special event, I'll go and get ready for bed, and then we'll all three of us spend the night in the Wellington Bomber. How's that?'

'Yes.'

'Yeah.'

'All right, you two prepare it for take-off while I change into my flying suit.'

It was the best she could manage, and it was popular with the boys, so she undressed hurriedly and donned her pyjamas and dressing gown before joining them with an eiderdown that would cover all three of them. Then, with both boys almost asleep, she settled down between them, adjusting to the awful knowledge that Vincent had narrowly escaped death, only to lose his right arm. It was too much to cope with after an emotionally draining day, and before long, she too, was asleep.

Her telephone call the next morning elicited little more news other than that the patient had spent a comfortable night – which she doubted – and that he was as well as could be expected.

Isabel, an old colleague from the Ministry, arrived to look after the boys while Hazel took a taxi to Stepney, where she rescued Vincent's car and, trying not to look at the damage to the embankment caused by the explosion, drove it to the hospital in time for visiting.

She found him immediately and kissed him, fighting back her tears as she did so.

'I'm all right,' he told her somewhat feebly.

'I left the boys with a friend. They're peeved at not being allowed to visit you, but they accepted my explanation. Last night was quite a night. In the end we all slept in the stair cupboard.'

He smiled weakly at the thought. 'Tell them I'll be back just as soon....'

His voice tailed off.

'Does it hurt horribly?'

'Some of the time. There's a limit to the morphia they can give me. They say it's highly addictive, but all I know is that it makes me daft. Still, all the time it's healing, the pain's bound to....' The word eluded him.

'Something you should know, is that Ali Barber was a trouper yesterday. He stayed with me in casualty reception and kept me sane. I've told Commander Todd about him.'

Surprise and concern crossed his features. 'Commander Todd?'

'Lieutenant Commander Ghyll wasn't available, which was just as well, because I might have told him exactly what I thought of him.'

'It wasn't his....'

'I was in such a state,' she confided, 'I'd have lashed out at anyone.' To take her mind off the events of the previous day, she stroked the sleeve of his remaining arm and said, 'These hospital pyjamas are awful. I've brought yours in. I brought your washing and shaving kit as well.'

He smiled oddly. 'One of the nurses shaved me this morning.' He raised his hand to feel his face, but thought better of it.

'Is it painful now?'

'Only when I move.' He went on. 'They do what they can, but shaving a man's face is different from... what they're used to.'

'If I shave you,' she said, 'you'll find out what a woman can do.'

'Don't,' he said wearily, 'I bled enough yesterday.'

'All right,' she said, changing the subject, 'you may as well know that you're the best uncle the boys have ever had.'

'How many have they?'

'You're their first.'

'Even so, it's quite a.... What's the word?'

'An accolade?'

Suddenly, he was serious. 'Hazel,' he said, 'what we discussed the other day....'

'What did we say the other day?' She thought she knew.

'About getting married. I mean, I'm a hopeless case now, with only one arm.'

'You've still got one left,' she reminded him, 'your left, as it happens.' It felt like a ridiculous thing to say, but she was trying to make light of his objection.

'You know what I mean.'

'No, I don't. I can't see how losing an arm can possibly make you less than the man I want to marry.'

'Are you sure?'

'I'm sure. "In sickness and in health, to love and to cherish.... And thereto I plight thee my troth." There, I've said it. Well, some of it, anyway.'

His expression changed from concern to relief, and then he became pensive.' "Plight" is a funny word, when you think about it. If you can think, that is, and I'm struggling.'

'Not where I'm sitting, Vincent. I'm taking your plight very seriously indeed.'

He relaxed a little and smiled. 'I meant funny-peculiar, of course. As a noun, it is distressingly appropriate, I have to admit, but as a verb….'

'As a verb, what, darling?'

'As a verb, and as you used it a minute or so ago, it eased my plight and made me much happier than I was.'

She kissed him, being careful to avoid touching his chest. 'Just get well again, darling, and I'll let you off the task of carrying me over the threshold. I never fancied it, anyway.'

30

June

Wittgenstein Had a Brother

That first visit had been a promising start, but Hazel was dismayed on the next occasion to find Vincent in very low spirits; in fact, he seemed to be in the grip of utter hopelessness. She was so alarmed that she asked to see a doctor, and Sister arranged a meeting later that day.

'He's suffering from post-operative depression,' Dr Littlewood told her. He was a young man with an engaging nature and what appeared to be a club foot, which was presumably the reason he wasn't in the armed forces. 'He came to us in a state of shock, and we treated that as best we could. In normal circumstances, Mr Goodwin would have waited longer before operating, but urgency overrode that precaution, and now, your fiancé is in mild post-operative shock. Also, he's yet to come to terms with his disability, he feels, quite irrationally, that he's let the side down, and on top of everything else, the morphia, which was highly necessary, does tend to act as a depressant.'

It was a shocking catalogue. She asked, 'What can be done?'

'We're encouraging him to eat, which is important, but not as easy as it sounds; we're careful to sound positive, and that's something with which you can help. Also, exercise is important. I know that sounds ridiculous, but he will soon be ready for physiotherapy.'

'What's that?'

'Exercises to get him moving. For one thing, he'll have to learn to walk again.'

'What?'

'Oh yes, the arms help to balance the body. Take one of them away, and standing upright isn't as easy as you'd think.'

'Thank you, Dr Littlewood. I'm finding communication with him more than difficult, but I'll persevere.'

'You do that, Miss Wythenshawe, and we'll do our share as well.'

One of the nurses came to Vincent's bed to say, 'You have a visitor, Lieutenant Reid.'

'I don't want to see anyone.' It would have been difficult at that moment, as his eyes were firmly closed.

'I think you'll see this visitor. He's a naval officer, and you're likely to be in trouble if you don't do as you're told.'

'They can bloody-well shoot me, for all I care.'

A familiar voice asked, 'What's this, Reid? Mutiny?'

Vincent opened his eyes to see Lieutenant Commander Ghyll. 'I'm sorry sir.' He uttered the words with no real conviction.

'I'm the one who's sorry, Reid. I'm truly sorry to find you in this condition and I'm abjectly sorry that it occurred after I'd sent you to an incident, knowing you were short on sleep and exhausted after working most of the night.'

'Tiredness had nothing to do with it. Everything on that mine was seized up tight.' Details had been returning to him with distressing clarity, usually at night, when the ward was quiet and the world seemed to stand depressingly still. 'I had to use the hammer, and I was just ham-fisted.'

'Clocks have been known to survive worse shocks than that.'

'I suppose my time had come.' He'd thought about that, too. 'Unfortunately, there are mines out there waiting to be made safe, and I can't do a damned thing about them. I've rendered myself unfit for duty and incapable of pulling my weight.'

'You've pulled much more than your weight, Reid.'

'That's easy for you to say, but I know how I feel.' Incredibly, he didn't care if he offended a senior officer.

'It seems to me that your experience has turned you into an

argumentative bugger, but I'm not the only one who's impressed by your record. There's one man whose opinion you wouldn't dare challenge.'

In spite of himself, Vincent was curious. 'Who's that?'

'His Majesty the King. He seems to think your record is worthy of official recognition.' In a friendlier tone, he said, 'I believe you're engaged to be married.'

'Yes, sir.' He still wasn't sure it would go ahead, but he was disinclined to argue about such a thing with an outsider.

'Well, you need to hurry up and marry the lady, and then she'll receive an invitation to the Palace.'

It all sounded very Lewis Carroll. 'What for, sir?'

'So that the pair of you can have your photograph taken, with you holding your new George Medal, you chump. It was confirmed yesterday, and well-deserved, I'd say. Congratulations, Reid.'

'Thank you, sir. It was completely unexpected, and Hazel would enjoy the occasion. He owed her that for being so horrible to her. Suddenly, he was overcome by guilt.

'Take it easy, old chap,' said Ghyll, taking Vincent's left hand. 'You're going through a rotten time, and you don't owe your country a thing.'

Several days later, Vincent was able to greet Hazel on foot. He could now manage a few steps without falling over, and he was beginning, just beginning, to feel that he was his own man.

'Hazel, I'm sorry I've been so difficult.'

'So you keep saying. It doesn't matter, darling. I'm just thrilled to have you back.' She kissed him, still being careful to avoid his ribs. 'Could you bear to see the boys? They're desperate to see you.'

He didn't understand. 'How…? I mean, they're not allowed in the hospital.'

'As we're on the ground floor, Sister says I can bring them to the window, as long as there's no physical contact.'

'That would be…. Yes, bring them over.'

'I shan't be long,' she promised.

It was an odd feeling, and Vincent sat on his bed, composing himself. Hazel and the two boys had been through an awful time made worse, particularly for Hazel, by his foul moods. It was time to make amends. He took a deep breath and walked to the opened window. They'd left the car and were walking, at least, Hazel was, towards him. The boys had run ahead and were almost at the window.

Typically, Reggie spoke first. 'Hello, Uncle Vincent. When are you coming home?'

'Just as soon as they'll let me.'

Eric said, 'Auntie Hazel says you're learning to walk again. Did you hurt your legs?'

'No, but you need arms to walk.'

'Only if you're a monkey,' said Reggie, who was a keen student of wildlife, both real and mythical.

'Or Tarzan,' said Eric.

Vincent obliged them with a Tarzan call, remembering not to beat his chest. 'Listen, boys,' he said when they'd stopped laughing, 'there's a special job I want you to do.'

Reggie eyed him suspiciously, but Eric asked, 'What is it?'

'I want you both to look after Auntie Hazel, to help her and make sure she doesn't do too much. I want you to be very good, as well, because she has an awful lot on her mind. Will you do that?' He felt an awful hypocrite when he thought of the anguish he must have caused her.

'Yes,' said Eric.

Reggie merely nodded confidently. The task was evidently in safe hands. It was as well, because Sister arrived at that moment, to advise him that time was up.

'Come and see me again,' he told them, waving as Hazel took them back to the car. In future, they might have to come by tube or taxi, because the source of petrol was no more.

'Come and sit down, Lieutenant,' said Sister. 'That was nice, wasn't it? Are they your children from a previous marriage?'

'No, they're orphans, but they have a home with us, now, and my fiancée is their guardian. They lost their father in the war, their mother recently to cancer, and they came close to losing me as well, but you're right. It was very nice to see them again.' Before she moved away, he said, 'Sister, I'm sorry I've been such an ill-tempered brute.'

She laughed and said, 'Don't give it a moment's thought. We've coped with your sort before now, and we'll do it again.'

Vincent had a succession of visitors in the next week or so, beginning with Ali Barber. His arrival was most unexpected, but it was doubly welcome; he'd always enjoyed Ali's company, and his visit gave Vincent an opportunity to thank him for his kindness on the day of the accident. He was also able to assure Ali that he hadn't forgotten his offer of a reading list.

The second surprise visitor was Jack Andrews, who'd heard on the grapevine about the accident and taken the opportunity during a rest period to call in and see him. His greeting was typically robust, yet philosophical.

'Vincent, you old bastard, what a turn-up this is. Still, it beats a premature trip to the Pearly Gates, and you're better off without a crook arm, anyway.'

'Except that I make my living with music, Jack.'

'I'm sorry, mate. Me and my big mouth, I'd forgotten that.'

'Don't worry. You could make up for it by doing me a big favour.'

'What's that, mate?' He sounded genuinely keen.

'Will you be Best Man at my wedding?'

Jack's delight was undisguised. 'If I can get leave, it'll be a pleasure, mate. When is it?'

Vincent gave him the details. 'I imagine they'll allow you a day off, Jack.'

'I don't see why not. I mean, fair goes, I've put in enough time for HM, so I won't be asking a lot from him.'

It was a happy visit that did much for Vincent's recovering spirits, and his next reunion was to have a far-reaching effect.

'Jimmy! It's good to see you.' Vincent offered his left hand.

'I came as soon as I heard about it, sir. What a catastrophe.'

'But I'm on the road to recovery. How are things with you, Jimmy?'

'Life is busy, but rewarding, sir.' As if he were sharing a confidence, he leaned forward to say, 'My work with RMS has encouraged me to keep up the clarinet. Unless I'm falling asleep, I practise after a defusing. I find it helps me to relax.'

'Good. Don't forget to come and see me at the Institute when all the fuss has died down, and do some work on the piano when you can. It's important.'

'I will, sir.' Jimmy looked uncomfortably at the place where Vincent's arm had been, and then looked away.

'Let's not ignore it, Jimmy. That won't make it grow back.'

'No, sir. It was the most awful thing to happen.'

'I'm told it probably saved my life by cushioning my head against the stone steps when I fell. Anyway, I'll just have to be satisfied with chalking and talking from now on.'

'I don't know, sir.' Jimmy was looking thoughtful.

'What's on your mind, Jimmy?'

'Does the name Wittgenstein ring any bells, sir?'

'Ludwig Wittgenstein, the philosopher? "The meaning of a word is its usage." That's about all I can remember about him, and I must say, I'm not bowled over by that intellectual gem.'

'There was a family of them, sir.' Jimmy was almost impatient. 'Wittgenstein, the one you mentioned, had a brother. I think he had several, but the one I'm thinking of is Paul Wittgenstein, the concert pianist. I believe he's living in America, now.'

'I believe so.'

'The thing is, sir, he lost his right arm in the last war, and he persuaded several composers to write music for the left hand.'

'So he did.' The half-forgotten story was coming back to Vincent. 'If I remember, he was very rude about Ravel's "Concerto for the Left Hand", which I think was ingratitude at its worst, as well as an admission of his appalling taste, considering the concerto stands out from the rest as the masterpiece it is.'

'It's a superb concerto,' agreed Jimmy, 'and it deserves to be heard again, along with a lot of other left-hand repertoire.'

'Jimmy, you're being sly.'

'But in a good cause, sir. Aren't you glad that, as well as a philosopher, the Wittgenstein family produced a pianist?'

At the very least, it was something to consider.

31

July

The Real Thing

The summer of 1941 was a special time. The battleship Bismarck was sunk at the end of May, almost coinciding with the news that the Nazis had invaded Russia. Early bulletins were received cautiously at first, but restraint gave way to a growing sense of confidence that the invasion of Britain was, if not cancelled, at least postponed. Meanwhile, the nation welcomed the on-going respite from the Blitz. As if in celebration, the sun seemed to shine more brightly than ever before, and from mid-June to mid-July, scarcely a drop of rain fell.

Into this season of cheery optimism, Vincent emerged from physiotherapy, now steady on his feet and with a new sense of purpose.

First on the calendar was the wedding. Being a spinster of St George's Parish in Bloomsbury, Hazel naturally chose to be married there, and she and Vincent made the arrangements accordingly.

On the day, the select gathering arrived at St George's Church, with Vincent somewhat anxious at the non-arrival of his Best Man, but Jack appeared in good time, having just dealt with a Type 'B' in Southwark, and then gone home briefly to change into his best uniform.

The organist was playing Bach's 'Chorale on the Prelude "*Wachet Auf*" ' when the electric lamp on the organ console flashed to inform him that the bride had arrived at the south door. Improvising deftly, he made a seamless transition into Wagner's 'Bridal March', thereby earning Vincent's fleeting approval, even though it was likely that he'd been obliged to do the same kind of thing many times before.

In a gorgeous frock fashioned in silk from an undisclosed source, Hazel processed up the aisle on her father's arm, followed by Isabel from the Ministry as her Matron of Honour, although she preferred to be called a bridesmaid because it made her sound younger. To complete the entourage, Eric and Reggie were pageboys. No one really knew what the duties of a pageboy were; the important thing was that they were included, and so far, they had been on their best behaviour.

The vicar spoke the time-honoured words, 'Dearly beloved, we are gathered together here in the sight of God, and in the face of this congregation, to join together this man and this woman in Holy Matrimony....' and the ceremony had begun.

Vincent listened to the familiar text as he might to a favourite piece of music, such was the appeal of the seventeenth-century language, but when the vicar came to, 'the dreadful day of judgement,' it was as if some unseen force had seized him, and he was transported immediately back to Stepney, to the muddy casing, the stubborn plate and the whirring clock. Suddenly, he felt horribly cold and he shook, clenching his jaws to prevent himself calling out. Sensing that something was wrong, Jack put his hand on Vincent's shoulder and whispered, 'Steady, mate. Hold on.'

Hazel looked at him in concern, but he simply shook his head and smiled. He knew she wasn't convinced.

The vicar asked, 'Are you all right, Vincent?'

'Yes, thank you. I'm fine.'

'Good.' He went on to challenge the assembled company, and hearing of no lawful impediment why this man and woman should not be joined in Holy Matrimony, proceeded to guide Vincent and Hazel through their vows.

From feeling intensely cold, Vincent was now perspiring and he was conscious of his heart beating rapidly, but he heard the vicar's words and answered, 'I will.' Then it was Hazel's turn, and he made a determined effort to tear his mind away from Stepney and the horrors associated with it, as the ceremony continued.

'...I pronounce that they be man and wife together, in the Name of the Father, the Son and the Holy Ghost. Amen.' The vicar led them to where the Register lay open, and in a welcome demonstration of sensitivity, provided chairs for the bride and groom.

Hazel asked, 'Are you all right, darling?'

'Yes, don't worry about me.'

The vicar asked, 'Are you sure, Vincent?'

'Absolutely, Reverend. Please don't give it a moment's thought.'

As if some explanation were necessary, Jack said, 'The poor bugg…. The poor bloke's had a tough time recently, Reverend. I can vouch for that.'

'I quite understand. If you're both happy to continue, we'll attend to the signing of the register.'

Vincent remembered little of the remainder of the ceremony; he was vaguely aware of walking down the aisle to Mendelssohn's 'Wedding March' and standing with Hazel outside the church, but the fleeting horror that had afflicted him during the service had left him reeling, whatever he told Hazel and the vicar.

As they greeted everyone and accepted their best wishes, something happened to restore Vincent to reality, and that was the appearance of Jimmy, who had only just arrived, having been obliged, as Jack had before him, to attend to a mine that morning. It was equally delightful to see Daisy at his side.

'Jimmy and Daisy,' said Vincent, 'I'm delighted you could come. You will join us at the reception, won't you?'

'Of course, sir, but not before I've wished you and Mrs Reid much happiness.'

'Thank you, Jimmy.'

Hazel added her thanks, saying, 'That's the first time I've been called "Mrs Reid".' In the circumstances, she neglected to mention Ali's innocent question when they met on the day of the accident. In any case, distraction intervened when she overheard a conversation between the vicar and the pageboys. He was asking them if they'd enjoyed the wedding. She never heard Eric's reply, but Reggie's was all too audible.

'We thought they were married already, because they were living in the same house, but they said they were only practising for when they really were married.'

If the vicar disapproved, he made no mention of it, presumably taking the enlightened view that the day was one of celebration rather than recrimination.

They held the reception at Emil's in Covent Garden. It was a joyful affair, with the choice of venue making it almost a family event, and their pleasure was made greater still by the late arrival of Ali Barber. The family was now assembled, and telegrams from Commander Todd and Lieutenant Commander Ghyll provided the final touch.

At home afterwards, Hazel could contain her concern no longer. She asked, 'What happened in church, Vincent. You looked awful.'

'I'm sorry, darling. It's the face I was born with, admittedly with more wrinkles, but I'm told it's much the same.'

'This isn't a joking matter. What happened to you?'

He had to be honest. 'I don't really know. It was like a nightmare, except that I was wide awake. The vicar mentioned the "dreadful day of judgement", and that seemed to act as a trigger, because suddenly, I was back on the Thames at Stepney, with everything happening in awful detail. I was listening through a stethoscope, and I could hear the clock running. To be honest with you, it was harrowing, but it passed quickly enough. It did leave me wobbly, though.'

'I'm sorry, darling. As soon as you can, you really must see a doctor about it.'

He shook his head very definitely. 'No, not until I'm back in civilian life.'

'But why?'

'When they discharge me,' he explained, 'it must be because of my physical handicap, and not because some naval psychiatrist has decided I lack moral fibre.'

'Vincent,' she said, palpably shocked, 'that's an awful expression, as well as being patently untrue.'

'It's the official term,' he explained. 'In the last war, men suffered from shellshock, and the term eventually received official adoption, although sympathy was hard to find. In this war, the language, at least, has changed, and it's generally agreed that "lacking moral fibre" sounds much better than "war neurosis", especially to those who only experience a heart-stopping moment when they realise they're down to their last box of paperclips.'

'Promise me,' she demanded earnestly, 'that, if this thing happens again, you'll consult a doctor as soon as you're discharged from the service.'

'Scouts' honour.'

'And please take it seriously.'

'Oh, I do. Believe me, I do.'

Unable to leave the subject alone, she asked, 'In the meantime, is there anything you can take that's likely to help at all? I don't know if that kind of medication is available without a prescription.'

'My prescription is music, which "hath charms to soothe a savage breast".'

'Are you sure?'

'Yes, and Congreve evidently thought so, too.'

'I thought that was Shakespeare.'

'He would probably have agreed with the sentiment. He was pretty sound on human nature, and he'd already identified music as the food of love.'

'You're impossible,' she said.

'Don't give up on me on our wedding day, darling.' He put his arm round her and kissed her.

'I'm certainly not going to give up on you, but I really don't understand how music is going to protect you from the kind of thing that happened today.'

'You don't have to be a musician to understand it,' he assured her, withdrawing his arm to take her hands in his. 'Whenever I've had a problem that seemed insurmountable or that refused to be dismissed, I've always made a bee-line for the piano. It's the most calming influence I know,' he said, adding quickly, 'apart from being with you, obviously.'

'So, you're saying you'll play your troubles away.'

'That's right.'

'But you've only one hand.' As she spoke, tears were forming in her eyelids.

'You'll see. Trust me.'

With their marital status now official, the application for adoption could go ahead, and that meant as much to Vincent as it did to Hazel.

The next excitement would be the visit to Buckingham Palace, but the date was not yet known, so Hazel put her new hat away in its box and waited for events to develop.

Two days after the wedding, she was preparing dinner when she heard music coming from the drawing room. She wondered at first if Vincent might have put a record on the gramophone, but the sound seemed to have an altogether more immediate and real quality than that. Even so, it was such a full, rich sound that, overcome with curiosity, she went to the drawing room to find out what was happening.

She stood for a while at the door, watching him play and listening to the extravagant, romantic sound he was making, until he realised he was no longer alone. He stopped playing.

'I wish you hadn't stopped, Vincent. That was so beautiful, but…. I'm no expert, but it sounded, incredibly, as if you were playing with both hands. I know that sounds ridiculous, but that's how it seemed to me.'

'Thank you. That's the acid test, you see. If it sounds as if I'm playing with two hands, my left hand is obviously doing a good job.'

She leaned over to kiss him and hold him in her arms. Tears were coursing down her cheeks at the knowledge that, after all that had happened to him, he could still make beautiful music. 'I'd love to hear it again,' she said. 'What is it?'

'Alexander Skriabin's "Nocturne for the Left Hand".'

'Will you play it for me? I'm dying to hear it again. It sounded so much like the real thing.'

'Oh well, there's a perfectly good reason for that.'

'I don't follow you.'

He smiled reassuringly and said, 'You will, because from now on, it *is* the real thing, and if that doesn't call for celebration, rather than regret, I'm sadly mistaken.'

The End

www.ingramcontent.com/pod-product-compliance
Lightning Source LLC
Chambersburg PA
CBHW032141020726
47496CB00003B/669
9781636830339